WITCHING FIRE

A Wild Hunt Novel, Book 16

YASMINE GALENORN

D1714616

A Nightqueen Enterprises LLC Publication

Published by Yasmine Galenorn

PO Box 2037, Kirkland WA 98083-2037

WITCHING FIRE

A Wild Hunt Novel

Copyright © 2021 by Yasmine Galenorn

First Electronic Printing: 2021 Nightqueen Enterprises LLC

First Print Edition: 2021 Nightqueen Enterprises

Cover Art & Design: Ravven

Art Copyright: Yasmine Galenorn

Editor: Elizabeth Flynn

A Nightqueen Enterprises LLC Publication

Published in the United States of America

ACKNOWLEDGMENTS

Welcome back to the world of the Wild Hunt!

Thanks to my usual crew: Samwise, my husband, Andria and Jennifer—without their help, I'd be swamped. To the women who have helped me find my way in indie, you're all great, and thank you to everyone. To Kate Danley in particular, for running our author sprints that have helped me regain my focus in this current pandemic. To my wonderful cover artist, Ravven, for the beautiful work she's done.

Also, my love to my furbles, who keep me happy. My most reverent devotion to Mielikki, Tapio, Ukko, Rauni, and Brighid, my spiritual guardians and guides. My love and reverence to Herne, and Cernunnos, and to the Fae, who still rule the wild places of this world. And a nod to the Wild Hunt, which runs deep in my magick, as well as in my fiction.

You can find me through my website at Galenorn.com and be sure to sign up for my newsletter to keep updated on all my latest releases! You can find my advice on writing, discussions about the books, and general ramblings on my YouTube channel. If you liked this book, I'd be grateful if you'd leave a review—it helps more than you can think.

Brightest Blessings,
~The Painted Panther~
~Yasmine Galenorn~

WELCOME TO WITCHING FIRE

As the Winter Solstice approaches, Raven faces a difficult choice. She's dragged before the Queen of the Ante-Fae in a no-win situation, forced to choose between her people and her friends. On top of that, her grandfather presents her with an ultimatum that drives a wedge between Raven and her father. And the problems keep coming. Vixen, the gender-fluid owner of the Burlesque A Go-Go, asks for her help. An astral entity is draining the life from Vixen's web designer and Raven may be the only one who can help. As she searches for answers, Raven's investigation leads her to Kipa's homeland to meet with one of the Force Majeure—Väinämöinen. And there, the ancient bard offers her another choice. He offers her an opportunity that—if she accepts—will change her life forever.

Reading Order for the Wild Hunt Series:

- Book 1: The Silver Stag
- Book 2: Oak & Thorns
- Book 3: Iron Bones

CHAPTER ONE

WHEN I WALKED INTO THE LIVING ROOM, I SAW BOTH KIPA and Raj sprawled on the sofa, snoring up a storm. Dishes sticky with maple syrup cluttered the coffee table, and the TV blared away with a reality show. Contestants had to make their way through an obstacle course that looked like a drunken engineer had designed it. Most of them ended up in the water or mud, struggling to return to the course before they were disqualified.

Raj snuggled under a throw—a Hello Kitty throw, at that. He had recently discovered the world of Hello Kitty and now my otherwise sleek, minimalist house was littered with Hello Kitty plushies and Hello Kitty comic books. Much to my dismay, Raj had begged for a Hello Kitty collar as well, and I'd had to fashion one to fit him because nobody made Hello Kitty collars that would fit a gargoyle. But I loved him, and if wearing a pink cartoon collar made him happy, so be it.

I glanced around the living room. Beyond the dirty dishes and the Hello Kitty toys, the place was a mess. The floors needed sweeping, the sofa cushions were scattered everywhere, and generally, chaos ruled. Kipa had stayed at my house all week and his things were everywhere. He tended to leave his things lying around. Raj had slacked off, too. They both seemed under the misconception that I was going to happily skip around in a French maid's apron, cleaning up after them. Kipa was getting better about his sloppiness, but the Lord of Wolves was an alpha at heart and he was still coming to grips with being in an equal partnership.

Frustrated, I debated on whether to squirt them with the plant mister, or to be nice and just yell them awake. Before I could make up my mind, my phone blared out "Flight of the Valkyries." That meant one thing: my mother was calling me.

"Hey," I said, answering. "What's up? Please don't tell me you can't make my party."

Kipa and I were throwing an open house for Yule that night, which was one reason I was so pissed off about the dirty house. I wasn't about to clean it *and* do all the cooking myself.

As usual, my mother—Phasmoria, Queen of the Bean Sidhe—wasted no time with small talk. "I'm coming in early. I'll be there at three o'clock. We have important things to discuss. And don't worry, I'll help with the party tonight."

I barely managed an "Oh" before she hung up. Staring at the phone, I mulled over the news. I loved my mother but she could be abrupt, bordering on brusque. Turning back to Kipa and Raj, I decided to go with the most expedient route, even though it would be fun to blast them with a shower of water.

"Wake up!" I shifted into high gear, yelling so loud that neither Raj nor Kipa could sleep through my command.

"*Wha*— What's wrong?" Kipa asked, jerking awake as he bolted to his feet.

Raj, on the other hand, gave me a lazy blink, staring at me with bleary eyes as he barely moved his head off the sofa. "Is Raven okay?"

"Raven is fine, but the house is *not*. Not only do I need to cook for the party tonight, but this place is a pigsty and I'm not about to be stuck with the cleaning. Add to that, my mother's coming in early. She'll be here at three and I will not have her walking into this mess, so both of you get off your asses and clean up this mess, *now*!"

Kipa ducked his head. He knew I meant business. "Raj needs to help Kipa," he said, stretching and yawning. "Raven will tan Raj's and Kipa's hides if they don't do what she says."

"Very observant," I said. "Raven wants Raj to put his toys away and turn off that television. Then he's to sit and watch TV, and not make any more messes. And you," I turned to Kipa, "for fuck's sake, please clean the kitchen, the hall bath, and straighten up this living room. You *promised* you would be responsible for cleaning them when you stay here and *newsflash*: they're all filthy. You and Raj made most of the mess in this room. There's an entire day's worth of dishes in the sink. Don't dawdle— get moving!"

Kipa saluted. "Yes, ma'am." He was grinning, but he had gotten the message. "Sorry I've been slacking. You said Phasmoria's coming early?" He knew better than vex my mother. Even though he was a god, she was Queen of the Bean Sidhe and she scared the hell out of him.

"She'll be here at three. It's *noon* and I still have to do the shopping. You have three hours to clean this place until it's spotless. And I might add, I expect this to *stick*. I hate micromanaging people. You've been teaching Raj bad habits."

He sighed. "I'm sorry."

"I should hope so. You know I hate clutter. I don't keep a messy house, and I expect both of you to do your chores without complaint. Got it?" Hands on my hips, I stared them down. That was one thing about man-boys and gargoyles. Give them an inch and they'd take a mile.

Both gargoyle and god lowered their eyes and whispered another "Yes ma'am" before kicking it into high gear. As I headed into the bedroom—which, I might add, was clean since I had made the bed when we got up, and dusted—they attacked the mess like industrious worker bees. Sometimes you had to give people a kick in the ass, lovingly so.

HALF AN HOUR LATER, after cleaning the bedroom bathroom and tending to the ferrets, I grabbed my purse and keys. "I'm going shopping. Keep working while I'm gone." I turned to see that Raj had already dragged out several of his toys again and left them on the floor. I knelt, holding them up. "Did Raj forget what Raven asked him to do?"

Raj hung his head. "Raj is sorry. Raj doesn't mean to make a mess."

"Raven knows that," I said, giving him a hug. He was about the size of a rottweiler and as heavy as one, but he was a sweetheart. Most of the time, if he hurt someone, it was an accident. "It's usually okay for Raj to make a mess, as long as he cleans it up without being reminded. But Raven and Kipa are having a party tonight, so the house needs to *stay* clean today. Does Raj understand?"

"Raj understands," he said, his gloom lifting. He gave me a smile that was as innocent as a child's. "Raj will do better for Raven. Raj loves Raven."

"And Raven loves Raj," I said. That was our pattern. Whenever I left, Raj always told me he loved me and I reaffirmed it back to him.

In some ways, he was very much like a child. In gargoyle years, he was still young. I doubted that Raj could ever fend for himself—not fully. He was in his formative years and growing up away from his own kind. He had had his wings cut off by a demon, and so he was unlike his brethren. And one thing I *did* know about the gargoyle world was that physical imperfection was considered unacceptable. They'd never take him back, given what the demon had done to him. Gargoyles weren't kind to their disabled. So I made myself a promise that I would always take care of him, and we had been together for over fifty years.

Next, I kissed Kipa, who wrapped his arms around me. He was so gorgeous and charming it was hard to stay irritated at him.

"Are you *sure* you need to go to the store?" He leaned down to nuzzle my ear. "Hmm? Do we have time for—"

"No, we do not," I said, even though the thought of running off to bed with him appealed to me far more than grocery shopping. "I'd love to, but there's nothing in the cupboards and we promised people a buffet. Also, if I don't go shopping, we're not going to have anything to eat beyond a few cans of soup."

"Then go, wench! Rip your beautiful self away from me and leave me yearning for your touch," Kipa said, throwing his hand across his forehead. He squinted at me from below the shade of his arm. "Is it working?"

"Oh go on, fly." I swatted him lightly. "You're just being a drama queen now."

"Drama *king*, my love," he said, laughing. "I'm your king, and you're my queen. So is it working? Won't you stay for a while?"

"No, it's not. Though that bulge pressing against my thigh is tempting. Now, get your handsome ass back to work. I'll be home in a while." I pressed against him for another long kiss, then broke out of his embrace and headed for the door. "And don't give Raj any more sugar. You two gorged on waffles this morning and you used up the maple syrup. That's *enough* sugar for now."

"We had sausages and eggs, too," Kipa called behind me, but I shut the door, ignoring his protests.

As I headed toward my car, my breath froze in puffs in front of my face. It was thirty-one degrees, and there was snow on the ground, as well as patches of black ice on the road. As I slid into my car, I was grateful that Kipa had put on snow tires a week ago when the snowstorm was first predicted. And one glance at the clouds overhead was enough to know that we weren't done yet. The sky shimmered with that silver frozen look that whispered "incoming snow." Not a big fan of heat, I welcomed the winter weather.

As I pulled out of the cul-de-sac, I waved at Meadow O'Ceallaigh and her brother, Trefoil, who were building a snowman in their front yard. My neighbors—we lived on opposite sides of the end of the cul-de-sac—worked for LOCK, the Library of Cryptic Knowledge. They were in the paramilitary side of the organization, though I wasn't entirely sure what they did. Their work was classified. Both were gay, and they were friendly, but they also maintained an aloofness…a certain air of "You're better off not knowing about us." They waved back, laughing.

The trip to the store proved to be more hazardous than I anticipated.

People were slip-sliding everywhere. Nobody in the Seattle area knew how to drive in snow. Beyond the fact that snow wasn't a regular event here so there weren't enough snow plows to effectively clear the city streets, the topography of western Washington didn't lend itself to navigating snow and ice. A number of streets both in Seattle and here, on the opposite side of Lake Washington, on the Eastside, had anywhere from an 18 percent grade to a 21 percent grade. Basically, Seattle was built on a series of rolling hills, thanks to the fault lines in the area. So snow and ice meant conditions that were nearly impossible to navigate.

At the store, I found a cart. We were out of most everything so I tossed whatever looked good in the cart, along with a variety of staples including pasta, breads, eggs, milk, and any number of canned goods and jarred sauces. I also added a number of delicacies and found what looked like an incredible fifteen-layer chocolate peppermint torte. I picked up five of them, given that everybody coming had hearty appetites. I was planning on making a huge vat of clam chowder for dinner, and decided that fish and chips would be a good addition, so I added several boxes of premium battered fish, a couple big bags of frozen fries, and French bread that I would smother with butter and parmesan.

Because I felt guilty for yelling at Raj, I added a case of cat food to the cart. He loved it and I kept it for special occasions since he tended to eat more of it than was good for him. He usually ate what I was eating, unless it had onions or garlic or peppers in it—or pineapple. Pineapple made him sick. But I knew he didn't care for fish, so cat food it was.

After one last stop at the flower section to buy several bouquets of red roses with white carnations, baby's breath, and fern fronds, I checked out. I glanced at my phone. *1:35 P.M.* I had time enough to run by A Taste of Latte to buy some pastries and a triple-shot mocha. I needed more caffeine like I needed a hole in my head, but with caffeine, *want* mattered as much as *need*.

BY THE TIME I got home it was almost two-thirty. I stepped out of the car, about to summon Kipa to help, when he came darting out of the house and motioned for me to go inside. The temperature had dipped again—it was now twenty-nine and a few flakes were starting to fall. I shivered, but Kipa, who was originally from Finland, had no problem in the cold. In fact, he loved it.

"Go inside and warm up. It's supposed to start snowing heavily this afternoon," he said, motioning for me to head out.

I entered the house and paused. Every surface of every table gleamed. The floors were freshly washed and mopped. There was no dust anywhere, and everything had been put away. The air smelled crisp and clean and it was obvious they had aired out the house. The soft sound of the washer running told me that Kipa had started a load of laundry.

Raj was sitting politely on the sofa, watching TV, a bowl of popcorn by his side. He glanced up as I came in.

"Raven's home! Did Raven bring food?" He had such a plaintive note in his voice that it made me want to pinch his cheeks and indulge in baby-talk with him, but I restrained myself. His cadence might be odd, and while he liked TV shows targeted toward children, he was a deeply intelligent being who happened to have a gargoyle's perspective on life.

"The place looks wonderful," I said, smiling. "Good job! Raj really helped Kipa out. And yes, Raven brought food. Raven's mother should be here soon, so Raven's very happy that the house looks good."

Raj grimaced. "Will Raven please stop Phasmoria from making Raj try to sit at the table for dinner?"

Last time she was here, my mother had gotten the idea that, since Raj was actually intelligent and not a pet, he should sit properly at the table during mealtimes. I had let it go a couple times until it was obvious that Raj was uncomfortable. I had promised next time she tried to make him sit in a chair with a napkin tied around his neck, I would put a stop to it.

"Phasmoria won't make Raj sit in a chair anymore when he's eating," I said. "Remember, Raven talked to her about that several weeks ago? If Phasmoria forgets, Raven will remind her."

"Raj thanks Raven." He went back to watching his

show. He had switched loyalties from *Acrobert and the Alphas* to *Captain Ghost*—a cartoon about a ghost sailor superhero who sailed the oceans, helping people avoid pirates. Raj had a deep, abiding love for cartoons and comics. They made him happy, and that's all that mattered. He didn't like opera or ballet, which suited me fine. I liked *The Nutcracker*, and I would occasionally watch a play, but I had no love for opera or the symphony.

Kipa carried in the groceries. "Everything look good?"

"Everything looks perfect," I said. "Thank you." I followed him into the kitchen and started putting away food as he brought in the rest of the bags. As I was debating on whether to put the apples in a crystal or a china bowl for the table, I suddenly felt dizzy. It was as though something blew past me so fast that it spun me around.

"What the hell?" I muttered, looking around. I closed my eyes and reached out to see if any ghosts had come through, but my wards were strong and nothing was in sight. I kept the house and my car heavily guarded, given the run-in I'd had with Pandora.

While the Elven therapist I was seeing had helped me move past the PTSD, I remained wary. The chaotic goddess was still out there. I had thwarted her plans and her fun by escaping her torture chamber. While I wasn't sure she'd be out for revenge, I didn't want to take any chances on leaving the door open for her to waltz in.

But there was no sense of a spirit, nor of anything out of the ordinary. Frowning, I went back to putting away the food, but in the back of my mind, I couldn't shake the feeling something big was barreling my way, and I was right in the center of the road.

CHAPTER TWO

I spent the next half-hour making the chowder. After it was done, I poured it into a slow cooker to keep it warm. The extra time would blend the flavors even more. While I cooked and simmered, Kipa sliced the French bread loaves in half, buttering them and then wrapping them in foil. He stowed them in the fridge, then made turkey and provolone sandwiches for lunch. We cleaned the kitchen again, together, and had just finished when the doorbell rang.

I glanced at the clock. "Three P.M., precisely. That's my mother."

Phasmoria was seldom late, but she never overstepped her boundaries when it came to my privacy. She rang the bell, knocked at the bedroom door when she stayed over, and didn't try to snoop in my mail.

Beyond that, I knew that she was always a step ahead of me. But I didn't mind because she was on my side, and that was the *one place* you wanted the Queen of the Bean Sidhe.

I opened the door.

She was leaning against the doorpost, clad in black leather—both jacket and pants—with knee-high platform boots. Beneath the jacket, she wore a blood-red tank top. Her hair was perfectly straight, falling to the curve of her lower back, and it was black, streaked with silver. My mother was a little taller than me—at five-eight—and far more muscled. She looked like a classy biker chick, and was tougher than any biker you'd ever meet. Her fingernails were painted blood red, and her lipstick matched both her top and her nails.

She swooped me into her arms for a quick hug. We weren't a demonstrative family, but Phasmoria and I had gotten chummier over the past few years and we now willingly exchanged hugs when we met. I had noticed that, ever since Pandora had abducted and tortured me, my mother had kept a closer eye on me.

"You're looking good," she said, eyeing me up and down. "How are the memories?"

I shrugged. "They're there, but…I'm all right. Wary, but okay. I'm having a lot fewer flashbacks."

"Good." Phasmoria sighed. "I'm glad that you're feeling better, because I have some news, and…you'd better sit down for this one, because it's big."

A shadow passed over her face. For her to look so concerned made my blood run cold. The Bean Sidhe weren't afraid of anything except their goddess. As I walked her to the living room, I wondered if Pandora was on the move again. And if so, was she gunning for me?

So, I'd better start with an introduction. I'm Raven Bone-Talker, one of the Ante-Fae—the predecessors to the Light and Dark Courts. While my mother eclipses me, I'm definitely developing my own style. I stand five-seven, and I'm curvy in a plump sort of way with big boobs and big hips. Humans call me goth, though it's truly just my nature.

I've got long brown hair streaked with purple—all natural—and my arms, torso, and back are covered with scrolling birthmarks that look like intricate tattoos. I'm a swirl of curls and spirals, and the markings on my back are wing-shaped. My amalgamation of birthmarks are from my mixed parentage. As I said, both my parents are Ante-Fae—my mother is Queen of the Bean Sidhe, and my father is the Black Dog of Hanging Hills.

And me? I'm a bone witch. I walk with the dead, and I'm a priestess of Arawn—Lord of the Dead—and Cerridwen—Keeper of the Cauldron. Mostly, I work fire and death magic, read fortunes, exorcise houses, and clear out the dead who should not be lingering. My mother has hinted that I have other powers that haven't manifested yet, and so I wait, not pushing the envelope because when you encourage Fate to move too quickly, it usually implodes.

I'm hundred-plus years old, barely legal in my world, in love with a god, and trying to help out my friends who are on the front lines of a war against the dragons. If I were to encourage Fate to intervene again, I'd be dumping one too many things on my plate.

And of course, the moment that thought crossed my mind, I realized I had just jinxed myself.

Phasmoria glanced around, spotting Raj. Before doing anything else, she walked over to plant a big old smooch on his head. "How's Raj doing?"

"Raj is good. How is Raven's mother?"

I wasn't sure why, but he seldom called her by name. He was wary of her because my mother treated him with the same buck-up attitude she treated everybody else. My mother was hard to ignore when she told you to do something.

"Phasmoria is doing well, but she needs to talk to Raven alone, so would Raj please go play in another room?" She turned to Kipa, whom she had a grudging respect for. She wasn't thrilled I was dating a god, but she also had seen him stick by me during a very rough time, and she respected loyalty. "Kipa, hello, and would you go with Raj? We can all chat afterward, but I need to talk to her right now; and what I have to say needs to be said in private, at least to start." She shooed them off the sofa.

"Raj and Kipa will go watch TV in the bedroom," Kipa said, motioning for Raj to accompany him. He had a worried look on his face, though, and he glanced back once, frowning. As soon as they were in the bedroom and the door had closed, Phasmoria turned back to me.

"What's going on?" I asked. "What's happened? Is Da all right?"

"As far as I know. Sit down, Raven. As I said, this is... concerning news."

Wondering what was going on, I sat down on the sofa and she joined me. "Is this about the dragons?" We were in the middle of a war against Typhon, the Father of All

Dragons. Or rather, the gods were going up against him. Those of us who were puny and easily crisped by dragon breath were taking care of the collateral damage, which included a massive number of dead rising, and all sorts of delightful fallout like that.

But Phasmoria shook her head. "No, actually it doesn't. Did your father ever tell you about the Banra-Sheagh?"

The name sounded familiar, but I couldn't remember where I'd heard of it. "No, I don't think so. What…who… are we talking about?"

She took a deep breath. "I wish your father hadn't been so remiss in his duties. Granted, he's one of the Exosan, like you, but he owed it to you to tell you more about your heritage."

"My heritage? You mean his family…your family?" I was confused now. If we had a relative named the Banra-Sheagh, I'd never known about it.

"Not exactly." Phasmoria paused, biting her lip. "All right, do you even know that our people have a queen?"

That was a new one. "Nope. I thought that we Ante-Fae are mostly…anarchists, so to speak. We don't have a ruling government like the Light and Dark Fae do."

"Yes, we do, though some of the youngsters like you don't know about her because you're being brought up in a human world. The Banra-Sheagh is Queen of the Ante-Fae. She's ancient—far beyond reckoning. Like Arachana, she's almost a goddess." She paused, still looking troubled.

"What's going on? Why does this matter to me?"

"Because the Banra-Sheagh has commanded you to come before her." When Phasmoria grimaced, I realized this wasn't exactly a good thing.

"*Me*? How does she even know about me?" I was thoroughly confused now. I knew the Light and Dark Fae—who had evolved from the Ante-Fae and were technically our descendants—had their twin courts. But I had no clue about a governing council of the Ante-Fae.

"Unfortunately, your grandfather—Dougal, Curikan's father—still communicates with the court. I believe that he put the bug in her ear." My mother leaned back, crossing her legs. She swept her hair back into a ponytail and wrapped an elastic hair tie around it. "I'm not as much of an Exosan as your father, but even I believe we've outgrown the monarchy."

"What could the Ban... What's her name again?"

"The Banra-Sheagh."

"Thank you. What does the Banra-Sheagh want with me?" I had no clue why an ancient queen would be interested in meeting me.

"I don't know, but I have a bad feeling about this, Raven. You can't ignore it. To do so would be suicide. The Queen can execute any member of her court who pisses her off. So you have to travel to Reímseil-Tabah, the realm in which she lives, and go before her."

I could sense Phasmoria's worry, and when my mother was worried, there was always a good reason. She wasn't the type of woman—or Ante-Fae—to be scared of anything. I tried to think of every possible reason the Queen might summon me, but couldn't come up with any. I kept to myself for the most part, and yes—I was Exosan, meaning I liked the human world and hung out with humans—but there were plenty of Ante-Fae who were Exosan now.

"Maybe it has something to do with Pandora?"

"I don't know, child." Phasmoria bit her lip—a gesture alien to her. "I met the Banra-Sheagh one time when she summoned me to court. She wanted to congratulate me on being promoted to Queen of the Bean Sidhe. The meeting was short and to the point. I walked in, knelt before her. She bade me rise, said a few words of how I was making the Ante-Fae proud with my actions, and then boom, the guards escorted me out again." She shivered. "I can tell you, even that short a time was creepy as shit."

"That doesn't bode well. When do I have to go?"

"I'm not sure—she's sending an official escort. I'm friendly with one of her personal guards and that's the only reason I know about this. He told me what he could get away with. And now you know everything I know. He did mention that the Banra-Sheagh wasn't in a good mood when she gave the guards their orders. You'll probably get the summons tomorrow. I'll go with you, of course. I'm not letting you walk in there without me."

Grateful once again that my mother was who she was, I stared at the floor. "What's she like?"

Phasmoria hesitated for a moment, then said, "I don't want to scare you, but… She…reminded me of an insect. She was round. Not fat—not in the way you'd think of being fat—but…round. She's probably seven feet tall, and reminded me of an odd mix of humanoid and a scarab beetle. I can't explain it any better than that. When I try to think back to our meeting, my mind can't pin down an image to go with it. It has to be her glamour. Which, by the way, will work on anyone except the gods."

"That makes me even more nervous. How do I get there?"

17

"She'll send guards to accompany you. They'll pave the way." My mother took my hands. "I'm going to stay here until you get the summons because otherwise she might sweep you away without warning. I refuse to let you stand before the Banra-Sheagh without me there to help." She brought my hands to her lips and kissed them lightly. It was right then that I realized I might be in big trouble and that, if I was, there wasn't much anyone could do.

PHASMORIA OFFERED to help finish cooking and decorating for the party. I had set up my Yule tree in the corner the week before Thanksgiving, and it had managed to withstand both Raj and Kipa and retain its beauty. The tree was exquisite—a shimmering vision of white and blue and silver and clear crystal. I had bought an artificial blue spruce that was eight feet tall, and with the tree topper—a blue faerie figurine—it came close to brushing the ceiling. Kipa and I had decorated it, though more me than Kipa, who preferred to sit back and watch me hang the ornaments.

While we were finishing preparations, I turned on *Frosty the Snowman* and several other seasonal shows for Raj. I had to interrupt at one point when he decided to twirl around the living room. To avoid a major disaster, I switched channels to a cookie baking competition, and now we could hear him shouting at the TV. Shouts of "Cinnamon! Peggy shouldn't use so much cinnamon or the judges will yell at her!" and "Doesn't Evan realize that he put the cookies in the oven too late? They won't bake in time!" echoed from the sofa.

Phasmoria broke out into a big grin. Lowering her voice, she said, "He's quite the character, isn't he?"

"Yeah, he definitely is." I began arranging cookies and pastries on several trays.

Kipa, who was stirring the chowder, asked, "What power does this Banra-Sheagh have over Raven?"

Phasmoria paused from organizing vegetables on a crudité platter. "The Banra-Sheagh—that's her title and name—has the power of life and death over any of the Ante-Fae. She can order any one of us to be executed, though those who work in service to the gods are exempt to that. Which means since Raven is an official priestess of Arawn and Cerridwen, the Banra-Sheagh can't take her life. But she can order punishment of many kinds. She can also reward those she feels deserve it."

"Can she order the Ante-Fae to go to war?" I asked. Now that I knew we had a queen, I wanted to know everything she could force us to do.

"I doubt it. She could try but given how spread out we are and how…different…we all are, that's not a likely scenario. The Banra-Sheagh seldom speaks out anymore, since a good share of the younger Ante-Fae still live in this realm. A large segment of the ancient Ante-Fae moved over with the Queen when she withdrew, but they're even less likely to obey if she tried something like a war." Phasmoria finished setting up the tray of vegetables and dip and moved on to slicing the tortes.

By five we were ready. Right on time, the doorbell rang. I went to change while Kipa answered it. I found Raj sitting on my bed, looking worried, his limpid brown eyes looking glossy as though he'd been crying. I sat down beside him and put my arm around him. He was sitting in the Scooby-Doo position, upright, with his back legs sprawled out in front of him, and his front legs bracing himself up. As I hugged him, his leathery gray skin felt smooth and cool. He leaned into my hug, resting his head on my shoulder.

"What's wrong with Raj? Why does he look so sad?"

Raj let out a long sigh. "Raj is worried about Raven. Raven's mother says Raven has to visit a queen. That sounds frightening."

"It will be all right. Raj doesn't have to go with Raven, so he'll be safe here at home."

"Raj isn't worried about Raj…Raj is worried Raven's in trouble. Did Raj do something to get Raven in trouble?"

I bit my lip. "Oh no, sweetie. Raj did nothing to get Raven in trouble. Raven's not sure why she has to go visit the Queen, but it has nothing to do with anything that Raj said or did. Raj isn't to blame himself. Does Raj understand?"

Raj looked bewildered. "Raj understands, but he's still worried about Raven."

"Raven's worried about Raven, too," I said. "Raven's not sure what to expect and she doesn't like that feeling. But…she's going to be brave about it, so Raj needs to be brave, too. Can Raj be brave for Raven?"

He nodded again. "Raj can do that. Will that help Raven?"

"That will help Raven a lot," I said, giving him a kiss on the top of his head. "Raj is a good boy. Now if Raj would go out and help Kipa, Raven's going to dress for the party."

Raj obediently trundled off the bed and headed for the door, shutting it behind him. I watched him go. Raj had picked up my mood, that was for sure. I wasn't certain what the Banra-Sheagh wanted with me, but it had to be something big.

Sighing, I picked out my party outfit—a black velvet circle skirt over a red petticoat, a red plaid corset that zipped up the front with black buckles and silver chains on it, and red and white striped tights. I added a silver fascinator, pinning it to my hair to keep it in place, and then a silver necklace that Kipa had bought for me. It had a ruby hanging from the chain that was as big as my thumbnail, and set into platinum.

I slid on a pair of platform knee-high boots, black with silver buckles, and a silver bracelet. Finally, I stood back and stared at myself in the mirror. I was ready for the party, but on the inside my concentration was shot. Regardless of whether the Queen's summons was for good or ill, I hoped that the meeting would be quick, and that it would happen soon, because I *really* didn't want to wait to find out my doom.

CHAPTER THREE

By the time I was dressed, Kipa had let in the first guests—Ember and Herne. I wanted to tell them what my mother had told me, but I didn't want to dampen the mood, so I decided to put it off until later. Enjoying the party would take focus. There wasn't much I could do about the Banra-Sheagh for now, so I tried to push all thoughts of the future out of my mind.

"Where's Angel?" I asked, looking around.

"She's on the way. She decided to drive herself so she could stop and pick up a package that got rerouted to the Express Delivery station instead of to our house," Ember said.

"How's she doing?" I had been there when Angel's boyfriend had been killed—in fact, I had witnessed the entire event, and so had Kipa. Neither one of us had been able to prevent a group of skeletal walkers from killing Rafé, and it wore heavy on our consciences, even though we had done our best to get him to medical treatment. I still felt guilty, though I knew guilt was futile, especially in a situation that had been as dire as the one we had been facing.

"She's all right. In fact, I wonder if she's overcompensating. She seems too...unaffected. I mean, look at all the changes she's been through. Rafé's death, finding out she's a quarter magic-born, and drinking the potion of life. I guess she's sorting things out the best she can," Ember said. "She'll get through it—she's talking to Marilee a lot. I don't think Angel ever believed she had much power. That she has a magical heritage to draw on opens up a whole new perspective."

"Big changes do that, and so does trauma. And good gods, losing someone you love always brings trauma. I know all too much about that." I paused as the doorbell rang. "Excuse me." Grateful to whoever had showed up, I moved to answer the door. I didn't want to talk about trauma tonight, given how on edge I was since my mother had told me about the Banra-Sheagh.

I opened the door to find Vixen and Apollo standing there. Both were Ante-Fae and both were also Exosan. Apollo—the Golden Boy—was Vixen's lover, and their sub. He was enrolled in college in a business management program. Apollo was stunning, with a perfectly symmetrical face and delicate features. His golden hair mirrored sunlight on a spring morning, and he had a model's body. He could have been a supermodel, outshining anyone in the business, but he chose to dance at the club and go to school instead.

"Hello, darling," he said, air-kissing my cheek. Apollo and I had developed a good friendship over the past couple of years and he occasionally watched Raj when I was gone. I made sure never to give the wrong impres-

23

sion, though, because Vixen was very possessive of their boytoy, and even though they were a good friend, I wanted no misunderstandings.

Vixen had chosen an androgynous form for the evening. A Taipan snake shifter, they had a deadly bite. Vixen was gender-fluid to the point of where they could change their looks, depending on their mood. Tonight, they chose a tall, lanky form, both beautiful and yet masculine, blurring the lines between gender. Vixen was also wearing enough sequins to blind a person.

"Raven, it's always a pleasure," Vixen said, giving me an air kiss. They glanced around as they entered the house. "So sorry we're unfashionably punctual tonight. Apollo has exams coming up that he must study for." They paused for a moment, then said, "Tell me, is your goth boy coming tonight?"

I sighed. Vixen didn't like Trinity, another of my friends. Actually, not many people liked him. "I invited him, yes. I expect you to be civil in my house, Vixen. Trinity's not to blame for his parentage."

Vixen let out a sigh, then said, "True that. He didn't have a choice. Very well, I'll be civil. Oh, I see Herne and Ember—I'll go say my hellos to them. But Raven, my dear, I want to talk to you later about a matter involving a possible possession, so pencil me in, if you would, when you have some time this week." They kissed me on the cheek and, picking up the golden leash that circled Apollo's neck, they headed over to greet Herne and Ember.

Kipa slid up behind me, his hands on my waist. He leaned in. "You have some interesting friends."

"I lead an interesting life," I whispered back.

"That you do. Vixen reminds me of a couple of the gods. The Ante-Fae are quite a bunch."

"We are, aren't we?" I grinned up at him. "We live on the outside of the world, even when we're smack in the middle of it."

The doorbell rang again and I kissed Kipa's cheek. "Be a good wolf and get that, would you? I'm going to set out the food."

He slapped my ass. "You sure I'm not the Big Bad Wolf?"

"Oh," I whispered back, "I *love* it when you're the Big Bad Wolf."

Laughing, he headed toward the door as I slipped into the kitchen, where my mother was organizing the food. I stared at her. She was wearing an apron over her leather jeans, and the juxtaposition of imagery threw me for a moment.

"You are the least domestic woman I know," I said. "Yet…somehow the apron fits with the outfit."

Phasmoria laughed. "*Right*. And I'm Tinkerbell. I didn't want to drop anything on my pants, and I wasn't about to let you do all the work." She paused, then asked, "You do love your friends, don't you?"

I nodded. "They're all good people. They're part of my family. They'd have my back if I needed help, without ever asking why."

Phasmoria paused. "I'm glad. I can't be here all the time, or even most of the time. And you're still…"

"Young, I know. But I do my best to stand on my own two feet—" I paused as Angel bustled into the kitchen, her arms filled with bags. "Angel!"

"I brought desserts. I know you probably already have goodies, but…"

As Phasmoria took the bags from her, I gave her a hug. "I'm glad you came, and we can always use more. Did you bake them?" I peeked in to see several varieties of pie.

She snorted. "You think I'd bring you *store-bought* pie?"

"Nope, just reassuring myself. Those will go fast. Come here, taste the chowder and tell me if I need to add anything."

Angel was a natural-born chef. As she obligingly moved toward the stove, I stepped aside, giving her room in which to work. Angel was gorgeous. Like Apollo, she, too, could have been a model. Her white maxi dress was held up by gold buckles on the shoulder straps, and the color stood out in contrast to the warm glow of her rich brown skin. Her eyes were brown, as was her hair that coiled down to her shoulders. She had gathered it back with cloisonne combs, which I remembered had been a present from Rafé.

I leaned against the counter, watching her taste the chowder.

"This is good, but a dash of lemon pepper would go a long way," she said. "Where's your spice cabinet?"

I pointed toward the narrow drawer at the end of the counter. I had a galley kitchen, large enough to do some decent cooking in but far from a gourmet kitchen. She found the bottle of lemon pepper and added a dash to the chowder, tasted it again, then added another shake.

"There, that's good." Turning around, she let out a groan. "I hope you don't think I meant it wasn't good to begin with—"

"No, you told me it was good. I believe you," I said,

laughing. "I'm not so vain about my cooking that I'm going to get my nose bent out of shape when you think of a way to make it better. You're like…the Cooking Channel incarnate."

She snorted. "Thank you. I love to cook and I've done a lot of it over the past couple of months. It helps me cope."

"I'll take these crudité platters out to the table," my mother said, delicately stepping around me with them. I waited till she was gone.

"How are you doing? Honestly?" Angel and I shared a special bond over Rafé's death. He had been her boyfriend, and he had been my late fiancé's brother, the one link I had left to Ulstair, who had been killed by a serial killer over a year before. Losing Rafé forced me to realize that Ulstair was truly gone. But I had Kipa to steady me. Angel had lost her lover.

She hesitated, then tilted her head. "I'm surprisingly okay, to be honest. I keep waiting for his death to fully hit. Oh, I've cried, but I keep waiting to have a breakdown that never happens. At first it was hard, but…can I tell you something I haven't even told Ember?"

"Of course."

Angel glanced around to make sure we were alone. The party was in full swing and nobody was in the kitchen but us. "I'm sad, but I don't feel…heartbroken. I feel like I *should* be, and I feel guilty that I'm not."

I let out a slow breath. "I understand. I felt the same way after Ulstair died. I missed him, and I still do. I loved him, and I still do. But now I wonder if I was ever truly *in love* with him, because my heart healed far faster than I expected. While I miss the *friendship* we had, I don't miss the *relationship*."

"You don't think that makes me a bad person, then?" Angel searched my face, and I realized she was looking for a way to forgive herself.

I took her hands. "Not at all. You loved Rafé, but he wasn't your forever-person. That doesn't mean you didn't care about him. It doesn't mean his death didn't matter."

She ducked her head, then smiled. "Yeah, that's a good way to put it. We had a rocky road—coming from different cultures, with him being Fae and me being mostly human. And then when he went through the torture, it changed him and even after counseling, he was never fully the same. I guess he couldn't be. He wasn't as present, you know what I mean? I always felt like he was standing outside of himself, watching the rest of us. And it couldn't just be the PTSD. Look at you—you went through something as bad, or worse, and you're *here*. You're not a million miles away."

"I got counseling—" I started to say, then stopped. "When Rafé lost his brother, that's when things first shifted. They were tight, you know. They protected each other. Something shifted back then and it just kept shifting."

"I'm glad you understand. Everybody expects me to be brokenhearted and to cover myself in black and they tell me I'm hiding from my feelings," she said. "Ember and Herne tiptoe around, like they're afraid if they kiss in front of me, I'll break down. I *wish* to hell they'd stop coddling me."

"*Tell them*," I said. "Ember's your best friend. You need to be straight with her. Don't let the resentment build up.

They aren't going to think you're a horrible person. Not at all." I wrapped my arm around her waist. "The truth can be difficult, but it's ten times easier than living a lie so you protect other people's expectations." I rinsed out the massive soup tureen—it was bone china with a cranberry and snowy woods motif. I jerked my head toward the living room. "Come on, help me serve the food before they riot."

I held the tureen steady as Angel filled it. Then she removed the bread and fish fillets from the oven while I retrieved the fries from the air fryer and emptied them into a bowl matching the tureen's pattern.

I recruited Kipa to carry the food to the table. We were serving buffet style and had set up two long folding tables so that we could sit in the living room and watch the tree as we ate. I changed the music over to a soft ambient background music—mostly instrumental—and we called people to dinner. My mother fed Raj his cat food without even a hint that he should join us as I made the rounds.

Llew and Jordan had arrived, along with Talia, Viktor and Sheila, Yutani, and Trinity. Vixen was good to their promise, and didn't cause a ruckus, and as we all sat down to dinner, I relaxed, trying to push away the worry over what my mother had told me.

THE LIGHTS of the tree and the candlelight on the table seemed to relax everyone. After we finished eating, the men cleared the dishes and folded the tables, and we all had dessert in the living room. I didn't have enough furniture so we had brought the chairs from the dining table over, and the folding chairs as well.

True to my prediction, Angel's pies disappeared at a rapid rate, and then people moved on to the tortes and the pastries. We were discussing anything and everything we could think of that would allow us to avoid talking about the war against the Dragonni.

"So, there I was, stripped down to my golden bikini briefs, when my ex-owner showed up and challenged Vixen to a duel," Apollo was saying.

"True, but what that scumbag of a demon didn't realize is that I'm a snake shifter and even a demon's no real match against the venom in my fangs," Vixen said, letting out a rich laugh. "Taipans are far more deadly than most people think."

The doorbell rang and I excused myself as they continued to spin out their story.

I opened the door. Four tall guards were standing on the porch. They looked almost Amazonian, but I knew they weren't Amazons—not with incredible tattoos that I recognized as Celtic in origin. The knotwork ran up their arms and the shortest one must have been six feet. The women wore silver winged helmets and black trousers with silver tunics, and they were carrying dirks, sheathed at their sides.

A shiver ran up my spine. They carried heavy magic. It rippled over my arms, making the hair stand to attention. The magic wasn't chaotic like Pandora's energy, but whoever they were, these guards weren't lacking for defense.

"Yes, how can I help you?" Even as I asked the question, I knew. They were sent by the Banra-Sheagh.

The one in the frontmost position straightened her shoulders. "By order of the Banra-Sheagh, I command you in the name of Her Majesty to accompany me to Reímseil-Tabah, to stand before the Queen and answer the charges brought against you."

I stared at her, unable to speak. *Charges brought against me?* What the hell had I done? Finally, finding my tongue, I turned around and called for my mother.

CHAPTER FOUR

I HAD NO INTENTION OF LETTING THE GUARDS WALTZ through my front door, but they had other plans and before I realized what was happening, they pushed their way into the house, firmly but quietly. *Crap*, I thought. Even if I told them I was in the middle of a dinner party, they weren't likely to apologize and agree to come back later.

Herne and Kipa immediately bristled. The cousins stared at the guards with suspicion and Kipa stepped around me, inserting himself between us.

"Who are you and what do you want with my *mate?*" he said. "You do realize who I am?"

One of the guards blinked, but the one who had ordered me to come with them barely even showed a response.

"Yes, you're Kuippana, Lord of the Wolves, and this is Herne, Lord of the Hunt. We know who you are. Now step aside. We're here to escort Raven BoneTalker to Her Majesty, the Banra-Sheagh," the guard said.

Herne paled, but Kipa seemed oblivious to the guard's words.

"You're royal guards to the *Banra-Sheagh*?" Herne asked.

The guard shifted from one foot to the other. "Yes, and we have been ordered to take Raven BoneTalker into custody."

Herne gave me a quick look. "What the hell is going on, Raven?"

"I don't know—my mother warned me today that they were being sent, but she didn't know what they wanted either," I said. My irritation was rapidly giving way to fear and I felt myself spiraling down a dark hole. I felt like a child, facing a big, bad monster. "Mother, what do I do?" I asked as Phasmoria pushed herself in front of Kipa.

"What do you mean, showing up like this and threatening to arrest my daughter?" She shook her finger at the lead guard, her eyes flaring. The guard held firm.

"Do not interfere, Queen of the Bean Sidhe. This is not your affair."

"It most certainly is my affair," my mother said, gritting her teeth. "Raven is my daughter and you will treat her with respect."

"Very well, you may accompany us. But if she doesn't come with us now, we'll drag her out in chains." The guard reached for her dirk.

Attached to her belt were silver cuffs. At least they weren't iron. "I'll go, but my mother's coming with me."

"That is acceptable," the guard said. "Two allies may accompany you."

I turned to Kipa, who was scowling. "Will you come?" I glanced at Herne. "Will you ask Angel to lock up, and ask

Apollo to look after Raj and the ferrets in case we're detained?"

Herne's eyes filled with worry. "Of course," he said.

My mother turned to the guard. "Give us time to dress for the weather."

The guard grimaced but acquiesced. "Be quick about it."

Phasmoria hustled me toward the foyer closet. "We don't dare take more than a few minutes or they will drag you out in chains. Hurry now, grab a jacket. I'll explain to Herne what I told you as we go."

I rushed to the foyer closet.

Angel came up, frowning. "What's going on? Are you all right?"

"Truth? No. And I'm not sure. My mother, Kipa, and I have to leave." I gave her a quick hug. "Herne can explain a little after we're gone. Tell everyone I'll be back as soon as I can. Give Raj a hug from me and explain I didn't have time to say good-bye. He worries so much ever since what happened with Pandora."

"Of course—" She paused as the guards moved toward me.

"I have to go," I said, hastily slipping into a vintage military coat in steampunk style. Glancing back at Raj, who was frowning, I hustled the guards outside so he wouldn't see them if they decided to handcuff me. My mother and Kipa were waiting. Kipa reached for me, but the guard stepped between us.

"Do not touch the prisoner," she said. "Are you ready?"

"Ready," I said. I had my purse with me, but I had left all weapons behind. It wasn't a bright idea to show up at a palace packing heat, blades, or anything else.

The guard held out her hand and right in front of her, a swirling vortex opened. I blinked—whoever she was, she was powerful. As she and another guard flanked my sides, and the other two brought up the rear, behind Kipa and my mother, we stepped through the vortex, into the portal, and everything seemed to shimmer and shift around me.

PORTALS WERE ALWAYS DISCONCERTING, even if you were used to them, and this was no exception. The world fell out from beneath my feet and everything began to swirl, blending into a blur of stars and motion, of energy tracers and glowing clouds. I felt like I was falling, but then my feet hit the ground and I opened my eyes, cautiously looking around.

Overhead, the moon was shining down onto a field of snow that glistened as though it had diamonds sparkling on the surface. The trees were tall, black silhouettes against the night sky that stood like solemn guardians over the woodland. Everything looked like the forests back home, except for a subtle difference that I could feel on an energetic level. There was magic in the air, the feeling of electricity that swam around me like at the height of a lightning storm. As I stared up at the stars, they seemed to blaze a path across the night sky, a thousand suns almost blotting out the moon.

I caught my breath, spellbound. I loved being out under the stars, but even in the years before light pollution had become such an impediment to seeing the night sky, I had never seen anything quite like this.

"Where are we?" I asked.

One of the guards glanced at me. "You're in Reímseil-Tabah, which is near Caer Arianrhod."

I froze. Caer Arianrhod was the home of Arianrhod, the goddess of the Silver Wheel. She was the original ice queen, sitting on her throne of stars as her realm rolled through the universe. That the Banra-Sheagh's realm was close to Arianrhod's didn't bode well for me, if the Queen of the Ante-Fae was anything like the goddess. Arianrhod wasn't evil, but she was aloof and near untouchable; she was as far away from humans and Otherkin as were the Force Majeure.

"You must walk," the guard said.

I glanced at her. "How long have you worked for the Banra-Sheagh?"

She hesitated, then said, "For as long as I can remember. Time moves differently here, when it moves at all. I have always been a guardian of the realm. I will always be a guardian of the realm. That is my existence."

I thought about asking her what she did for fun, but I had the feeling my query wouldn't be appreciated. And she probably wouldn't even understand the question. I was quickly getting the feeling that the Banra-Sheagh's guards were almost automatons. I watched them as we walked along the trail. They moved in sync—they strode along in rhythm. Even their subtle head movements were aligned. They didn't look alike, but I realized that none of the other guards had spoken. Were they some sort of hive mind creature?

"What are your names?" I asked.

Without a blink, the guard who I had been talking to said, "We are guardians of the realm."

The others said nothing. In fact they didn't even seem to acknowledge I had asked them a question.

"But do you have a name? I'm Raven—"

"Yes, you are Raven." The guard turned her face forward again and I realized the conversation was over.

Kipa and Phasmoria were behind me, but the two guards who weren't flanking me had interjected themselves between us. I wanted to drop back to talk to them, but one glance at the guard who was willing to talk to me told me that it was better I didn't try.

The night was cold—the wind blowing past us in a constant stream—and I was grateful I had put on boots and a coat. The snow was up to my shins, and it was so crisp that when I stepped into a fresh patch, it crackled like thin ice, shattering into small poofs.

I had no frame of reference for how long we had been walking. My muscles weren't sore, but then again, I could walk for a long time without hurting. I wasn't terribly cold—I had chosen one of the jackets I had charmed into being perpetually warm. No matter how cold it got—within reason—I would stay toasty. I had begun making similar jackets for my friends as well. Or rather, I would ask them to bring me one of their jackets and I enchanted them. I wasn't exactly good at working a sewing machine, and I didn't even try to pretend. I had once attempted to make a poncho for Raj, and it had ended up looking like a potato sack.

As we approached a thicket of tall fir and cedar, I shivered. I didn't relish the idea of walking into a forest during the night, in a realm that I wasn't familiar with. I wished I had tried to memorize the position of the portal—then again, Kipa was here, and my mother, and both could dimension shift if necessary. I tried to relax as we ducked under the boughs that were bowing, laden with snow.

The moonlight was so dazzling that it splashed through the trees to light up the forest.

Once inside the woodland, the noise level increased. Here, the wind blew through the limbs of the trees, howling as it rattled against them. And noises from all sides bombarded us as we trudged along. The sound of creatures rushed through the undergrowth, and beneath it all, I heard a heavy beat that reminded me of a heartbeat. I could also hear our breathing in the brittle cold, but as I listened, I realized that the Banra-Sheagh's guards weren't breathing. I squinted at the guard to my right.

Her chest neither rose nor fell, and I realized there was no puff of white in front of her face like there was in front of mine. She *wasn't* breathing. For a moment I panicked—thinking that somehow a group of vampires had interceded and they were leading me into some sort of trap. But then I shook it off. Vampires wouldn't go to this trouble for me, for one thing. And for another—I didn't have a problem with any vamps, not that I knew.

I was debating whether to ask why they weren't breathing when we emerged from the forest to yet another clearing, long and narrow like a spit of land.

Up ahead, across another barren field filled with snow, stood a vast structure. It looked like it was made out of sticks and thorns, and it was the size of a football field, but the proportions seemed out of sync, and every time I looked at it, I saw something else, as though it had shifted once again. I wondered if it was actually blending and changing right before our eyes. Was it alive? Was it in another realm of its own? Confused, I looked away because watching it gave me a headache.

"The palace," the guard said, shattering the silence that surrounded us. Her voice hung in the air, echoing faintly, before it was snatched away by the wind.

"Is that where the Banra-Sheagh lives?" I asked. "It's hard to look at."

"That's because the palace lives in the realm of Chaos. You must—all of you—listen to me and obey my orders lest you harm yourself or your friends when entering the palace."

I glanced over my shoulder, trying to see Kipa's and Phasmoria's faces. Neither of them, however, were standing close enough to the moonlight for me to see.

"All right," I said. "What do you have to tell us?"

"When you enter the palace, do not step off of the center tiles. Three tiles wide are safe. We will go ahead of you and behind you to keep watch. If you try to run, you'll step into the territory of the shadows. The shadow demons are living, breathing creatures and they are hungry. If you step into their space, they will drain you dry without a second thought and we won't be able to help you."

My stomach lurched. "What if we accidentally stumble?"

"Then you pay the price," the guard said. "When we come to the doors, enter behind us and keep silent until you are spoken to. Even you, Lord of the Wolves. You may be a god, but this is not your territory, and while you cannot be killed, you can be taken prisoner. The goddess Arianrhod is the patron goddess of the Banra-Sheagh.

You *don't* want to provoke a war with the Lady Arianrhod."

Kipa said nothing. Neither did my mother. I glanced back at them and Kipa gave me a tight shake of the head, a warning look darting across his face.

"Anything else we should know?"

"Do not attempt escape. Again, you would be overwhelmed by the shadow demons, and no one would step in to help." The guard fell silent again.

My stomach was tied in knots by now, and again I wondered what I had done to warrant this level of treatment. That my mother didn't know, either, was disturbing. Phasmoria was usually on top of everything. I wondered if the Morrígan had said anything to her, but the best course of action seemed to indicate keeping my mouth shut.

As we approached the structure, I caught my breath yet again. It was beautiful in a jarring way, and I could now see that it was built out of vines and brambles that had entangled so much that no one in the world could detangle it. The vines overlapped and entwined so tightly that not even a flake of snow could penetrate the walls, and the thorns that jutted out from the walls were three and four feet long—dangerous spikes that gleamed under the moonlight.

There was one entrance that I could see, and the guards in front of the opening looked very much like the guards escorting me. In fact, now that I looked at them closely, I could see a resemblance between them all. They weren't exactly clones, but they were so alike they could have all been siblings.

As we approached, the guards at the door saluted my

guards. Without a word, they moved aside to let us in. I could feel an undercurrent of discussion, but if they had anything to say, they kept it below the surface.

Yep, I thought. *Hive mind.*

As we entered the structure, the chill from outside vanished and the path changed to tiles, three wide before falling into shadows. I could hear wisps of movement and whispers from the hidden recesses and they made me queasy.

The light shining on the tiles came from overhead, from some fixture that shone straight down. It was impossible to tell how wide the room was—the shadows on the sides were so thick they might as well have been mud.

The two guards flanking me immediately moved to the front. As I glanced over my shoulder, Kipa and Phasmoria were directly behind me now, with the latter guards marching behind them. Kipa caught my attention and gave me a short shake of the head that I assumed meant: obey them for now. My mother's look underscored Kipa's, so I turned around to follow the guards who huddled together in the center of the walkway.

I began to understand why they avoided the side edge of the floor, when the shadow demons—who looked suspiciously like shadow men except that they weren't so clear-cut humanoid—reached out as we passed by, trying to reach into the light toward us. But the moment their arms hit the blaze of light, and with a flurry of shrieks and groans, they jerked away from the light. That didn't seem to stop the rest of them from trying, though.

Nervously, I made sure to walk in the exact center, and any thought I had of trying to run off vanished. I couldn't tell how many of the shadow demons there were, but there were far too many for comfort.

We continued down the center tiles until, up ahead, the path ended at a pair of huge double doors. I steeled myself as the guards opened them and continued through.

As I stepped up to the doors and then in, I hadn't a clue what to expect, but we entered a massive chamber. It seemed to be lit by the same starlight as the walk outdoors had been, and here the subtle clamor coming from the shadow demons fell away. But the power here frightened me more than the shadow demons had, because up ahead—on a throne forged of silver and rubies and garnets and obsidian—sat the Banra-Sheagh, and she was more terrifying than anything I had ever seen.

CHAPTER FIVE

THE BANRA-SHEAGH WAS BOTH HIDEOUS AND WONDROUS.
A queen, she was—but she was a round creature,
reminding me of a ladybug covered with spikes the color
of the night sky. Glittering patches formed bright circles
on her exoskeleton. The tips of the spikes flared with a
sickly green color, occasionally melting into a shimmer of
yellow.

Her head was out of proportion with her body, small
and set atop the rounded exoskeleton. Her arms were
human enough, but there were four of them. She stood on
two short, stubby legs, but even so, she towered over
everyone in the room.

My lungs tightened and I realized I was barely breathing. She looked like a queen of monsters, and yet—as we
approached—I saw there was beauty there too.
Monstrous beauty, alien to anything I had ever seen, but
still mesmerizing.

The Banra-Sheagh wore a crown made of silver and
rubies, and her eyes glowed with a deep internal light.

Whether she was wearing clothes was debatable. It was difficult to tell whether her exoskeleton—for lack of a better word—was her outfit or her body. And I didn't think it was wise to ask.

Behind me, Phasmoria caught her breath. I didn't turn around but she reached forward, patting me on the shoulder. Grateful for her reassurance, though I wasn't sure she could do anything if the Queen had it in for me, I followed the guards to the foot of the throne.

The throne was its own monstrosity, made of silver and oak. I knew it was oak because the wood sang to me —the throne was alive in its own right.

The guards stopped and stood to the side, motioning for me to approach the bottom of the throne. I wasn't sure whether to bow or kneel or curtsey, so I opted for curtseying.

As I stood, I remained silent, waiting to take my cue from the Queen.

Kipa and my mother closed the distance between us, so they were right at my back, with Kipa on my right side, my mother on my left. We stood there for some moments, the Queen watching us like a spider might eye a fly caught in her web.

Then, without warning, she broke the silence. "Raven BoneTalker. You *are* Raven BoneTalker?"

After my mother gave me a little shove from the back, I said, "Yes, Your Majesty. I'm Raven BoneTalker."

"You are the bone witch, daughter of Curikan and Phasmoria, Queen of the Bean Sidhe, yes?" The Banra-Sheagh's voice was terrifyingly rich, echoing through the chamber. I wasn't sure what I had expected, but it wasn't that. Her voice was enough to make me want to dive under the bed.

"Yes," I squeaked out, wishing with everything that I was only one of the background players in this drama.

She stared at me for a moment, her gaze burning a hole through me. I tried to look her in the eyes, tried to stand my ground but after a few seconds of her scrutinizing me, I quickly turned my gaze to the side.

"I see you brought a god and your mother with you for support." She paused again.

I wasn't sure if she was waiting for an answer so I stammered out, "Yes, Your Majesty."

One of the guards standing near the throne leaned forward and whispered something in her ear—or where her ear should be. I couldn't tell if she actually *had* ears.

"Yes, I'm aware of that. Very well, bring him in."

Him? Him *who?* Wondering who she was talking about, I heard a noise from the darkness to her rear left and then a door opened, a shaft of light blazing in. Two figures walked through, approaching the throne. To my shock, I saw my father, followed by a man who looked far older than that. But there was a resemblance between them and I knew—without a shadow of a doubt—this was my grandfather Dougal. The question was, what were they doing here, in the realm of Reímseil-Tabah?

"RAVEN!" My father's face brightened and he held out his arms to me, but I held my ground. I wasn't sure what would happen to any of us if I ran to him for a hug.

The Queen, however, cleared her throat and said, "You

may acknowledge your father, child. And your grandfather."

Nervously, I glanced at Phasmoria, who looked as confused as I did. I slowly moved forward to hug my father. I whispered, "Da, what's this all about?"

He pressed his cheek against mine. "Just do as you are told."

I stepped back after kissing him on the cheek, waiting for the Queen to speak again. This couldn't just be some elaborate family reunion. I was smart enough to know that.

Shyly, I turned to my grandfather and curtseyed, who exuded more power than any of the Ante-Fae I had met except for the elders like Arachana or Blackthorn. He couldn't hold a candle to the Queen's power, of course, but still, it was enough to make me walk a cautious line.

Dougal looked older, and being Ante-Fae, those who looked older were incredibly ancient. I had no idea how long he had been alive. Nor, for that matter, if my grandmother was still around. In fact, I hadn't ever thought about it, but I had no clue about her—or my mother's parents. The realization made me feel weird now that I thought about it, but as I grew up, none of the familial relationships had been particularly in the forefront and it felt like an unspoken rule never to ask.

Dougal wasn't as tall as my father, but he was stocky with broad shoulders, and muscular, and his wavy red hair seemed a stark contrast to his scowling countenance. His eyes were pale gray, and they seemed to pierce right through me as I stood in front of him. A shock of violet ran through his hair—a lot like the purple running through mine—and I could see scrolling tattoos on his forearms beneath the shirt that he wore. They looked a lot like my own birthmarks.

He crossed his arms across his chest and looked me up and down. "You're a sturdy-looking lass, you are."

I wasn't sure what to say. "Hello, Grandfather."

"So you've a tongue, do you?" Dougal's voice was gruff, and somehow, he made me feel five years old. "Well, we'd best get started." He glanced over at the Banra-Sheagh. "Let's get this court underway."

"Very well," she said and right then, I knew that my grandfather had sway with the throne. She motioned for me to step back in front of her.

I did, darting a nervous glance at my mother. Phasmoria was scowling, and so was Kipa. I wanted to edge over to stand beside them, but I knew better than to defy the Queen.

"Dougal of the High Crags, do you claim this girl as your granddaughter?"

"I do swear by the flame and the sword, and declare Raven BoneTalker to be my granddaughter." He barked out his words, and I had the sudden vision of him in his natural form—as black as pitch, with blood-red eyes. The Black Dogs were a form of hellhound. For the first time since I'd been born, the idea made me nervous. My father had played with me when I was young—both in his two-legged form and in his dog form, and I loved dogs. But there was something intimidating about envisioning my grandfather in that state.

"Curikan, Black Dog of the Hanging Hills, do you claim this girl as your daughter?"

Okay, this was getting weird. I was beginning to feel

like I was being marked. The next thing you'd know, they'd be challenging Kipa to a pissing match.

"I do swear by the flame and the sword, and declare Raven BoneTalker to be my daughter," Curikan said. He spoke more softly than Dougal but as they stood there, side by side, I began to see the resemblance.

"Very well then, lineage is set on the paternal side. Phasmoria, Queen of the Bean Sidhe, do you claim this girl as your daughter?"

Phasmoria fidgeted and I could tell she was getting impatient. "Of course she's my daughter. She came out of my womb, she rested inside me for months and then clawed her way out to make her way in the world, like one of my children should."

"Lineage is claimed on the maternal side," the Banra-Sheagh said, ignoring my mother's irritation. "Phasmoria, Dougal has asked that you give up claim on the girl, so she may take up the mantle of Chatelaine of the House of Dougal. Her grandfather wishes her to move to Scotland and take her place in the life of the Highland Crags Black Dogs Clan."

"You have to be joking!" My mother wasn't laughing. Her eyes grew darker and her voice was quickly edging up to Bean Sidhe level.

I started to gasp but the Banra-Sheagh turned back to me. "Raven BoneTalker, think carefully before you speak. This offer would mitigate your crimes in the Court of the Banra-Sheagh."

Unable to keep my tongue, I burst out with, "What the hell did I do? You say I'm accused of crimes. Well, what *crimes* have I committed?"

The Queen stared me down, looking absolutely unimpressed with my outburst. "Hold your tongue, girl. Very well, we'll leap to that portion of this trial. Tryx, read aloud the list of accusations against Raven BoneTalker."

A guard who looked almost exactly like the one who had talked to me stepped forward and held out a scroll, unrolling it, then raising her head after she spent a moment reading it.

"This list comprises the list of crimes against the bone witch, Raven BoneTalker, are these: One, the accused has befriended numerous human and Fae, and has not taken care to secret herself or her life in any way. Two, the accused has chosen to immerse herself in human society, therefore casting herself into the Exosan encampment. Three, the accused is entertaining a dalliance with one of the gods. Four, and most damning, the accused remains friends with Ember Kearney, a tralaeth who has openly admitted to murdering Blackthorn, one of the Ancient Ante-Fae. She is keeping company with the enemy.

"Let it be known that should Raven BoneTalker not break off any communications with the modern world and return to the bosom of her family, taking her rightful place as Chatelaine of the Clan of the Highland Crags, she will be forever cast out of the world of our people, and forever be considered pariah to our world. None of the Ante-Fae will speak to her, nor accept her presence in their midst. None of the Ante-Fae will lift a hand to help her, even should her very life be in danger."

I swayed, trying to take in everything, but the next moment, my mother stood by my side. She placed her hand on my shoulder and I straightened, grateful for her presence. I had no clue what to say, but my mother didn't suffer from the same problem.

"I will *never* willingly give up claim on my daughter. She will always be the daughter of the Bean Sidhe, who I might add are *all* Ante-Fae, and we *all* consort with the gods. The Morrígan is my goddess, and Cerridwen and Arawn are my daughter's gods, and they alone may decree what she is allowed to do." Phasmoria's voice echoed through the chamber loud and clear, leaving no mistake as to how she felt about the matter.

My father glanced at me, and I stared back at him. He was always the one who taught me to care about humans and to care about the people around me. Now, he was willing to stand here and listen to this garbage?

I had to speak. "Da, how can you hold your tongue? *You're* the one who taught me how to care about others, regardless of their heritage. You are the most tender-hearted man I've met and I always respected you for that!" I ignored the guard, ignored the Queen, and stomped my way over to Curikan.

But he merely stared at the floor. "I'm sorry, my child, but…the past month has taught me other ways. I never understood why my family—my father—was like he is. Now I do, and I have to say, I misunderstood my father's messages all these years. It's vital to keep the heritage alive, to keep to tradition."

I couldn't believe what I was hearing. My father was throwing away everything he had believed in. I whirled to face Dougal. "*You* did this! What did you say to him? What did you do to turn him into a clone of you? You're nothing but a monster."

My grandfather's eyes flashed. Without warning, he reached out and slapped me hard across the cheek. "How dare you speak to me like that!"

"Don't you dare hit my daughter," Phasmoria shouted, storming over.

With her beside me, I felt brave enough to respond, my cheek stinging. "I'll speak to you any way I like. My father is—*was*—one of the kindest men I've ever known and I looked up to him. I *respected* him. And you go and do this? What did you use to threaten him? Because the Curikan I know and love would never willingly turn his back on his beliefs."

"Raven, stop, please—*little bird.*" For a moment, the father I remember shone through the cool demeanor, and then the light in his eyes faded and his face hardened again. "Raven, respect your grandfather. Apologize."

I turned back to my mother. "What's wrong with him?" I pleaded. I couldn't bear to see my father acting like this.

Phasmoria motioned to Kipa. "Watch her for me. Dougal, Curikan—we need to talk. Now." She turned to the Banra-Sheagh. "I demand a recess."

The Queen paused, looking like she was about to say no, but then my mother glowered at her and the Banra-Sheagh let out a sigh. "Very well. Be quick about it."

My mother led Curikan and Dougal off toward the corner.

I turned to Kipa, feeling lost and afraid. He held out his arms and I slid into his embrace, resting my head on his shoulder as he gently rubbed my back.

"What's going on?" I whispered.

"I'm not sure, but I don't like any of it. Don't worry, love. You'll be fine. I'll make certain of it, and so will your mother. We won't let anything happen to you. I promise you that." He glanced up, over my head, scowling as he stared at the Banra-Sheagh.

A few moments later, Phasmoria and the men returned. She turned to the Banra-Sheagh. "I claim the right to speak to my daughter. You cannot refuse me."

The Banra-Sheagh looked like a storm was brewing. "Very well."

Phasmoria motioned to me and to Kipa and we followed her out of sight of the throne.

"What's going on?" I burst out, but she shushed me.

"Your grandfather has finally got what he wants—he's got his hooks in your father. He's been out to lure your father back into the fold ever since Curikan ran away from the family hundreds of years ago. It's not a magical spell, not a charm, but apparently, Dougal convinced the Banra-Sheagh that Curikan should be punished for leading you into an Exosan lifestyle. When he heard about Blackthorn's death, it proved the final catalyst, especially since word got around that you work with Herne and Ember."

I stared at her. "You mean that this was all a plot to drag my father back to the family clan? Why involve me?"

"Because Dougal wants you, too. As far as I can see, he stirred the pot with the Banra-Sheagh, and then once that was set, he convinced Curikan that the one way to keep you from being labeled pariah was for him to knuckle under. He dangled you like a carrot. Your father's trying to prevent you from being cast out of our people. They don't dare cast me out, or any of the Bean Sidhe, given we're under the Morrígan's direct orders, but your father's now afraid you'll become a casualty in this scheme that he believes the Banra-Sheagh thought up."

Phasmoria leaned against a wall. "His concerns are understandable, if misguided."

"I won't do it! My friends are all Exosan—"

"Yes, well, apparently the Banra-Sheagh took what Dougal said and ran with it. She's planning to banish every Ante-Fae who identifies as such from ever being part of our culture again. This is the point in history where the Exosan become a separate division of the Ante-Fae race. I imagine, though I'm not sure, that she'll declare the Exosan to be enemies of the crown. Even if we get you out of here, you'll be considered pariah, and they'll be in worse trouble if they communicate with you. I doubt if there will be a war, but the old guard are committed to keeping tradition alive, even when those traditions are to our detriment." Phasmoria glanced over her shoulder.

"Then I'm damned if I do and damned if I don't. If I give in to my grandfather, I'll live the rest of my life under his fist, cooped up in a massive house in Scotland, and I'll lose you. How on earth did my father think this would encourage me to—"

"He thought it would keep you safe. Your father's sweet but he can be very short-sighted." She straightened. "Raven, this is up to you. I'll stand behind you, regardless of your choice. If you want me to set you free so you can become the Chatelaine, I will."

Kipa turned me around. "Choose what you feel is best in your heart. We'll have to part if you choose to return to your family clan. I doubt your grandfather considers the gods a good choice for a paramour."

"Dougal has a strange hatred for the gods," Phasmoria said. "He feels they're worthless."

"I don't have to think about it," I said, my heart dropping. I wasn't willing to give up my mother, my life, my love, or my friends. I loved Curikan and I was proud of being Ante-Fae, but I wasn't going to turn my back on everything my father had taught me because my grandfather was pissed off. "I choose you, Mother. I choose to stay with Kipa. I choose my friends. I choose everything and everyone I love…except…I guess, my father." I turned to Phasmoria. "What will you do? You're Exosan, too."

"As I said, she doesn't dare mess with the Bean Sidhe, given we could bring the Morrígan down on her ass and regardless what the Queen thinks, there's nothing she can do that will prevail over my black-hearted winged goddess."

I dug in my heels. "I'm not giving up Trinity and Vixen and everyone I know, even if they can never talk to me again. Ember killed Blackthorn because he was going to torture her—he was a vile, wretched creep." I was young and part of the world, and I saw no problem with intermingling with other races and spirits.

"Are you sure? There may be no turning back," Phasmoria said.

I thought for a moment. "I'm sure."

"Very well, let's return. You'll have to tell the Banra-Sheagh, and be prepared for her to blow up and sound like she's going to rip you apart."

We returned to the others and slowly took our place in front of the throne.

I stood at attention, staring up at the Banra-Sheagh.

"Well?" came her imperious question.

"You leave me no choice." I turned to my father and Dougal. "Neither do you. I have no choice but to exile myself from our people. I choose my mother. I choose my friends. I choose my lover. I choose everything that is now my life, because I'm loyal to all of them. If the rest of the Ante-Fae can never speak to me again, then so be it. I choose to remain Exosan, and I formally disavow my father, my grandfather, and my heritage."

As I spoke, the Queen grew very quiet, and out of the corner of my eye, I could see my grandfather fuming. The next moment, my father let out a cry, but my grandfather grabbed him by the shoulders and shook him.

"She made her choice," Dougal said. He turned to me. "Raven BoneTalker, daughter of Phasmoria, you are no longer a member of the Clan of the Highland Crags Black Dogs. You are no longer my granddaughter." He gave my father a hard shake that made me want to smack him a good one.

My father turned to me and, with tear-stained eyes, whispered, "Raven BoneTalker, you are no longer my daughter. Our bonds are forever broken. You will return to me the money I paid for your house."

Phasmoria, hands on hips, faced my grandfather and my father. "This is your fault—this is your doing. I hope you lie awake at night tortured by it. Because you both deserve every heartbreak in the world this brings."

I met my father's eyes one last time, then turned away, feeling oddly free. So much had gone south, but I had made my choice. And now, I had to find a new way to reinvent my history.

CHAPTER SIX

AFTER THAT, THE REST OF THE MEETING BECAME A BLUR.
My father tried to say something but my grandfather
jerked him back. My mother hustled me back in front of
the Queen, who stood, then turned her back to me. One
by one, all the guards did the same, and finally, my grandfather and then my father.

"Hear me, Banra-Sheagh, and the Court of the Ante-
Fae," my mother said, her voice reverberating against the
walls.

Slowly, the Queen turned around again. "Speak, Phasmoria, Queen of the Bean Sidhe."

"I am proud of my heritage. But I claim my daughter's
side and as of this moment, I renounce my ties to the
Ante-Fae. I will make certain that the Morrígan hears of
what happened this day. I turn my back on *you*, the Banra-
Sheagh, and your entire court. You have no power over
me or my daughter."

And with that, she slid her arm through mine and—
with Kipa behind us—led us out of the throne room. As

soon as we were in the outer chamber, my mother motioned for us to lean close to her. "Close your eyes, Raven," she said.

Kipa seemed to know what she was doing, because he wrapped his arms around both of us. My mother closed her eyes and the next thing I knew, we were on the astral, though I wasn't sure what realm we were in. Another shift, and I opened my eyes, and we were home, in front of my front door. I took a look around, realized where we were, and burst into tears.

As we entered the house, I saw to my surprise that Ember and Herne and Angel were still there, along with Vixen, Apollo, and Trinity. Raj was asleep, curled up beside Angel. When I stepped into the living room he woke, jerking his head so fast he almost headbutted her, and then he bounded off the sofa, racing over to me.

I fell to my knees, opening my arms so that he landed smack in the center, almost knocking me over. I wrapped my arms around his shoulders and planted several kisses on his head. "Raven's home. Don't worry—Raven's home and she's safe." I knew he had been scared—I could feel the energy rolling off of him.

"Raj was so worried," Raj whispered, low enough so the others couldn't hear him. Of everyone who was there, only Kipa, my mother, Ember, and Angel knew he could talk. "Raj thought those bad people took Raven away from him."

"It's okay. Raven's okay," I said, wishing I was telling the truth. To be honest, I had no clue what being excommunicated from the Ante-Fae community would mean. I did know that Vixen and Apollo—any of the Ante-Fae, for that matter—were walking on thin ice if they continued to communicate with me, and I owed them the knowledge. They had to make an informed decision.

My mother paced, a scowl lining her face. Kipa looked angry too, and I knew that I was buzzing with nerves as bad as a beehive.

"What happened?" Ember said, a worried look on your face. "And don't tell us nothing—it's apparent from all three of you that something big went down."

"Oh, it went down all right," I said. I dropped into the rocking chair. "This concerns all of you, in a way. Ember, first, you should know the Banra-Sheagh is pissed at you for killing Blackthorn."

"Don't tell me there's a bounty on my head," Ember said, groaning.

"No, but you're considered persona non grata among the non-Exosan Ante-Fae." I grimly turned to Vixen, Apollo, and Trinity. "And you three…the Banra-Sheagh has declared me pariah. Any of the Ante-Fae who communicate with me are subject to losing their status, too. I've been kicked out of the Ante-Fae community." My heart dropped as I added, "I'll understand if you decide you can't talk to me anymore. I truly do." I bit my lip, hanging my head.

"What she's not telling you is that she was kicked out because she refused to stop being Ember's friend—because Ember killed Blackthorn in self-defense. And she refused to return to Scotland and live with her grandfather and father." Kipa's eyes narrowed. "I wanted to wipe that smug look off the bitch's face."

Ember gasped, stiffening. "Is this true? You were kicked out because of your association with *me*?"

I gave her a shrug. "Yeah. I think I'm being used as the scapegoat to remind the Exosan where their true allegiances are expected to fall. The Queen is feeling threatened by the Exosan's forays into the human communities. Anyway, my father and grandfather have disowned me. I won't be able to come to the Burlesque A Go-Go anymore, or I'll put all of your customers in danger," I said to Vixen.

Shaking my head, I sat down. "It's hard to take in. I still feel like this is a nightmare. I can accept my grandfather cutting ties with me, that doesn't surprise me. But my father…" I looked up at my mother, stricken. I loved my father and he had always championed me. "I feel like he kicked the world out from under me."

Phasmoria muttered something under her breath and sat down next to me. "I think your grandfather must be holding something over his head."

I leaned into her shoulder. "Thank you for standing by me."

"You're my daughter. Of course I stand by your side. I couldn't be there while you were growing up, but I never once abandoned you in my heart." She wrapped her arm around me. "I believe you're right, however. The Banra-Sheagh is terrified of the Ante-Fae growing too close to the human world, and so she is making an example of you to show the Exosan where their allegiances should lie. That's a dangerous game, though, since it can all too easily backfire."

A wave of exhaustion swept over me as I sat there and

I found it hard to even talk. My thoughts were such a whirl, I couldn't sort them out.

"Everyone, thank you for staying. But I need to sleep now," I said, still staring at the floor.

Ember gave me a long hug, whispering in my ear. "I'm so sorry, Raven. I never meant my actions to backfire onto you."

"You were protecting yourself. Blackthorn was dangerous and had the upper hand. You did what you had to do. I never once blamed you or felt you did the wrong thing," I whispered back. "And I won't abandon my friendship with you because you killed him to save yourself."

Ember gazed into my eyes, and even now, I could see that she was changing and growing into the goddess she would soon become. "I won't forget this. Maybe, when I go through the Gadawnoin—when I am a goddess—I'll be able to talk to the Banra-Sheagh and settle matters."

I wanted to tell her not to bother, that any such ritual would be fraught with nuances that could endanger the relationship between the Ante-Fae and the Fae, but that could wait for later. Instead, I kissed her cheek—and Angel's—and gave Herne a hug, then watched them leave.

Vixen, Trinity, and Apollo were still sitting in the living room. Vixen was gathering their things, but stopped for a moment to say, "I count you a friend. I will *always* count you a friend. The Banra-Sheagh has been trying to close down my club for years. This time, she'll probably excommunicate me as well but I honestly don't care. Most of my clientele are Exosan and most feel cut off from the monarchy, anyway. We're all a little bit of a rebel, aren't we?" They laughed then, a rich throaty laugh that sounded like a lounge singer who had been smoking too much.

Apollo, his golden hair hanging halfway down his back, gave me a quick hug. "Vixen speaks for me as well. I don't care about being on the outs with the old guard. I'm here if you need me."

"Can you drop by my house to talk about that case that I mentioned?" Vixen asked.

"Around one tomorrow work for you?" I asked, opening my phone's schedule.

They checked their own schedule. "One would be good. Come to lunch. Kipa, you're invited if you like, as well." And with that, they left, nodding to Trinity, who merely waggled his fingers at them.

Once Vixen and Apollo left, I turned back to Trinity. He was slipping his coat on, and as he headed for the door, he stopped to give me a warm hug, which was a surprise, given he seldom hugged anybody.

"Never let the bastards get you down," he said with a laugh. "You know I don't give a flying fig about the Queen. I have no desire to be part of the court. I'll be here for you, Raven. Know that. Whenever you need anything, just call me." He was the cutest goth boy when he smiled—he was older than I was but he looked young, and he had that timeless sense to him. For a while Kipa had been jealous of him, but we had moved beyond that.

I *did* find Trinity attractive, but I liked the friendship we had and when sex intervened, everything shifted, regardless of best efforts to keep the status quo. Also, the fact that Trinity was half incubus was problematic, and then—the most important reason to stay friends instead of lovers—Kipa. Kipa and I were exclusive.

At the beginning, I had realized that Kipa had always played the field—except for once. Yet he expected me to keep myself for him. That shifted quickly enough, and he understood that whatever we decided on went both ways, so we opted for exclusive.

But then, he told me about his one great love. She'd been human and he had stayed with her until the end. And he also told me that I was only the second woman he'd ever been with who had made him want to commit. We said the "L" word—and settled into seeing where the relationship was going to take us.

A fling with Trinity wouldn't be worth jeopardizing everything I had with Kipa. I had no clue if we'd be together forever, but for now, we were good. We fit together. He was the only man who had ever challenged me in the way he did.

After Trinity left, Phasmoria told us to go to bed. "I'll clean up. Don't worry about anything. It's been a long and difficult evening. You go rest."

Kipa fell asleep quickly, but my mind wouldn't shut up. After a while, I slid out of bed and into my robe and joined my mother in the kitchen. She had finished putting everything away, and the dishes were in the dishwasher. She poured herself a cup of tea as I entered the room.

"Can't sleep?"

I shook my head. "I'm exhausted but…"

"The adrenaline rush hasn't worn off?"

"Right again." I peeked in the fridge and found two slices of pizza that were still good. "Mind if I eat these?"

"They're yours. It's your house." She added, "Let me warm you some milk. It will help you sleep."

I carried the pizza into the living room where I sat

down, crossing my legs on the sofa. Raj had fallen asleep in his bed. I had bought a massive dog bed—the biggest I could find—for him, and he was curled under his blanket, snoring softly. As my mother joined me, she opened the curtains so we could watch the snow falling. The lights of the tree twinkled with a soft glow, and Phasmoria turned off the rest of the lights so we were sitting by the glow of the tree and the steady flicker of flames in the gas fireplace.

She motioned for me to drink my milk, into which she'd sprinkled some cinnamon and a hint of sugar. "Drink up. It will do you good."

I leaned back against the sofa, cradling the warm mug in my hand. "This is good. Da used to make me a drink like this when I was little."

"No, I was the one who made it for you. While I was still there, during the years the Morrígan gave me to be with you." She stretched out in the recliner. "This is lovely. You have good taste in decor."

I finished the milk, then picked up the pizza. Pausing, I asked, "Why do you think Da turned his back on me? I never thought he'd abandon me like…" I stopped.

"You were going to say like *I* did, right?" Phasmoria held my gaze. "It's okay. You know why I had to leave, but I know it felt like I abandoned you. But Curikan, he was always there for you. It has to feel like he betrayed you."

I sighed and ate a few bites of the pizza. I loved cold spaghetti too. I was odd like that.

"Yeah, it does. He set me up to believe he would always be there. You've always been there, but I never expect you to be—and I don't mean that in a bad way. I understand your life. That you schedule time to be with me means a lot. I know that you only have so much free time and when you choose me, I feel like I matter. But Da was my foundation. He's the one who was supposed to take my side. And damn him, he fucked up. He pulled the rug out from under my feet and didn't catch me when I fell."

Phasmoria looked ready to cry. I never saw her with tears in her eyes and the sight scared me more than when she was angry.

"I don't know what happened, Raven. But I *will* be talking to Curikan at the first available chance. I'll get to the bottom of things." She sputtered, "I know I've been the bad cop over the years, and he's always been the good cop, so I'm not sure how to behave now that the roles are reversed. It's going to take me some time to adjust."

I set my plate on the coffee table. "Tell me about the Banra-Sheagh. How old is she? Who gave her the power of command? Why didn't I know about her before?" I suddenly felt full of questions, but the one I wanted to ask the most—"Why did you throw me away?"—I couldn't, because my father wasn't here. And this time, the question was aimed at him.

Phasmoria sighed. "That's a lot of material to go over, given how late it is. Why don't we talk about it tomorrow? For now, you need your rest."

I yawned. The milk was making me sleepy. Frowning —hot milk had never had quite that powerful of effect on me before—I reluctantly agreed. "I am tired. And now I think I can sleep."

"Good. I'd tuck you in but I don't want to startle Kipa. Go to bed and we'll talk in the morning." She walked me down the hall, her arm around my shoulders. "I'll lock up and make certain the wards are set. Meanwhile, go to sleep and don't think about what happened. There's no use in borrowing more trouble than we already have."

I slipped into my room and flung my robe on the vanity bench. I stared at the snoring god in my bed for a moment and then, with relief that he was there, I slid beneath the comforter and snuggled up to him, wrapping my arms around him as I sought comfort in dreamless sleep.

THE NEXT MORNING, my mother was finishing up preparations on a massive breakfast for all of us, and she had fed the ferrets and Raj, who was happily slurping up another bowl of cat food. Kipa was helping her when I trudged in, still wearing my robe.

"That's too rich to feed him much of. He needs to get that for a treat." I paused, not wanting to sound ungrateful. "Thank you, though. I appreciate the extra sleep." I glanced at the clock. It was almost nine-thirty. Yawning, I added, "I can't believe I slept so late."

Kipa set down the platter of waffles on the table and swung me into his arms, giving me a long, lazy kiss. "You needed the rest. Your mother and I have bacon and eggs and coffee and waffles ready, and fruit, if you want it. Go dress and breakfast will be ready when you return."

I padded back to the bedroom. I had taken a shower the night before, so—given the rumbling of my stomach—I decided to forgo another one.

I slid into a short black tulle petticoat, then a flared pleather skirt, a sheer black long-sleeved blouse, and then a purple corset over the top. I was wearing a garter belt so

I added fishnet stockings, then platform patent leather knee-high boots that had so many buckles and chains they jingled when I walked. I brushed out my hair, did my face, and when I reentered the dining room, my mother and Kipa turned, staring at me.

"How did I get to have such a gorgeous daughter?" Phasmoria asked.

"Forget gorgeous daughter—I have a beautiful girl-friend," Kipa said, waggling a piece of bacon at her.

"Knock it off, you two. Thanks, I know you mean it but I also know you're trying to cheer me up. I dress like I feel, and right now, I feel decked out for war against the Banra-Sheagh." I stabbed a couple waffles with my fork and dropped them on my plate. Then, I added eight rashers of bacon, a scoop of scrambled eggs, and I filled my dessert bowl with the fruit salad. "Caffeine?" I asked plaintively.

Kipa jumped up and a moment later he returned with a steaming mug filled with peppermint mocha. "Here you go."

"Thank you." I leaned back. They were acting oddly today. "Look, I appreciate your efforts. I do. Yes, I'm in a state of shock about everything that went down last night, but…it's not like she ordered a bounty on my head. My father abandoned me and I'm kicked out of the special club I was born into. Am I upset? Yes, but it's not like when Pandora decided to use me as a guinea pig for how much pain she could inflict. Please, relax and enjoy break-fast with me?"

Phasmoria glanced at Kipa. "I told you this would be her answer."

"You were right," he said, laughing, and handed her a five-dollar bill.

"You bet money on how I'd react?"

I tried to scowl but the fact that my mother and boyfriend were taking bets on my reactions hit me as absurd but fitting, and I was already feeling on edge. I burst into laughter, which was quickly followed by a bout of tears, and then I managed to get hold of myself as Kipa handed me a tissue and I wiped my eyes and nose.

"Okay, maybe I *am* hypersensitive," I added after I took a long sip of my coffee.

"Better out than in," Kipa said. "That goes for food poisoning and for emotions, too."

Phasmoria gave him a long look. "Can we please not talk about vomiting at the table?"

Kipa lowered his eyes. "Yes, ma'am."

I took a long breath, then exhaled slowly. "All right, so my father's withdrawn his support. He's asked for all the money back he spent on me for the house over the years—"

"I've taken care of that," Phasmoria said. "I hope they choke on it."

"Thank you," I whispered. "You've come to my rescue a lot over the past year or so. I don't know how to show you how much I appreciate it."

"You don't have to. You needed help. I'm your mother. If this had been something incredibly stupid or flighty, I'd let you fend for yourself for a while before intervening, but it's neither. I find it incredibly vulgar of your father to ask for the money. But I know Dougal put him up to it. He may be Ante-Fae, but he's also a Scot and they can be…"

"Cheap?" I asked, laughing.

"I was going to say frugal, but yes, that's the gist of it." Phasmoria handed me the maple syrup.

I doused my waffles with it. "Good thing I picked up more syrup yesterday."

"So, what are you going to do today?" Phasmoria asked. "I'm sorry your party was such a bust last night. If I had known they were going to show up during it, I would have suggested you postpone it."

"Doesn't matter now," I said with a shrug. "I'm going over to Vixen's at one to see what kind of a mess they've gotten themselves into now. But Vixen's usually both careful and smart. If they're worried about a friend, I'm guessing the problem doesn't have an easy fix. Vixen doesn't exaggerate."

"Are you working at the shop today?" Kipa asked.

I glanced at the calendar. "No, it's Sunday and Llew has started closing the shop early on Sundays. He's open for about four hours now. But he's expanded his Saturday hours for classes and workshops on tarot, crystal magic, all sorts of things."

"That's enterprising of him," my mother said, handing me the platter of waffles. "Here, there are two left. You want them?"

I took one. "You can have the other, thanks. And yes, he's savvy. Business is going up and with the fears about the Dragonni, he's offering protection magic classes and talisman making classes. People are flocking to them in droves. Regardless of how approachable the dragons think they're being, there's a sizable section of the population who are afraid of them."

"With good reason," Kipa said. "That's smart of Llew. I

got to like him when we were helping out his friends. How are they doing, by the way?"

"Rain and Marigold? They're all right. It will take awhile before they fully rebound from that mess, but they're doing better and so are the kids." I finished my breakfast. "I should do the dishes before I head out—"

"Nonsense," Phasmoria said, jumping up. "I'll take care of them. I thought I'd stay around for a couple of days, if you don't mind."

"I don't mind," I said, but I knew that—as casual as she sounded—she wasn't hanging around to chat. She was worried about me, and she wasn't going to leave me alone till she knew I was all right. And for once, I appreciated the support.

CHAPTER SEVEN

VIXEN OWNED SEVERAL PROPERTIES, AND CURRENTLY THEY were all being rented except for their sprawling house on the outskirts of Redmond. The house wasn't a cookie-cutter McMansion, but rather a renovated ranch house like you might find in the Old Bridle Trails neighborhood.

I parked in the curving driveway and headed up the sidewalk. The lawn was covered with snow, but come spring, it would be a riot of colors. Another tidbit that few people knew about Vixen—they were an avid gardener and spent many an evening out in the yard, tenderly transplanting flowers and bulbs with an almost Zen-like focus.

As I rang the bell, Camilla—Vixen's new housekeeper —opened the door. She was dressed in a maid's uniform, and her long blond hair was caught up in a chignon, pinned behind a white cap. She was human, that much I could tell, and about thirty years old. She took my name and quietly led me through the maze of rooms and hall-ways to a back parlor.

The house was five thousand square feet and picture-perfect. The gourmet kitchen was swathed in muted tones of gray and quartz. The high ceilings were painted white, and the light fixtures were all crystal and chrome. Everything was refined and elegant, totally unlike what you would expect from such a flamboyant personality. But I knew one thing about Vixen that very few others—save for Apollo—did. Vixen needed a space in which to decompress and they valued their privacy. Vixen's home was sacrosanct against uninvited drop-ins.

The house was built in a U-shape, with two wings, and a courtyard between them. The parlor overlooked the courtyard, with a gas fireplace that sizzled and popped, and the room was decorated in a deep blue, with knick-knacks made of mother-of-pearl that shimmered as the flames reflected against them.

Vixen was sitting in a rocking chair, watching the fire as Camilla escorted me into the room. Today they were dressed in a green velvet bedjacket, a pair of peach lounging pajamas, and they looked very much like a rich retro housewife at a 1950s party. Very Joan Crawford, or Bette Davis.

They glanced over and a smile spread across their otherwise taciturn face. "Raven, you came! Here, sit across from me. That's a new sofa and it's so comfortable I'm thinking of having a bed made by the same company."

I smiled back at them. "It's lovely. The whole room is gorgeous. I don't think I've seen this room before." I had been over to Vixen's other places a number of times, but this house, I'd only been in once. I took the offered seat and leaned back, still feeling weary. Although I had slept in, the events of the night before were still hitting me hard.

"You look tired, girl." Vixen motioned to Camilla. "Fix us some peppermint tea, please." To me they asked, "Have you had lunch?"

"I had a late breakfast, thanks. But go ahead if you're hungry."

"Tea, and a tray of those mint cookies—the chocolate mint wafers." They motioned for Camilla to leave, and the housekeeper ducked into a brief curtsey and left the room. "So, how are you doing today? And don't BS me." They brought out what at first looked like an old-fashioned cigarette holder—one of those long affairs that the glamour girls used to use, but when I looked closer, it was actually a vape pen. Vixen still liked to smoke, but now they didn't bother most people with the smoke.

I let out a sigh. "I don't know, to be honest. I'm still processing. This whole mess came out of the blue—it struck like lightning. I'm heartbroken my father actually listened to Dougal, and I feel blindsided. If my mother hadn't warned me earlier yesterday that something was going down, I would have been totally caught off guard."

"You sound bitter," Vixen said.

"Of *course* I'm bitter. I got thrown under the bus in a game that isn't even my fight." I frowned. "You have to admit, it's a stretch to ding me for being Ember's friend. It's a stretch to try to force me to give up being friends with someone who killed one of the Ante-Fae in self-defense. What the hell was she supposed to do? Let him kill her…or worse. And believe me, I know what worse can be, thanks to Pandora."

I jumped up, waving my arms. "I love being one of the

Ante-Fae, but let's face it, Vixen—our kind can be terri-fying and ruthless. Blackthorn had it in for Ember ever since the first time they met. She told me about him. I wish Herne could have gotten to him first. The Banra-Sheagh wouldn't dare chastise a god."

"Sit down, love, you're going to give yourself a stroke." Vixen motioned me back to my seat. "You're absolutely correct, of course. Which is why I'm going to put up a notice that I won't be keeping you out of my club, and that anybody who chooses to enter may be subject to retaliation from the Queen—"

"You can't do that," I said, straightening up. "You can't jeopardize your club for me."

"It's more than that," Vixen said, frowning. "If I keep you out, I'll be tacitly endorsing what the Banra-Sheagh did. It sends a message and I don't want to send that message. And…" They paused, letting out a long sigh. "I realized that I'm doing the same thing to Trinity. I've never fully taken the time to know him. I went on appear-ance only. So I've invited him to the club to have a talk and to apologize."

Too shocked to respond, I suddenly remembered why I had come to visit. In the surprise of Vixen taking a stand against the Queen's ruling, I had lost the thought right out of my head. "Okay, then, you said you had a friend you think is possessed?"

"Yes, that's right. So, here's the problem. My friend Lenny—he's human—runs the club's website. He's one of those people you can set your clock by. He's reliable to a T. Never once have I had a problem with him in the past ten years."

I could feel something coming. "But?"

"Yes. But…the past couple of weeks he's been acting oddly. He's gone from sunny and annoyingly cheerful to surly and downright obnoxious. He's late on updates and that never happens, and in the space of less than a week, I'm thinking of changing computer techs. And I never expected to be saying that." The pain on Vixen's face was tangible.

"Lenny's been a good friend, hasn't he?"

Vixen gave me a reluctant shrug. "Yeah. I helped him through the death of his wife. I helped him avoid foreclosure after the medical bills for her cancer wiped him out. He's a contractor, so he didn't have catastrophic insurance. I put him on my payroll so that if—the gods forbid —he gets ill, that won't happen again. You don't know how many late-night calls we worked our way through during that time, and because of all that, we bonded in a way I never thought I could with a human."

"You love him," I said, holding their gaze. "Like a brother, maybe, but—"

"Maybe like a child, girl. Even among my kind, I'm unique. Usually, snake shifters bear live young, but I'm gender-fluid in the strongest of ways. My gender shifts with my moods, which is actually quite delightful. But I was born unable to breed. I can't bear young, nor can I impregnate anyone. I'm unique. One of a kind. My heritage will die with me." A look in their eyes told me that Vixen was lonely—in a way most people could never understand.

"We're all unique," I murmured. I had known about Vixen's gender-bending, but I hadn't realized they were sterile.

"Most, yes, but most of the Ante-Fae can engender

young. I cannot. So I adopt. I gather my family in other ways. Apollo is part of my family—my lover and my mentee. You're part of my family, a delicious young witch. Before you ever worry, I would never overstep my boundaries with you because you seem so very young to me. And Lenny is part of my family as well. Unexpected, but not unwelcome." Vixen sat back, crossing their arms. "I'm unsure of what to do about this. I tried to ask him what was wrong, but he snapped at me."

"Is there anything else that makes you think he might be possessed? He could just be having a bad month. Or maybe he's on a new medication—"

"I know the signs of possession, child."

"Well, I'll have to meet him to tell whether he's being possessed. I might be able to uncover something with my cards, but for a definitive answer, you have to bring us together." I held up my bag. "You want me to pull a few cards?"

Vixen perked up. "Yes, please. Meanwhile, I'm going to try to figure out a logical reason for you two to meet."

While they thought, I pulled out my cards and began to shuffle, keeping the nebulous Lenny in mind. I usually didn't need a picture to go off of, given I was so attuned to the cards. But it would have been much easier if Lenny was here.

I shuffled the cards, keeping the situation in mind, then laid them out. I turned over the first card, then the others. The eight of Chalices, then the Death card. The third was the two of Discs. The fourth and fifth were the High Priestess and the Tower cards. And the sixth card—the outcome card—was the Sun.

Vixen waited, watching my face anxiously.

I glanced up at them. "Well, first, the eight of Chalices points to codependency—to a psychic leech or an enabler. Given you think we're dealing with possession, I believe the card indicates that someone is definitely feeding off of his energy. The Death card in the second position is the core of the problem, so I'm thinking you may be right and we're probably looking at a spirit. Usually the card signifies that transformation is on the way, but something is whispering 'spirit activity' to me, and I'm going to trust my instinct. The third card is the two of Discs, which could mean several things—it could mean that things are on a downturn now, but will rise again when we get into the thick of things. It's yin/yang. Life/death. Good/evil."

I gasped as a feeling of dread swept over me. I could feel it from the tips of my toes to the top of my head. Whatever was attached to Lenny's energy was clammy and malignant and filled with hunger.

Vixen looked at me. "What's wrong?"

"Whatever's going on, it's not good. Lenny's in trouble, Vixen. That much I can tell you."

"Read the rest, please," Vixen said, contemplating the cards on the table.

"The fourth and fifth cards are the advice cards. The High Priestess indicates that I'm the one to deal with this, given I'm a priestess. The Tower card indicates that destruction and tearing down of old structures is the only way to change the outcome. But even with my intervention, I'm not feeling optimistic."

Sitting back, I stared at the spread. The last card—the potential outcome—was problematic.

"Why? What's wrong?"

I looked over at Vixen and sighed. "Okay, the Sun is

usually a good card, but this spread…there's something more than the cards speaking to me. At times—rare times —the sun can indicate sudden death."

"Oh." They sat back in their seat, looking lost. "Is there any wiggle room?"

"There's always wiggle room," I said, nodding. "Right up till the end. Nothing in life is sure and we always have a chance to change the outcome, at least until a certain point. If somebody decides to jaywalk and doesn't see a car barreling down on them, there's still the chance they'll suddenly notice their shoe is untied and stop, or look around when someone calls their name and prevent the accident. But once the car is seconds away from them, and there's nowhere to run, well…the accident *is* going to happen. As far as Lenny's concerned, I feel we still have time to go back to the curb. But I'm not sure *how much* time or what's involved."

"So there's a chance to help him. Then we have to start as soon as possible. Can you stick around? I'll call and ask him to come over." Vixen pulled out their phone.

"Sure, I can stay for a while. But I can't stay too long." I stood and walked over to look at the series of paintings Vixen had lined one of the walls with. The art was tropi-cal. Beautiful, but so warm and lush that it almost made me cringe. I wasn't sure what I didn't like about it, because the artist was incredibly talented, but try as I might, I couldn't work up enthusiasm.

While Vixen talked to Lenny, I crossed to the bay window and stared out into the courtyard. The snow drifted down lightly, and a sudden explosion of color blinded me as all of Vixen's outdoor decorations blazed to life. There were stars and moons and a shimmering field of blue twinkling lights spread over the yard. I clapped softly, the light show was so ethereal.

Vixen was arguing with Lenny. "I'll do what I can...I will...I promise..." After a moment, Vixen hung up and turned back to me. "Lenny will be here in a little while."

"All right, but I don't want to stay too late." Accumulating snow wasn't fun to drive in.

"It was a hard sell, but Lenny finally agreed. I told him I needed to talk to him about a website emergency, but I'm worried that whatever's commandeering him will put up a fight when he meets you. He sounds so angry. I think he agreed because he knew I'd fire him if he said no." Vixen paused, eyeing me up and down. "Maybe you can get him to loosen up. You're definitely in the wheelhouse of what he likes."

"What?" I almost dropped the figurine of a cat that I had picked up, and that would have cost me at least a thousand dollars, according to the price tag that was still on the bottom. "I'm not offering myself as bait, whether in the soul department or the honeypot aisle." I paused, lowering my voice. "Ever since Pandora, I've been very leery of volunteering myself up to anybody who might decide to exact pain for fun."

Vixen took a deep breath, then ducked their head. "I forget you went through that. I'm sorry. I wouldn't for the moment suggest that you pimp yourself out. I was joking —well, maybe not all the way, but I didn't mean it." They focused their gaze on me for a moment. "It was bad, wasn't it? What she did to you?"

I hadn't told Vixen or Apollo how bad it had been. They knew that I had seen an Elven therapist for the trauma and they had seen a few of the scars, but I never fully expanded on how helpless I had been, and how Pandora had tortured me.

"It was bad," I said, holding Vixen's gaze. "It was so bad that I'll never be the same. There's a part of me who will forever be wary, who will forever question motives or agendas. I don't think that I can ever go back to trusting anybody the way I did. I've never been a sucker—you know, PT Barnum said there's one born every minute. But now…" I paused, stiffening.

Vixen waited patiently, but I could see the anger welling up. "If Pandora was here now…"

I let out a long breath. "Even though the therapist took away the triggers, the memories remain. And on occasion, the memories—even detached from the feelings—overwhelm me. I've never been that helpless or hopeless before. The pain she inflicted on me was beyond anything I've ever experienced. It changed me, Vixen. It changed me for good."

"If I ever get my hands on that bitch, no matter that she's a goddess, she will pay. The gods may be immortal, but they aren't immune to pain. And trust me, my dear, I can make someone wish they were dead." Their eyes turned jet black, with a tiny ruby light where the pupil was, and for a moment, scales rippled on their skin, and their teeth lengthened into curved fangs that gleamed with a wicked sheen.

I must have jumped or moved without realizing it, because the next moment, Vixen looked like Vixen again. They held out their arms.

"Come, dear girl, come here."

I hesitated a second, then reminded myself that Vixen was my friend. Vixen was willing to risk losing their place in the Ante-Fae community because of me. I stepped into their arms and let them hug me for a moment.

After Vixen let go, I stepped away. "Thank you."

"No, thank you. You remind me of what it means to be young in the world—young and at risk. I'm far older than you, and far more jaded. But I've never been hurt like you were, and it does me good to remember how vulnerable we can be. Knowing you makes me a better person." Vixen motioned for me to follow them to the massive tri-panel bay window, where we sat down on the banquette that fit into the nook. They took my hand and held it as we watched the snow fall and waited for Lenny to arrive.

CHAPTER EIGHT

LENNY ARRIVED AROUND TWO. BY THEN, VIXEN AND I HAD demolished the entire package of mint cookies and they kept fretting, glancing at the clock.

"I can't stand being made to wait," they said.

"You'd go nuts with Kipa, then. He's always running late. I swear, I have to tell him we need to be somewhere a half hour earlier than we do so we manage to get there on time," I said, laughing. "He's trying, though."

"You bedded yourself a wild one. I always knew you were a fireball," Vixen teased.

I had long suspected that if I hadn't been so much younger, Vixen might have made a play for me, but though my age didn't bother Kipa, for some reason it bothered Vixen. I wouldn't have taken the chance, though. As much as I liked Vixen, they could be ruthless when they were angry and I had seen them browbeating Apollo now and then. Part of me wanted to intervene, but Apollo had a mind of his own, and he belonged to Vixen—he was their boytoy and the pair of them had some sort of agreement about what was and wasn't acceptable.

"Kipa's wild, in some ways, yes. But there's a side to him that not many people are allowed to see. And that side…is the side that makes me want to hold him when he's upset, and that makes me trust him with my heart." I paused as the doorbell rang. "Don't tell Lenny who I am. You can tell him my name if he doesn't know I'm a bone witch. But if you have talked about me, introduce me as just a friend."

"No, he doesn't know your name," Vixen said. "Are you ready?"

"Yes, but I'll need some time alone with him because your energy can interfere with my reading. So make up some excuse to leave us alone for about ten minutes." I returned to the seating area and sat down in an armchair that had a good view of both sofa and loveseat.

Vixen joined me, sitting in the rocking chair. A moment later, Camilla escorted in a man who looked to be around mid-forties, with short hair that was bleached blond. He was medium height, his eyes were pale gray, and he looked fit, but not overly athletic. But his looks were the least of my concern. I shuddered as he entered the room, a malevolent aura following him. His shadow loomed larger than it should, and as I watched, it moved in directions that it shouldn't. Crap, I'd never seen that before.

"Lenny, this is my friend Raven. Raven, this is Lenny. Raven dropped by to return something she borrowed from me," Vixen lied smoothly. Vixen was good at lying, at underplaying a situation, and like all snakes, they could be charming all the while they were sizing you up.

Lenny stared at me warily. He didn't extend his hand, so I stood up and thrust mine out at him. He couldn't ignore it without being rude.

"How do you do?" I said. "Any friend of Vixen's is a friend of mine."

Lenny stared at my hand for a moment, then took it. His skin felt icy, but I could feel his pulse racing through his fingers, so I knew he wasn't a vampire. He squeezed a little too hard, his eyes lingering on me a little too long. It took everything I had not to pull my hand away too fast. I could already tell he had an attachment.

Something was siphoning energy off of him, but it was more than a simple psychic leech. Whatever was back there was watching me, sizing me up, and so I raised my shields, blocking its view. That would put it on alert, but better it be leery of me than see through to how much power—and what kind of power—I actually had.

"Where do you live?" Lenny asked.

As he spoke, I could tell that something was using him as a puppet, making his mouth move. I wondered if Lenny was still in there. In some cases, a Walk-In would obliterate the original soul. In other cases, the original soul wasn't strong enough to wrest back the body from the intruder.

"I live around," I said, returning to my chair. "Vixen, I need my hair dryer back that you borrowed?" That was one thing I absolutely knew Vixen had. With the elaborate hair styles that they wore, they had to have every gadget and product in the world.

"Of course. I really like it, but I think I'll stick with the one I have." Vixen stood, giving me a wry look. "I'll go find it." They exited the room with one last look back at Lenny and me.

I waited for a beat. Then, clearing my throat, I said, "So, how do you know Vixen?"

"I'm their web designer," he said, abruptly turning to stare out the window. "But I'm getting bored with the job. I'm thinking I might pick up stakes and take off." His voice was gruff and he shifted in his seat.

"How long have you worked for Vixen?" I tried to pursue the conversation. If I could keep him talking, I could observe him. That was my best bet of deciphering what was going on.

"No more questions," he said, turning around. For a human, his eyeshine was intense.

I stiffened, narrowing my eyes. "Sorry—I didn't mean to intrude."

But Lenny leaned forward, squinting at me. "I know that Vixen called me over here to set us up. Don't even think about it, toots. I'm not interested. I don't need arm candy."

I suddenly realized that Lenny—or whoever was manning Lenny's helm—thought that Vixen was trying to set us up. I could work with that.

"*Busted.*" I hung my head and forced myself to blush. "I'm sorry they troubled you. Trust me, given how surly you are, I'm definitely *not* interested. And don't blame Vixen. I was the one who pushed them to see if they had any single friends—"

"Wait a minute. You're one of *them*. You're one of the Ante-Fae, aren't you?" Lenny's expression took on an interesting look, one I didn't care for. He was sleazy and menacing, and that he had perked up when he realized I was Ante-Fae also set an alarm bell going.

"Yeah, I am," I said. I wondered if I should come out and confront the creature, but that might not be the best idea. It would surely cause him to run for cover and then Vixen would be out of a website designer and a friend.

"So, you were looking for a date? Why are you interested in someone who's human?"

The Walk-In was testing me. I scrambled, trying to think on my feet. "I'm not, per se. I lost my fiancé a year and a half ago. I'm just now feeling ready to date again and I'm looking to get back into practice." It wasn't exactly the truth but it wasn't an outright lie, either. I had lost my fiancé, and if it wasn't for Kipa, I probably wouldn't be dating even now. We had instantly hit it off and that didn't happen very often.

"Hmm, what are you?" he asked.

I had no intention on telling him that I was a bone witch, but I was stuck on what to say. I could stall but—

"I know Vixen owns the nightclub. Do you work for them?" His interruption gave me a reprieve.

I quickly said, "I read tarot cards for a living." I left the exorcisms out of the conversation.

Lenny pulled back, relaxing. As he did so, I managed to catch a glimpse of something shifting yet again in his expression. And in that moment, I saw the face of a tired, frightened man, staring at me with pleading eyes. *That* was Lenny. It was so quick that I would have missed it if I had blinked, but long enough to confirm that Lenny was still inside, being held hostage. But it also told me that I had been talking to the attachment. The glimpse also told me that—whatever it was—it was stronger than he was. He couldn't fight his way around it.

At that moment, Vixen returned, carrying a canvas bag. They were followed by Camilla, who was carrying another tray with a teacup and saucer on it. "Here's your blow dryer."

I took the bag. "Thanks. I'll be going now. I'll call you in a bit." I turned back to Lenny. "It's been nice to meet you," I said, but this time I kept my hands to myself. The entity was on guard and any further touch might give it more information than I wanted it to have.

Lenny leaned back and stared at me, crossing his arms over his chest. "Yes, you too."

And on that lie, Camilla led me out of the room and I left, after secreting the bag back to her.

ONCE OUTSIDE, I took a long breath to clear my thoughts. It was cold and snowing, fine thin flakes coming down fast with no signs of stopping. I paused at my car, using the device that Yutani—who worked for the Wild Hunt— had created for everybody in the agency. He had also made spares for a few friends, like me. A quick scan of the car told me there were no explosives, magical or otherwise, on my car. It also scanned for other magical traps waiting to happen. We had learned the hard way that when you're in a war, whether it be against the Dragonni or the Fae, you double check on things like that.

As I drove home toward the UnderLake District, I decided to stop off at the lake. It was a cold afternoon, but

I wanted the chill to clear my thoughts. The light was waning, but I still had time for a brief outing.

I found a bench that was free of snow—it was nestled under a canopy of fir trees—and sat down, leaning back as I tried to relax. The water was restless today and I imagined the Elementals were having a blast with the weather. Ember would be able to tell, but unless they chose to show themselves to me, most elementals were difficult to see, even for witches. I could see spirits no problem, but then again, I was a bone witch and that was my specialty.

Lake Washington was covered with choppy waves, and the seafoam scattered on the strip of dirt and grass that edged the lake as they rolled in toward the shore. Lake Washington was a massive lake, as far as lakes go, and had been known by several different Native American names long before 1854, when incoming white settlers had named it after George Washington. At twenty-two miles long and six miles wide, the lake plunged down to a depth of 210 feet. Fishing was good in it, and motorboats tore along the surface on a regular basis. At this time of year, boats decked out in holiday lights leisurely sailed over the surface.

Two bridges crossed the lake—the I-90 floating bridge, and the other was the 520 floating bridge, which had recently been replaced. Given the old 520 bridge had a one-in-twenty chance of going down in a big quake, and also given the area was prone to powerful quakes due to the fault zone that wove a web beneath the greater Seattle metropolitan area, the authorities had managed to push through a bill that allowed them go ahead with replacing it. The new bridge, formally known as the Evergreen

Point Floating Bridge, was both the widest and longest floating bridge in the world.

From where I was sitting, I could see both bridges, one toward the southern end and one near the northern end. I huddled back on the bench, watching the water churn along, and content to let my mind drift. I was processing what I had seen at Vixen's. Lenny was definitely carrying an attachment, but I still wasn't sure what it was. And even more important—could I remove it from him? That depended on what I was facing, so I was still in the dark.

As I was sitting there, watching the waves, I happened to glance to my left, where I saw a young man. He was wearing an open shirt over an undershirt, and a pair of blue jeans. I couldn't figure out how he was possibly warm enough. As he turned around and saw me, he froze. I glanced around, thinking maybe he was looking at someone behind me, but there was no one else in the park.

I tried to return to thinking about Lenny's case, but the guy was annoying me. He wouldn't stop looking at me. Then I paused, turning my attention to him again. I stared at him for a moment, then closed my eyes. I could see his aura better that way.

Oh, he's dead. Now that I looked closely, I could see the telltale signs.

The man's aura flared with purple around the outer edges, and there was no silver cord to be seen anywhere. He wasn't threatening, though. In fact, I felt sorry for him, though I didn't know why. Opening my eyes again, I patted the seat beside me. He cocked his head like a puppy, then began to walk my way. When he was standing about two yards away, he stopped again.

"Are you all right?" I asked aloud.

He paused, as if listening to something intently. With his left hand, he reached for his shirt and as I watched, he opened it fully and I saw a patch of red there, spreading across the area where his heart was. It wasn't blood, but an energy residue. He crooked his finger and motioned for me to follow him as he turned to walk toward a thicket of trees in the park.

I reluctantly followed, knowing and yet dreading what was next. And sure enough, the moment we came to the trees, he pointed toward a mound, recently covered with snow. I knelt beside the mound, still keeping myself alert for any sudden noises or movements, and as I brushed away the leaves and snow, I saw a hand sticking out from beneath the clumps of sodden, icy leaves.

"Crap," I said. Just what I needed now—a dead body on my hands. With a low sigh, I pulled out my phone and called the police.

THE OFFICERS ANSWERING the call were Fae. Light Fae, if I was correct. They took down my name and address and I was able to tell them I had seen the spirit and he led me to his body because the Fae, for the most part, believed in— and understood—the spirit world.

"Is he around now? Is there anything he can tell you about his death? Was he murdered? Or did he just drop dead?" The woman officer's name was Deaylia Larens. "We shouldn't move the leaves till the coroner gets here."

"I can try," I said. I turned back to the spirit, who was standing a ways back, watching. I motioned for him to approach. He slowly inched forward, nervously eyeing the exposed hand on the ground.

Can you hear me? I projected silently, to see if he could catch my words without me talking aloud.

He jerked his head up, staring at me. There was a certain puzzlement to his look, and I realized that he wasn't sure what was going on. Which meant he wasn't clear on the fact that he was dead. That happened a lot, and it was a pain in the ass to deal with, but it had to be done with compassion as well. When the dead were pissed or startled, they could act out in all sorts of unpleasant ways, even if they didn't mean to.

What do you want? He mouthed the words but I could catch them because even though he might think he was talking aloud, he was projecting them with his mind.

What happened to you?

He frowned again. *What do you mean?*

I glanced at the hand sticking out from beneath the leaves and pointed to it. *What happened?*

I don't know. I found him like that, whoever he is.

Okay, so he didn't realize that was his body. Now came the hard part. *What's your name?*

Josh Fine. Who are you?

I'm Raven BoneTalker. Um, Josh, what's the last thing you remember before you saw me in the park?

Well, I was walking through those trees. I like taking an early morning walk when it's snowy. I... He paused, looking confused. *I remember thinking that today was going to be a good day because...there was something I was going to do, but I can't remember now. And then I must have pulled a muscle because something hurt and...then...I saw you.*

Josh, where did you feel the pain?

My chest. Why?

That made sense, given the red energy spreading across his heart area. I turned back to the officers. "His name is Josh Fine. He doesn't remember what happened to him. He doesn't even know he's…"

"Dead?" The male officer blurted out the word so loud that Josh jumped and turned to me, a panicked look on his face.

I'm dead? *What's he talking about? I'm standing right here!*

"Idiot," I said to the cop, then turned back to Josh. *It's all right—you're still here. But...yes...he's correct. That's your body. You led me to it because your subconscious knew that you needed for us to find it. Did you have any heart trouble that you know of?*

He began to blink in and out, which could happen when a spirit was startled. But he seemed to gain some control after a moment. *My doctor said that I was asking for trouble. I smoke. And he keeps badgering me to stop. My blood pressure's too high and I forget to take my meds most of the time.*

I sighed. Poor man. There was no reason to chastise him for not taking better care of himself—that was a moot point. *Well, you're all right now. Do you have information for your family in your wallet, so we can get hold of them?*

Looking more morose than I had seen anyone look in a long time, Josh ducked his head. *Yeah, I do. My wife lives a couple blocks over. Damn it, today was our anniversary. This is going to kill her. Would you tell her I love her? That I'm so sorry? That I'm okay?*

I promise. What's her name?

Suzette. Suzette Fine. I hope she's okay. He paused, then added, *Tell her to ask Morty about my hidden stash. When we got married, I was worried, so I created a secret account. My buddy Morty knows about it. He'll be able to help her get situated. She may have to pay taxes on it—I haven't yet—but there will be enough to keep her comfortable for a while.*

Josh began to fade at that point. Now that he knew about his condition, he seemed to be making the transition toward the Veil well.

I raised my hand. *Have a good journey, Josh. I promise to tell your wife you love her and about the money.*

He started to say something, but the next moment, he vanished.

I turned back to the cops. "He's gone. Once he realized he was dead, he started fading out. His wife's name is Suzette Fine, and today's their anniversary. He asked me to talk to her—to tell her that he said he loved her. But I can't do that until you notify her."

"We can't notify her till the coroner examines the body and we find some evidence of what killed him." Officer Larens pulled out her notebook. "If you'll give me your contact info, I'll call you and tell you after we've talked to her."

"Raven BoneTalker." I gave her my number and address, and then, seeing Josh was truly gone, I headed back to my car. I was getting cold and the clouds were socking in for a good blow. The fine mist of snow had turned into a snow shower, and the flakes were bigger, and I wanted hot chocolate and cookies and the cheer of the Yule tree.

As I eased out of the parking lot, back onto the street,

it occurred to me that all over the world, the dead were wandering. Some might not know they were dead, but others were going about their days and nights as usual. The world was a crowded place.

CHAPTER NINE

BY THE TIME I GOT HOME, MY SPIRITS HAD DIPPED AGAIN. Everything seemed topsy-turvy, and I wasn't sure why I was depressed—whether because of my father's betrayal, getting kicked out of the Ante-Fae world, seeing the malignant force that had taken over Lenny, or the incident with Josh. At least Josh had managed to transition once he learned he was dead and I promised to talk to his wife. The other three, I had no clear answer for.

"Hey love," Kipa said, swinging me into his arms for a kiss after I'd taken off my coat. "What's going on? How was Vixen?"

"Their friend is possessed by a very nasty spirit. I was able to ascertain that for a fact. Then, on the way home, I met a ghost who didn't know he was dead and I had to break the news. I promised to tell his wife he loves her and he's sorry about their anniversary, which was today, and that there's a stash of money he hid from her. Oh, did I mention that I found his body? Or rather, he led me to his body but he didn't know it was his until some damned fool cop blurted out that he was dead in front of him?"

Kipa arched his eyebrows. "Sounds like you've had more than enough to fill one day."

I sighed, leaning my head on his shoulder. "It is, and it's not over yet. I'm trying to remember if we had anything on the calendar for tonight." The holiday season was usually jam-packed with parties, and I prayed that I hadn't agreed to anything tonight because I was exhausted. "I feel like I've been body slammed. I don't know why. Maybe I'm coming down with something?"

"Last night's activities are catching up to you," Phasmoria said, peeking around the kitchen corner.

I was about to answer when my phone rang. I answered. It was the officer from the park, telling me they had located Suzette Fine. I took down the information and made a note in my calendar to talk to her as soon as possible.

My mother waited till I was off the phone and then said, "Sit down. I made your favorite from when you were young."

I cocked my head, confused. "What favorite? I don't ever remember you cooking."

"This, your father made. But I remember how much you used to love this, so I looked up a recipe for it."

The moment she said that, my heart sank. My mother was one hell of a fighter, and she could Bean Sidhe with the best them, but a cook she was not. She would make a great sous chef, as long as you told her what to do, but she had no patience for cooking.

"And what was that? I honestly don't remember." I settled in at the table, bracing myself for some gods-awful combination of cabbage and fish or some such food. But when she carried in what looked like a perfect lemon meringue pie, my salivary glands set to work in overtime.

"You made me a *lemon meringue pie*? That looks delicious."

My mother placed it in front of me, then started to laugh. "I give up, I can't keep up the charade. You know perfectly well that if I made a lemon meringue pie it would be soupy and have a soggy crust. I bought it, though, and I hope that counts."

"You remembered," I said with a smile, staring at the pie. "That's all that matters."

She was right. When I was a little, I always asked for "lemmy ming pie" and my father would make the best lemon meringue pie in the world for me. And Phasmoria had remembered.

I teared up, thinking about how things were so askew. My father had always been my rock, and now the positions had reversed. Phasmoria was cushioning the blows and my father had abandoned me. But in all the time I was young, I never felt like Phasmoria didn't care.

"Why did he do it? Why did he let Dougal bully him? I'm his *daughter*." The words burst out before I could stop them and I started to cry.

Phasmoria pulled up the chair next to me. "I'm sorry— I didn't want you to cry. I didn't mean to make you cry."

"*You* didn't," I said. "My father's the one who made me cry." I looked over at her. "Why did he do it? Is he that weak-willed? Does he not care? Was my entire life a lie?"

Phasmoria glanced over at Kipa, who took the chair on my other side. "I don't know, child. But I plan on finding out. I intend on having a long talk with Dougal and Curikan, trust me."

Frustrated, I said, "I want to know why the Banra-Sheagh picked on me. Surely other Ante-Fae have been friends with someone who killed one of our people. And surely some Ante-Fae somewhere has killed another? I mean, our hands can't all be clean of blood against our own kind."

"Oh, they aren't. Trust me. Why she's targeting you is also a good question." Phasmoria stared off into space for a moment, then told Kipa, "Take care of her. I'll be back, hopefully by tonight, but if not tonight, then tomorrow." She stood, kissed me on the forehead and said, "Enjoy your pie," and then headed for the door.

I thought about stopping her but once Phasmoria made up her mind, it was set and there was no calling her back. As the door closed behind her, I picked up my fork and began to eat directly out of the tin. I looked over at Kipa.

"Want some? Grab a fork."

Kipa stood. "I'll leave this one to you. I'm going to take Raj for a walk. When we get back, you can tell me what happened to Vixen's friend." He left me alone with the pie, calling to Raj, who bounced over to his side so Kipa could put on the leash. We had to harness Raj because he had a tendency to wander off if he saw something interesting, and that wasn't good for anybody.

After they left, I locked the door and made sure the wards were working. Then I carried the pie into the living room and curled up on the sofa and ate my way through an episode of *Finland's Best Wild Spots*—a show that Kipa had downloaded from Zort, a streaming service. He wanted to take me to Finland, but I wanted to bone up first, so I would know what to look for.

The northern lights were incredible, scintillating across the sky. As I watched the show, my tension began to unravel. Maybe I needed some "me" time, or maybe time to give my brain a rest, but the more of the pie I ate, and the more I watched the gorgeous countryside, the more I relaxed.

I had finished two-thirds of the pie before my stomach warned me that maybe I had eaten enough, so I set the tin on the coffee table and stretched out so that I could see the TV. Before I knew it, the voice on the TV grew fainter, and I fell asleep to the soft fall of snowflakes.

"RAVEN? RAVEN? HONEY, WAKE UP." I pried my eyes open to see Kipa staring at me. He swept my hair back and then pressed his lips to my forehead and kissed me.

"Hey love, how are you?" I murmured, shifting as I sat up. I yawned and blinked against the light. Raj was curled up at the bottom of the sofa, right below my feet. He was already snoring.

"Fine. Raj needed a chance to run and work those muscles so I took him to the Field."

There was an empty lot nearby that we called the Field and we took Raj there to let him run off leash. It wasn't easy for him to dash out of eyesight there, since the lot was so open, so the entire neighborhood used it as an impromptu dog park. Luckily, people picked up after their pets and we picked up after Raj, and nobody complained.

"How long was I asleep? What time is it?"

"It's almost nine-thirty. When did you go to sleep?"

"Shortly after you left. I must have needed the rest." I had been out for close to three hours. My stomach rumbled. "I'm hungry. Apparently the pie didn't give me much to work on."

"Emotional shock can wreak havoc on the body—it can use up so much energy." Kipa slid in beside me and draped his arm around my shoulders. I leaned against him. "Truthfully, how are you? I know you're not all right, even if you try to put on a brave face."

I stared at the TV, which was showing reruns of *Golden Girls*. Raj had discovered the show recently and he was in love with it, always begging for cheesecake so he could eat "with the girls." I was grateful he hadn't discovered that more than one channel ran reruns of it.

One thing I had discovered about being with Kipa—I couldn't lie to him. He saw through my attempts to keep him from worrying, saw through my "I'm okays" when I wasn't. Licking my lips, I assessed how okay I actually was. I hadn't wanted to face the feelings, but my Elven therapist would trip me up on that next time I saw him. I had gone down to one session a month, but that session was like gold for me.

"How am I? I'm hurt, and I'm angry. And weirdly, embarrassed. My father, who was my rock all through the years, up and disowned me. If he hadn't gone back to Scotland to live with his father, he wouldn't have done that. I know Curikan, he loves humans. He loves people, and now he's siding with the Ante-Fae? Against someone who would have most likely killed my friend. He met Ember and he really liked her. Now…"

"Now, he's suddenly done a 180?"

"Yeah. He's a hypocrite. Why would he do this to me? Curikan always talked about how rigid his father was, and how he left Scotland when he was very young because he couldn't stand how oppressive his life was. And yet, he goes back there—"

"I'm not making any excuses for him," Kipa said, "but you and your mother engineered his move."

I glared at him. "I know. We did what we thought would be the best chance to save his life. You know as well as I do that moving to Annwn alone would have been the death of him. My father's not prepared to survive in a forest like Y'Bain. He would have been killed."

"I understand. I do. But did you ever think he may be playing along with his father to avoid something worse?" Kipa pulled me so that I was sitting across his lap.

"What do you mean?"

He shrugged. "I'm not certain, but it keeps needling the back of my brain that maybe there's more going on than you know."

I ran my fingers through Kipa's hair. He was so incredibly handsome that he took my breath away. His hair was long, trailing down his back, and it was a deep brown. His eyes matched his hair and neatly trimmed beard. He had a dolphin-bite piercing on his lower lip, and his skin was a rich, warm golden color. He was swarthy and sexy. Even in his wolf form, he was gorgeous.

"You're trying my patience," I whispered. "But I forgive you. You asked how I was—I'm hurt by my father's actions, pissed at the Banra-Sheagh's decree, and embarrassed that I was dragged before her for such a petty charge."

"You should contact Sejun and ask for an appointment," Kipa said, tracing my cheek with his finger. Sejun was my Elven therapist.

"You may be right," I answered. My body was tired, but his touch set me on fire. I shifted so I was sitting right over his cock, which was growing harder with every moment we sat there. I could feel his arousal through his jeans and my skirts, which meant he was really turned on. And without my mother there, I thought that maybe the best remedy to my angst would be sex. It was a good way to get emotions out. "Listen, my mother's gone…"

"You sure?" Kipa said, immediately picking up on what I was asking.

"Yeah, I'm sure." I wrapped my arms around his neck as he stood, picking me up. "Raj needs to watch TV and eat his snacks while Raven and Kipa go play games in the bedroom."

Raj knew very well that when Kipa and I were "playing games" he wasn't to bother us. I wasn't sure how much Raj understood about sex among humanoids—he'd never expressed any urges to find a mate of his own, at least not that I could see. I had no clue when gargoyles entered puberty, but it was actually something I should look into, now that the thought came to mind.

"There's a *Golden Girls* marathon on. Raj is going to watch until he falls asleep," Raj said, opening one eye.

"Okay, that sounds like fun for Raj."

As Kipa carried me down the hall, Raj immersed himself in the exploits of Blanche, Dorothy, Sophia, and Rose. I leaned against Kipa's chest, my pain and my desire blending into a mix that only my Wolf God could satisfy.

I WAS DEEP ASLEEP, totally satiated and feeling much less angry, when something startled me awake. I sat up. Had I heard a noise? Sensed a movement? Had Raj knocked something over and broken it? Unsure of what was going on, I slipped out of bed and pulled on my robe.

Kipa was breathing deeply, snoring in that stop-start sort of way. I debated waking him, but the wards hadn't gone off, so it couldn't be one of the Dragonni, or Pandora. They were set to announce the arrival of any unwanted visitor who tried to break in.

Still, wariness was a good idea and I cautiously opened the bedroom door, peeking out as I flipped on the hall light switch. But no one was there. I peeked in on the ferrets but they were all snuggled up, asleep, so I padded down the hallway, my feet freezing on the hardwood floors. It was cold outside and—as I entered the living room—I saw through the window that it was still snowing heavily.

I glanced around for Raj. He was asleep in his cushioned bed, and I saw that he had flipped on the heating pad. It was low wattage, but it helped Raj whenever he got cold, and he could turn it on and off by himself. Seeing nothing afoot, I peeked in the kitchen.

Nothing out of place.

I decided that it must have been a dream and turned to head back to bed when a sudden noise echoed through the hall and something grabbed me around the throat. I couldn't see what had hold of me, but whatever it was, it was squeezing my windpipe. I reached up, flailing to try to pry it off of me, but there was nothing for me to grab hold of. At that moment, Raj woke up, leaping out of his bed.

"What's hurting Raven—no! Bat monster no hurt Raven!" The next thing I knew, his eyes turned red in a way that I had only ever seen one time before. He shot a beam of light, aiming directly at me. The next moment, the chokehold eased up and then, something shifted and I could breathe. Raj relaxed.

At that moment, Kipa came racing down the hall, looking confused and concerned. "What happened? What's going on?"

I gasped in a shaky breath, rubbing my throat. It felt raw and sore.

"What—your neck is bruised, all the way around it. Are you all right?" Kipa gathered me up and carried me over to the sofa.

"Some monster tried to hurt Raven. Raj stopped the monster." Raj yawned. "Raj tired now. Very tired." He was heading over to his bed.

"Raj, come over here a moment, please," I said, clearing my throat as best I could. "Raven thanks Raj so much— Raj saved Raven's life."

Raj leaned against me, looking sleepy and ready to go back to sleep. "Raj loves Raven."

"Raven loves Raj, too. Can Raj tell Raven what the creature looked like? Raven couldn't see it." I was puzzled. I could usually see spirits, and that something got past the wards was troubling.

"Big bat had a long curling tail with a heart-shaped tip on the end. Horns on its head. It was a purple-red color," Raj said.

"And Raj could see it?"

"Yes, Raj could see it." He paused, then, looking confused. "Wait—what is Raven talking about? Raj is tired."

"We're talking about the monster that Raj saved Raven from," I said.

He yawned again. "Raj doesn't remember a monster. Raj needs to sleep," he mumbled.

"Go ahead, then." I watched as he walked over to tumble into his bed. Immediately, he started to snore. This had happened the last time too. He had forgotten what had happened—and to this day he had never mentioned the laser-beam eyes, and when I had asked him about them, he denied having any such memory.

I turned to Kipa and lowered my voice. "He won't remember this tomorrow. This happened once before. He saved the day and hasn't a clue about it. I'm not that conversant about gargoyle powers, but until now, I thought that might have been a fluke. Now, though…"

"You didn't see what attacked you?"

"No, and the scary part is that the wards didn't catch it," I said. "I must have tuned into it during my sleep because when I woke up, I knew something was off. I didn't expect anything like that, though, because the wards didn't go off."

"They're set to someone physically breaking into your house. The creature was probably on the astral plane. You need to rework those wards so that they alert us to anything coming in from other planes as well." Kipa examined my neck. "I don't think anything is broken, but that's one hell of a bruise, and it could have crushed your windpipe. If it does look like Raj described, it probably had its tail wrapped around your neck. Don't you have some sort of grimoire?"

"Yes, actually, I have a copy of *Beltan's Bestiary*. Come on, it's in my office." As I made certain everything seemed normal, it occurred to me that Curikan might actually demand the book back, and I decided that I'd better make a copy of it before he had the chance. I left the living room light on as we headed into my office. I was tired and sore, but still in the grips of the adrenaline rush, and I knew I wouldn't be able to get back to sleep yet.

As we began flipping through the pages of the book, I kept thinking about the creature. If this was a random attack—an attack of opportunity—then it would amount to carelessness on my part. But I couldn't get past the feeling that there was more to it. And that I suddenly had a target on my back from several different corners.

CHAPTER TEN

By three a.m. we hadn't found any mention of the creature so I bookmarked our place in the massive compendium and we went back to bed. Or rather, I went to bed. Kipa insisted on sitting up to keep watch over me.

"I'm a god. I don't need sleep—not much, anyway." He sat in the armchair near the bed, his sword across his lap, watching me until I asked him to please quit staring so I could get to sleep. After another ten minutes, I finally fell asleep.

Morning came all too early, but I managed to drag myself out of bed by eight. Still exhausted, I took a long shower, then dressed. I was feeling tired and draggy, and my throat felt like it had been rubbed raw. I decided to go with simple and picked a pair of warm black fishnet leggings, then a mid-thigh sweater dress. I belted it and—feeling as if I were somehow dressed like Peter Pan—I headed to the kitchen. There I found Kipa. He was making breakfast, and he glanced up, smiling at me.

"I'm glad you got some sleep, but you still look tired.

You want to go back to bed for a while?" he asked, cracking eggs into a bowl.

"No. I need to tend to the ferrets and I want to—" I paused. I'd been about to say that I wanted to talk to my father about the creature. He was heavily steeped in lore and good about figuring out what different entities were. Sighing, I added, "I'm going to talk to Llew. He might know someone who understands astral entities. That wasn't a spirit last night, or I would have seen it."

"Raj still doesn't remember what he did," Kipa said.

"That's another thing. I need to find out more about gargoyles. I know a few things, but this eludes me. That's twice now he's saved my ass, the first from Jim Morrison's whack-assed spirit, and then, whatever this is. And both times, he's almost immediately forgotten what he did. I don't know if that's a common gargoyle trait or if it's unique to Raj, but I need to find out because if that power ever gets out of hand, I need to know how to deal with it."

"Go sit down, breakfast will be right up." Kipa motioned me out of the kitchen and, after giving him a kiss, I returned to the living room and sat down.

Raj was watching TV. It was some game show with a lot of lights and confetti and I suddenly realized that it was in Japanese.

"Why is Raj watching that show?" I asked.

"Raj likes the show because Raj thinks it's funny," he said. "The game show host makes *hee-lar-eous* jokes."

I stiffened. "Wait a minute…can Raj understand what the host is saying?"

Raj nodded, gaze glued to the TV. "Raj can understand. The words sound funny compared to Raven's words, but Raj knows what they mean."

Flabbergasted, I sat back. My gargoyle understood Japanese and had never mentioned it. I guessed he thought it was normal.

"Raven doesn't understand the host?" he asked, glancing over his shoulder at me.

"Raven doesn't understand the host," I said softly. Then, crossing to where he was sitting, I picked up the remote. "Raj, can we change the channel for a moment? Raven wants to ask Raj a question."

"Okay," Raj said, looking glum.

I quickly changed over to Univision. A soap opera was on and I could pick out pieces here and there. "Can Raj understand what the actors are saying?"

Raj listened for a moment, then bobbed his head. "Raj can understand. He's angry at her for sleeping with the hot man downstairs."

I began to flip through channels, finding a Korean station. "What about now? Can Raj understand the man speaking now?"

Once again, Raj listened for a moment. "The man's talking about money. He wants a lot of it."

I turned back to the game show and handed Raj back the remote. "Raven thanks Raj. Raj can watch his show now." I gave him a quick hug and headed back to the table, where Kipa was arranging my plate, along with a mega-vat of espresso, chocolate, and milk.

"I've already eaten, and so has Raj. Take your time," he said, sitting down on the opposite side of the table.

The bacon and eggs were hot, the toast smelled all yeasty-buttery good, and the fruit salad looked bright and colorful. My stomach rumbled and I realized how hungry

I was, so I dug in. After a few bites, I sat back, setting down my fork on the edge of my plate.

"So, Raj can understand Japanese, Korean, and Spanish," I said.

"Oh? I knew he could understand Finnish, although his inflection leaves something to be desired," Kipa said. "But considering he's a gargoyle and Finnish is one hell of a language to learn—"

"Finnish? You knew he can understand Finnish and didn't tell me?" I stared at him.

Kipa looked surprised. "I thought you knew!"

"Of course I didn't know…" I paused, catching myself. "I'm kind of astounded. It appears Raj was born multilingual. There's so much about him that I need to learn. What else can that twerp do?" Shaking my head, I picked up my fork and began to eat again.

"I might be able to help you," Kipa said. "If you don't mind a trip to Annwn, we can visit one of my buddies there who has made a career out of studying Crypto species. When do you next work at Llew's?"

"I'm working Wednesday and Saturday this week, but not today or tomorrow, so I'd love to go." I had been to Annwn a number of times, but mostly to my therapist's office, which was at Cernunnos's palace, Herne's father and Ember's soon-to-be-father-in-law. I didn't envy her. Cernunnos was gorgeous, he could be incredibly polite, but he was overwhelming.

Kipa pulled out his phone. "I'll call Quest to see if she's home."

Quest Realto lived on the Eastside, like I did, and she was one of the portal keepers. She guarded a portal that led to Annwn for Cernunnos. A coyote shifter, she and I had become friendly over the months I had been traveling to the Celtic Otherworld for my therapy sessions.

I finished eating while he chatted with her on the phone.

"You'll be there until one? All right, is it okay if we come over in about an hour?"

I glanced at the clock. It was going on eleven.

"Thanks," Kipa said. "We'll see you then." He hung up. "I should have asked you first. Will noon be good for you?"

"It's fine. I'm dressed and I don't have many errands to run today." My phone rang and I glanced at it. *Vixen.* I answered. "Hey Vixen, how are you?"

"I'm fine, dear heart. I wanted to check on you and to ask what you thought about Lenny. You didn't call me back last night. I'm hurt," they said in a melodramatic voice.

"Oh, I imagine you're so butthurt." I laughed. "I'm all right, actually. Last night I had a bit of a meltdown, but today I'm okay. As far as Lenny, he's got an attachment plugged into him. I don't know whether it's a spirit or a Walk-In, but I'll try to figure it out. Meanwhile, I was attacked in the middle of the night by some astral nasty that managed to slip through my wards. Raj saved me, and later today I'm headed over to Annwn with Kipa."

Vixen paused, then—their voice suddenly serious— asked, "You were attacked, girl? Are you all right?"

"I'm okay, though without Raj, I'd be dead now." I was about to tell them that Raj had told me what it looked like, then stopped. Vixen didn't know that Raj talked, and we wanted to keep it that way until Raj was ready. Raj had a right to his privacy.

"Do you know what it was?" Vixen asked.

"No, but I'm hoping to find out from Kipa's friend—apparently they're knowledgeable about all sorts of Cryptos and I know this creature wasn't a spirit. I think it was an astral entity, but maybe it had the power of invisibility." For some reason, I felt skittish about telling Vixen anything more about the incident, so I promised to call them later and got off the phone.

"I'm not sure why, but I didn't want to talk to Vixen," I said.

"Did you two have a scuffle?"

I snorted. "Dude, if Vixen and I got into it, that would be the end of me. Taipan snake shifter and a Charmer as well? Nope, I wouldn't stand a chance. I feel very uneasy about their friend—Lenny. The one who's got the… thing…attached to him. When I met him yesterday, I felt like he was watching me. Not Lenny, but whatever it is has hold of him."

Kipa paused. I could practically see the wheels turning in his head. "Do you think that whatever it is realized you knew about it?"

"I have my suspicions, but I don't know for sure."

Kipa pulled his hair back into a ponytail and held it fast with a hair tie. He leaned back in his chair, staring at me with a contemplative look. He was truly gorgeous. We had said the "L" word a couple months back, but now and then it occurred to me that falling in love with a god was fraught with landmines. He was immortal, and while I was Ante-Fae, that didn't mean I'd live forever. But I also reminded myself that he had spent decades with a human woman he had fallen in love with, and he stayed by her side until she died. And that…that was the story that had made me admit to myself that I was in love with him.

"I have a thought," he said. "What if the attachment is what attacked you last night?"

I shook my head. I had been so tired that the thought had never crossed my mind. But the moment he said it, I could feel an alarm going off inside. "Fuck. Fuck me hard."

"Glad to oblige, love, but what do you think about my idea?" He was still grinning, but his eyes told me he was taking this completely seriously.

"You may have something there. I don't want to believe it because that means that Lenny's creature is onto me and managed to find out where I live. Being stalked by an astral creature—if that's what it is—isn't my idea of fun."

"Neither is being killed by one," Kipa said, his smile vanishing. "We have to find out what that thing is so we know how to deal with it." He paused. "Before we go, we need to beef up the wards so that Raj is protected. Although he seemed to hold his own last night."

"True, but we can't take a chance on the hope that he can do that again. He seems to have no control over the power. We can't rely on it and if anything happened to him, I'd never forgive myself." I glanced at the clock. "Crap, I need to feed the ferrets—"

"Already done. While you were sleeping. But you should run in and say hello to them. Elise seems to be feeling neglected. I'll clean up while you do that, and then we'll head over to Quest's place. Make sure you're dressed for walking through the snowy woods. My friend in Annwn lives in a cottage on the edge of Thicklewood."

I'd never heard of Thicklewood. I knew all about

Cernunnos's palace, and Y'Bain—the massive forest that spread through Annwn. I also had some knowledge of Brighid's castle. But I had no experience with the lesser-known places.

I hurried down the hall and entered the ferrets' room. I had three ferrets, except they weren't really ferrets. They were human spirits who had been bound into ferret form when I tried to free them from a tree they had been trapped in. The spell had gone awry thanks to a curse placed on the tree. Ever since then, they had lived with me, sliding more into their ferret natures with each year that passed. They'd been with me since the 1980s, and I had no idea how long they would live, but until then, I would keep trying to find the spell that kept them trapped. In the end, though, even if *I* wasn't able to free them, they'd eventually age and die, and that would free them to move on.

Elise, a beautiful white ferret, was the most aware. She always managed to keep hold of her core nature. Gordon was still trying, but he was having trouble maintaining his memories of his former life. Templeton was almost fully ferret now, and I didn't hold hope that he would be able to talk to me much longer.

I let them out of their cage. Templeton meandered over for a few head scritches before heading back to curl up in his bedding for a nap. Gordon began to zoom around the room, bouncing off the walls and wrestling with toys. As usual, it was Elise who came over for me to pick her up. I set her on the table in front of me and stroked her back. She leaned into my touch, sighing happily.

I missed you the past few days.

"I'm sorry. I know I've been AWOL, but I hope you haven't been too lonely."

Actually, your mother spent some time with us yesterday. She's a lovely...Bean Sidhe. I've always wondered about the Bean Sidhe. When I was alive, I used to study mythology, you know. I pictured hags—terrifying and reaper like.

"You haven't seen my mother when she's working," I said with a laugh. "She's not nearly as pleasant. When she goes into full Bean Sidhe mode, her shriek can kill. Anyway, I wanted to check in and see if everything's okay."

What was the commotion last night? I felt something in the house, but I couldn't tell what it was. It frightened me. And I felt you were in danger but I couldn't figure out a way to tell you.

I stared at her for a moment. That Elise had felt it too meant that the creature who attacked me was powerful. Elise wasn't particularly psychic.

"You felt it?"

Yes, I did. So did Gordon and Templeton, but they weren't easily able to verbalize what they felt. They huddled up near me and kept talking about "the monster."

If the ferrets were all feeling what had attacked me, that meant it had a great deal of power and I had to make certain the house was warded. I took my responsibilities as protector for Raj and the ferrets seriously, and I couldn't imagine someone hurting them because of my carelessness.

"All right, thank you for telling me. I'll try to make certain the creature can't return. I have to go, but I'll try to spend some time in here tonight or tomorrow. I'd let you run around the house while we're gone, but I don't trust Raj not to accidentally step on you."

I picked Elise up and cuddled her for a few moments, then shooed them back into their cage and secured the door. The entire back wall was one massive ferret complex so they had plenty of room to play inside the cage, and they had hidey-holes and a couple wheels to run on and space to be alone if they wanted to.

As I left the room, it occurred to me that if Kipa and I ever moved in together, we might want to buy a bigger house with a family room that I could turn into the ferrets' sanctuary. Realizing what I was thinking, I tried to clear my thoughts. I wasn't ready for a ring yet. Or a permanent roommate.

CHAPTER ELEVEN

BEFORE WE LEFT, I LOOKED THROUGH MY RITUAL ROOM, trying to find the most powerful wards I possessed. I thought I had installed the strongest ones to guard against Pandora, but on the off chance, I decided to look anyway. I was glad that I did because in the back of one of the altar cabinets where I stored all my spell components, I found a super-charged crystal that I had forgotten about. Fire and ice quartz—the spike was incredibly beautiful, with hundreds of fractures running inside the clear crystal. A multitude of prisms shimmered inside the spike.

I had charged it under a Black Moon a few years back, dedicating it to Arawn—the god of death, to whom I was pledged—and then put it away and promptly forgotten about it. But the crystal was still humming, and I realized that maybe sometimes we forgot we owned things to save them for a time when we'd need them more.

Carrying it out to the space in an étagère where I had arranged the spell grid for the wards, I added it to the center and immediately the energy of the house shifted. It was as though I had muffled the outer world, on both the physical and the magical levels.

"Whoa, that made things tighten up," Kipa said, coming to my side.

"Yeah, it feels like I raised the drawbridge over the moat." I glanced up at him. "That's the best I can do for now. I'm going to run and change quickly, then we'll head out."

"Don't be too long," he said as I dashed down the hallway. "I promised Quest we'd be there by noon."

I didn't answer but darted into my bedroom, where I stripped off my dress. I kept on the leggings, but slid on a pair of gauchos in black. I pulled on a hunter green V-neck sweater and belted it with a silver belt. Then I slid my feet into boots that came up to my knee. They were black leather, with a half-inch heel, and I would be able to walk through the woods in them. Despite my love for hardware, I had chosen a pair with rubber soles. They had a single buckle and strap across the top of my foot. Hardware made noise, and I wasn't sure how dangerous the Thicklewood forest was.

I shrugged into the jacket I had enchanted for warmth, and then added a pair of leather gloves, and draped a blue scarf around my neck. Another moment and I transferred everything in my purse to a backpack, added a bottle of water and half a dozen protein bars, and I was ready to go. I stopped in the living room to bribe Raj to be good and not get in trouble, then headed to the door.

There, I saw that while Kipa was still wearing his jeans and rust-colored sweater, he had added a windbreaker to the mix, and he, too, had a pack slung over his shoulder. He handed me a pair of earmuffs and slid his over his ears. They were fuzzy and warm, but I could still hear perfectly well.

"Ready?"

"Let's go," I said, as we headed out.

IT WAS SNOWING, and the flakes were piling up for real now. Seattle got snow every now and then, and it usually didn't last long when we did, but every few years we got a massive punch. It wasn't as bad as it had been the year before, but the inches were slowly creeping higher and I had the feeling the storm would be around for a week or so before moving off.

The air was so crisp and cold it hurt my lungs and I started to cough, then covered my nose until we were inside the car and the heater was blowing out cool air. It would take a few minutes for it to warm up, so we waited. By the time Kipa had finally de-iced the windshield, the car was warm and toasty.

The drive to Quest Realto's place usually took fifteen minutes from my house, but today it stretched out to twenty-five minutes thanks to how slick the roads were. We pulled into her driveway promptly at the stroke of noon. She was waiting inside, but when we stepped out of my car, she opened the door and hustled down the porch steps. Like most coyote shifters, she was thin to the point of being gaunt, and she had a weathered look to her. She waved us over toward the massive oaks that stood in her front yard.

"It's blowing up a storm," she said. "I know we were supposed to get a few inches, but another cold front is sweeping down into the area and it's going to bring subfreezing temperatures. I can feel it in my bones. So make sure you've got candles and flashlights ready, because that kind of storm brings outages."

I paused, frowning. "Should we go now? If the temperatures are dropping—"

"Everything will be all right. We'll be back by tonight, so Raj will be fine." Kipa wrapped his arm around my shoulders and kissed the top of my head. "I promise, everything will be fine."

I wasn't sure about that, but I decided to trust him. I turned to Quest. "When did they say the subfreezing temperatures are supposed to get here?"

"By tomorrow morning. They're moving in overnight. The weather forecasters are saying it's an arctic front like we haven't seen in years. I don't think it's supposed to bring much more snow, but we may have freezing rain or ice storms. So I suggest whatever you have to do over in Annwn, you hurry it up and get back as soon as you can."

Kipa glanced at the oak trees. "Is the portal ready?"

Quest jammed her hands in the pockets of her parka. "Yeah, it is. I won't be here when you get back, but I think it should be set fine for your return. Good luck with whatever you're doing."

Kipa took my hand and we headed toward the portal. This was the one I used when I went to see my therapist, and I was familiar with the vortex.

As I looked up, I could see a giant spider's web of energy between the trees. The glowing strands crackled and snapped as we approached. The trees themselves were sentient, like all portal trees, although not many people knew that. They could sense us, and if they didn't want us to go through, they could stop us. But most often, portal trees paid no attention to who used them, or why. Only when their energy was harnessed by one of the gods or a powerful magician did they keep a watchful eye on the travelers passing through.

"Ready?" Kipa asked.

"Let's go. Let's get this over with."

Holding hands, we stepped through the portal, into the mist beyond.

As we exited the vortex, we landed near Cernunnos's palace. We were on a road that led directly to it, first passing through a small village that I was unfamiliar with. Most of the inhabitants were Elves. As Kipa and I stepped onto the cobblestones that surrounded the portal, forming sort of an entry pad, the portal keeper stepped forward. He took one look at Kipa and bowed.

"Welcome, Lord of the Wolves." He glanced at me, and acknowledged me with a silent nod.

Kipa looked at him, frowning. "Since when did Cernunnos begin stationing portal keepers to greet visitors?"

"Lord Kipa, he ordered us to begin doing this about a month ago, should any of the Dragonni decide to try to invade Annwn."

It was then that I noticed the portal keeper was heavily armed. He had a bow on him that looked like the equivalent of an elephant gun, and the bolts in his quiver were massively thick. I couldn't help but wonder how strong he had to be in order to cock the bow string.

Kipa must have been thinking the same thing because he said, "Those must be poisoned bolts, then?"

Not poisoned," the portal keeper said. "They're allentar."

Kipa whistled. "Then yes, they could take down one of the Dragonni. Not kill them, but take them down for a while. Good thinking on Cernunnos's part." He wrapped his arm around my waist. "Let's get moving. We don't want to waste any time."

"What's allentar?" I asked. The word sounded familiar but I couldn't recall what it was or where I had heard of it.

"Allentar is ilithiniam that has been fortified with dragon scales."

I whistled. Ilithiniam was a magical metal that was incredibly strong and it held magic better than any other metal. The dwarves mined most of it. Combine it with dragon scales and it had to be almost invincible.

The path from the portal sloped downward, through an open meadow toward the village ahead. There was snow here in Annwn too—massive amounts of it compared to Seattle. The pathway had been shoveled, but it was still slick and to the sides were mounds of snow.

Beneath the banks of snow that had been shuffled off of the pathway, there was at least three feet of snow spreading across the field. To either side of the field stretched the great forest of Y'Bain. It bordered most of Cernunnos's lands and the massive trees grew so tall they almost blocked out what light there was. The forest proper was always gloomy except for sporadic clearings where the light shone through. Cernunnos's palace was on the other side of the village, probably two miles ahead.

Even in my enchanted jacket, I still shivered because

the rest of me could feel the cold. We came to a steep spot on the path where the slope had at least a 15 percent grade. I stared at the descending trail.

"Dude, I'm not sure I can navigate that without falling flat on my butt. My boots have good tread on them, but that's a steep slope and I'm not exactly the most graceful person in the world."

Kipa grinned, shaking his head. "True enough. Tell you what," he said. "It would be easier on both of us if I shifted into my wolf form and you rode on my back."

"That might be best, since you seem to have good traction when it comes to snow." I stood back as Kipa shifted into his wolf form. It was like watching a movie that had been sped up, to where his movements were almost a blur. The gods didn't have to disrobe before changing form, which was a definite advantage.

A moment later a great gray wolf appeared, almost up to my shoulder. Kipa's eyes were an intense blue when he was in wolf form, and he was both beautiful and terrifying. When we went on camping trips, he would transform and I would ride on his back like Ember did on Herne's back when he was in stag form, and we would traverse the back paths of the forest where most hikers never set foot.

He lay down beside me so I could climb aboard his back. I took hold of the fur on his neck to brace myself and then swung my leg over his back. As he rose, I held on to the fur. It didn't hurt him, and it gave me a way to balance. Kipa let out a bark. We had established a way for me to understand him, and I knew that meant he was asking me if I was ready.

"Ready, love," I said.

And then, we were off. He ran so fast the snowbanks

to the side of the path were a blur, shimmering like crystal as we raced along. I leaned forward, holding on tight, the wind and snowflakes gusting past me. The slope was daunting, but Kipa's paws were surefooted and his stride even. When we reached the bottom, he kept going.

Instead of heading through the village toward the palace, he turned to the right and we ran parallel to the town. The houses were made of stone, and smoke rose from their chimneys. Their yards were covered with snow, but barren oak trees were plentiful, as were conifers, and it reminded me of the rural areas back home, with more of a magical feel.

A few people were out and about, but they hurried along, the chill of the winter keeping outdoor interactions at a minimum. Most of the villagers were Elves, with a very few humans in their midst. From what Kipa had told me, over the millennia, some humans had migrated to Annwn and set up their homes here—usually at the behest of friends who were Fae or Elven.

We continued past the village, running parallel to the great trees of Y'Bain, through the open clearing. A small thicket up ahead loomed. It wasn't part of the forest, but a copse separate to itself, and was a mix of fir and cedar, birch and oak and maple. The barren limbs of the latter spread like webs through the sky, and the white bark of the birch stood in stark contrast to the trunks of the other trees.

Kipa paused at the trailhead and at first I thought he wanted me to get off, but when he didn't kneel, I said, "Are we almost there?"

He let out a warning bark. I stayed where I was and didn't try to scramble off. It would have been difficult to get off his back anyway, since he was still standing. He raised his muzzle to the sky, his nose twitching as he tested the scents in the air, and then, after a moment, he began to walk again, giving me time to once again grab hold of his fur before he took off, running along the path, lightly jumping over root and branch and stone.

The first thing I noticed about the copse was that the snow was thick here as well, but the path seemed fairly clear. Which meant either someone came out here and shoveled it, or some magical force was in action. Snow didn't decide where to drop by itself. I made a note to ask Kipa once he had shifted back.

As we loped along, we saw other animals in the thicket. I saw a great deer to one side and it made me think of Herne and his father. And we also passed foxes chasing rabbits, and dozens of birds who were hopping from branch to branch, looking for food.

I began to wonder how long we'd keep going when another clearing up ahead caught my attention. There were two houses in the meadow, with smoke swirling from both chimneys, and the cottages looked snug and well-made. To one side of the meadow was what I assumed was a shed, and next to it, a fire crackled beneath a frame that held row after row of fish, skewered on metal sticks. The fire bathed the fish in smoke.

Kipa came to a stop in front of the first cottage and knelt so I could slide off his back. I winced—his form was so massive that it always strained my thigh muscles when I rode his wolf form. I was standing on a path that had been shoveled clear. It led to the other cottage, then to the shed, and in the other direction it led back out to the path through the thicket.

As Kipa emerged from the mist that always swirled around him when he transformed, he motioned for me to take his hand. "Hey love, what do you think of Thicklewood?"

"It's beautiful," I said, looking around.

"Yes, it is. Y'Bain is an ancient forest, and Thicklewood is a remnant of it, divided from the main woodland. Once Y'Bain covered this entire part of Annwn—a sprawling woodland, until Cernunnos moved in and took over, building his palace and the villages surrounding it. The forest pushed back, and he made an agreement with the massive devas of Y'Bain that he would keep his people from destroying more of the woodland, and he and the other gods would stay out of its borders."

I frowned. "So the gods can't enter? What happens if they do? Is Y'Bain an entity in itself?"

"Exactly. Y'Bain is more than a forest. The entire forest is an entity, and it's capable of acting through any of the smaller woodlands around here. Through the animals, through the trees, through other, more sinister methods. Y'Bain has eyes and ears everywhere within its borders, and it's an ancient and crafty soul. If the gods enter, Y'Bain will make it rain hell on their followers." He stopped at the door and knocked.

A few seconds later the door opened and the man standing there looked at us, then he clapped Kipa on the shoulder. "Kuippana, what are you doing here? Come in. And who is this?"

"Dek, how goes it, you old salt?" Kipa grabbed his hand and pulled him in for a hug, in the way brothers in arms hug each other, giving him a thud on the back. "Let us in out of the cold, man."

Dek ushered us in, then shut the door. Kipa immediately aimed me for the fireplace where there was a cushioned bench in front of the flames.

I glanced around the cottage. We were in what looked to be the living–dining area, and it was spacious, with the massive stone fireplace as the focal point. A table to one side looked like it could seat ten, with long benches replacing the chairs, and there were two sofas along with a rocking chair near the fireplace. There were three other doors that led to what I assumed were other rooms, and through an open archway I could see what appeared to be the kitchen, with a massive wood cookstove.

"Dek, this is my mate, Raven BoneTalker. Raven, this is an old friend of mine, Dek. He's a bear shifter, and has lived out here for years."

"How do you do, miss?" Dek said, scrutinizing me. "You aren't an Elf."

"No, I'm not," I said with a laugh. "I'm one of the Ante-Fae."

His eyes widened. "I've heard of your kind but never had the opportunity to meet with any of you." He glanced at Kipa. "You're running with a dangerous crowd, my man."

I wondered if Dek knew Kipa was a god, but there was no reason to think he didn't. And it was true, the Ante-Fae *were* known to be dangerous.

"I can handle it," Kipa said. "How about a drink?"

Dek glanced at me. "Would you care for a brandy?"

Brandy sounded like a good idea. "I would welcome a drink. It's cold out there." While he was pouring brandy into three very ornate goblets, I asked, "Who lives in the other cottage?"

"My daughter and her husband and my grandchildren. My wife was killed several years ago," he said, his expression stoic. But beneath it, I could hear the edge of pain.

"I'm sorry," I said.

"Hilde was killed by a hunter. He mistook her for game when she was in bear form," Kipa said, his voice soft.

I winced. That was one danger all shifters faced, no matter where they lived. It was a hazard almost unique to their species—shifters always ran the risk of being killed by non-shifters. Most shifters could tell when someone was one of their kind, even if it was a different variant of animal form. But humans, Fae, and Elves weren't quite so clear sighted when it came to the subtleties that went into discerning shifter from animal.

Dek turned around. "Yes, and that hunter paid blood money to me, and has done his best to make up for the mistake…but all the *I'm sorrys* in the world won't bring back my wife. Anyway, yes, my daughter and her family live next door." He let a soft breath whistle between his teeth. "Tell me, Raven, what are your skills and strengths?"

That was one of the more formal ways in Annwn of asking what you did for a living.

"I'm a bone witch. I'm pledged to Arawn and Cerridwen. I live over through the portals, and I read fortunes, clear spirits out of houses, and other odds and ends like that." I accepted the crystal goblet. The warm scent of strong brandy rose to tickle my nostrils.

"Then a toast, to long years and many of them for all of us," Dek said, raising his glass.

Kipa and I followed suit, then I took a sip of the brandy. It was like fiery silk trickling down my throat.

Smooth, yet with a punch that clouded my senses. This wasn't any generic brandy, that was for sure.

"This is good," I said, my voice cracking from the alcohol. "What is it?"

"It's a special blend that I get from an Elf I know who makes it. Knocks your socks off, doesn't it?" Dek said, settling into one of the chairs near the fireplace. "So, old man, I don't often get to see you. What brings you to my doorstep today?"

Kipa swirled the spirit in his glass. "I'm sorry it's been so long. I've been embroiled in quite the mess back home. But that's for another time. We need to know about a particular entity, and whether it's a Crypto, or an astral creature, or what. You're the expert on the subject, so I figured, go to the best, first. And Raven needs to ask your advice on gargoyles."

"And so they *all* come to my door for answers," Dek said, grunting. "All right, suppose you describe this creature to me?"

I described what Raj had told me about the astral entity, and told Dek what had happened.

"So, a bat-like creature with a pitchfork tail and horns? And it probably used its tail to try to strangle you? That sounds like a barrel of laughs," he said, standing and heading for a bookcase that spanned half a wall on the other side of the room. He searched through row after row of books, and then finally pulled out a thick volume with a black leather cover. He carried it over to the table and motioned for us to join him.

"It's easier to skim through the pages here," he said, lighting the table lamp—an oil lamp that gave off a surprising amount of light. Kipa and I joined him, sitting opposite.

Dek handed me a notebook and a pen. "Can you sketch what the creature looked like?"

I stared at the paper and pen. "You didn't get these over here." The notebook was a college-ruled theme composition book and the pen was a gel-ink pen, common on Earth but not in Annwn.

"No, actually. A friend of mine returned from over on your side of the portal with a massive stash of goodies, and these were a gift. He knows how much I enjoy drawing, so he outfitted me with notebooks of all kinds, these wonderful ink pens, some colored pencils and paints—basically enough to last me for several years of sketching and writing." Dek beamed. "I envy your easy access to these sorts of things, but I don't envy what he tells me of the crowds in your lands, and of the pollution."

"Well, you're right to not envy that," I said, taking up the pen. I began to sketch out what Raj had described. "Mind you, my gargoyle saw it, not me—so this is based on what he saw."

"You have a gargoyle living with you?" Dek asked. "You get more and more interesting with every minute."

I glanced up at him. "Yes, and I wanted to ask some questions about gargoyles, if you happen to have any answers."

"Has he ever attacked you?" Dek asked.

I paused in my drawing. "No, never. I love him dearly and he loves me."

"Then you have an unusual gargoyle. They can be highly volatile and dangerous, Raven. I'm surprised he hasn't broken bones or scratched you bad enough for stitches." He motioned to the paper. "Finish the drawing, please."

I went back to my work, but in my heart, I was worried. What he said about gargoyles didn't mesh with Raj at all. I needed to know more—and I needed to know sooner rather than later.

CHAPTER TWELVE

WHEN I FINISHED, I HANDED THE NOTEBOOK BACK TO DEK. He stared at it for a moment, then snapped his fingers and began thumbing through the massive book.

"What's the name of that book?" I asked. "Have you ever heard of *Beltan's Bestiary?*"

He glanced over at me. "Beltan was an impatient man and when he copied the texts from *my* book, he skipped a lot of them. I never understood why he didn't want all the information. As you can see, this volume has twice what he ended up with."

I stiffened. "You *knew* Beltan? He wrote the definitive guide on Cryptos—"

"I'm sorry to burst your bubble, my dear, but Beltan was nothing more than a copycat. And a bad one at that. I've seen what he published in your world and it's a poor imitation of what I have here. I'm the one who researched and gathered this information over the centuries. When he accidentally came through a portal, I happened to be the first person he ran into."

"How did he end up with your grimoire?" I asked.

"He landed through a portal in this wood and I saved his ass. I brought him home and he stayed with us for a bit. Not only did he steal my work, but he tried to seduce my wife, the asshole. Before he made moves on her, though, he happened to see me working on the compendium and asked if he could have a copy. I told him he'd have to copy it, but sure. He did, but he grew impatient and skipped vast numbers of entries. And then he laid hands on my Hilde and she beat him senseless and told me to get rid of him. I escorted him back to the portal. I didn't give him permission to claim the work as his own, but he did anyway. Since he did so outside of Annwn, there's not much I can do," Dek said. "I do begrudge that he made a fortune off of my work and didn't even think to give me credit."

Sitting back in my chair, I said, "That's not right. But I don't think there's much I can do about it. But…I wish I could have time to read through your grimoire."

So Beltan had plagiarized his entire book and done a bad job of it at that. The thought made me simmer. I valued having the resource at hand, but he could have at least thanked Dek in the acknowledgments.

"Here, is this your creature?" Dek turned the book around and pushed it over to me. The language was one I didn't understand, but the shape of the creature matched what Raj had described to a T, and my inner alarm began to ring.

"Yes, that's it. I'm certain. My instinct is shouting that's what tried to kill me."

Dek ripped out a piece of paper from the notebook

and handed it to me. "Since I doubt you can read my scribbles, let me dictate to you what you need to know."

I took the pen and paper and waited. "All right."

"This creature is known as an *aztrophyllia*. It lives in the astral plane most of the time, but it can emerge into the physical realm if it finds a host. Usually the host will be weakened through grief or illness, to where it doesn't have the will to fight off the aztrophyllia. The creature feeds on life force, and will drain the host dry over a number of months—it's a slow feeder. Then, once the host dies, it will either return to the astral plane or it will look for yet another host."

I jerked my head up. "Lenny." I turned to Kipa. "I'll bet this is the thing that attacked Lenny." Looking back at Dek, I asked, "So, can it dislodge from the host and then return to it?"

He nodded. "They're actually great tactical creatures. Yes, it can do that, and it can also remain invisible when it enters the physical plane. But when it attaches to the host, it does so from the astral. Aztrophyllias are common in the astral plane—think of them as psychic leeches. But it can attack on the physical level as well, and the attack you described is its primary mode. You're lucky, though."

"Why?" I had a feeling there was more coming than I wanted to know.

"The point on that tail? When it's in the astral plane, that's how it attaches to the host, by inserting the tail into the back side of the heart chakra. However, when it materializes on the physical plane, not only can it become invisible, but the tail contains a venomous stinger. I'm surprised it didn't sting you, which would have allowed the creature to drain your magic and life force. For some reason, it saw you as a threat that it needed to dispose of quickly."

"It knew that I was onto the fact that it was attached to Lenny," I said. "So did Raj kill it?"

"No, I doubt very much that he managed to kill it. It's like the cockroach of the astral plane. Not much can eliminate it. You *can* wound it with a silver weapon, however. That requires stabbing it with either a silver weapon when it's in physical form, draping the host in silver—which will dislodge it astrally. Another physical attack is to immerse it in a saltwater bath or a pile of salt like a slug." Dek leaned back. "So, you say this thing has a friend in its power?"

"Yeah. I thought it was a Walk-In at first."

"The aztrophyllia can control its host, but that's not its main focus. The creature's primary goal is to thoroughly drain every ounce of energy out of the host. It's a predator, and a parasite. And they're clever."

"Then it definitely could have sensed that I knew something was wrong with Lenny and come after me to protect itself and its food source?" The thought of an astral leech that was also intelligent and that could recognize a threat was daunting.

"Yes, I believe that it could."

I glanced at Kipa. "Well, at least we know what we're dealing with. How do I go about detaching it from Lenny, though? And how do we keep it from reattaching itself to him again?"

Dek frowned. "That's a tough call. You'll have to go out on the astral to do that. Once you're out there, you'll have to wound it enough to keep it away while you fix a seal of protection on your friend. That's your best bet. If you try to destroy the creature, I'm thinking you'll end up in a fight you may have trouble winning."

"What about me? I'm a god. I should be able to stop it." Kipa leaned back, crossing his arms over his chest.

Dek laughed. "Oh, my brother, you know too well that the gods can't solve all problems. You would do well to help your lady, though. I think you should go out to the astral to fight it and keep it occupied while she casts the seal of protection on her friend."

"Good idea," I said. "I'm not familiar with seals of protection, but I'll do some research to find out how to cast them. Llew might know, or he'll know someone who can teach me."

Kipa shook his head. "No, Llew won't. This is a powerful spell and very few of the magic-born know how to wield it. But I *do* know someone who can teach you," Kipa said. "He belongs to the Force Majeure."

I took a deep breath. The Force Majeure was a group of master sorcerers and magicians. There were twenty-one of them at any given time, and all of them were thousands of years old. They ranged from Taliesin to Rasputin to the Merlin and more. In fact, the Merlin was Herne's grandfather. The chance to meet one of them was both tempting and terrifying. They were the rock stars of the magical world.

"Who?" I asked.

"Väinämöinen, the first bard," Kipa said. "He's the oldest hero in all of Kalevala. And he's a master sorcerer."

The thought of just being able to say hello to such a powerful magician was exciting, but to actually learn from him? That was a carrot I couldn't refuse.

"How do we get in contact with him?" I asked.

"I'll take you to him. We'll have to journey to the realm of Kalevala. That's where Väinämöinen lives. It will be a cold trip, though, far colder than this one." He flashed me a smile. "I'll get to show you my home sooner than I thought."

I had been looking forward to seeing the miles of forests and the thousands of lakes he had told me about. While the thought of going in there to face one of the oldest members of the Force Majeure was as daunting as it was exciting, I wasn't going to let fear sway me.

"All right. When can we go?"

"Tomorrow." Kipa winked at me. "You'll love it, and the first bard won't turn you into a toad. I promise."

"Well then, it sounds like you have a plan to take care of the problem." Dek pushed the book aside and stretched. He was truly a burly man and I could easily see the aura of the bear around him. "Are you hungry? I have bread and the sweetest, creamiest cheese you've ever tasted. I also have a pot of soup on the stove that's been simmering since morning."

I realized that my stomach was rumbling and now that he mentioned it, I could smell the soup. I had thought the cottage smelled good, but now I knew that it was the smell of rich broth and beef and tomato.

"I'd like that," I said, before Kipa could answer.

"Then lunch it is," Dek said, crossing over to the stove.

"Do you need some help?" I asked.

"Nay, lass. You're a guest. Sit and be comfortable. We'll have a chat about gargoyles as we eat." He methodically began to ladle out soup into stoneware mugs, and then opened a breadbox on the counter near the massive iron cookstove. As he was lifting a loaf out of the box, there was a knock on the door and it opened, a lovely, tall redheaded woman peeking around the corner.

"Da—can you… Oh, I didn't know you had company," she said, slipping inside the room. She was wearing a long green gown with knotwork trim in yellow, and over the gown she wore a heavy cloak in winter white. Her hair was down to her lower back, held in place by braids on both side of her temples that met in the back, fastened with a crystal barrette. Behind her, a small boy peeked at us around her skirts. He was the spitting image of her, and had his left thumb jammed in his mouth as he held onto his mother's skirts with his right hand.

"Come in, Nettie. Do you remember Kuippana?" Dek waved her in, his face brightening.

"Of course," Nettie murmured, curtseying to Kipa. "Lord of the Wolves, you honor us with your presence."

Kipa was suppressing a laugh, I could see it in his eyes. "Mistress Nettie, well met yet again. Allow me to introduce my lady, Raven BoneTalker, the Daughter of Bones. And is this one of your young ones?"

Nettie glanced at me and curtseyed again. "Yes, Lord Kuippana. This is my son, Avan. How do you do, Lady Raven?"

I wasn't used to the formality, but realized that here, Kipa's godhood was taken more seriously than back in our world. People—humans especially—didn't seem to realize how powerful the gods could be. They seemed to think they were like superheroes or entertainment celebrities rather than vast immortal beings. Granted, the gods weren't omnipotent, but they were far more powerful than most people understood.

"I'm well, thank you for asking. What a cute child," I

said. I wasn't that interested in kids, except if they needed help, but the boy was adorable. He stared up at me with sparkling eyes.

"Ghos'—" he said, pointing at me.

Surprised, I walked over to his side, kneeling. "That's right, I'm a bone witch and ghosts follow me everywhere," I said. "But they're okay—don't be afraid." I turned my head to Nettie. "He can see spirits?"

"Yes, it's a gift he has." As she stared at me, Nettie let out a gasp and took a step back, then caught herself. "I don't mean to offend but…you're one of the Ante-Fae, aren't you?"

I stood. "Yes, I am. Please don't be afraid. I'm not nearly as dangerous as some of my race."

There was a lot of fear of the Ante-Fae among some of the Crypto communities, and with good reason.

"Yes, Lady," Nettie said. She turned to her father. "Da, I was going to ask if you could watch Avan for the afternoon? I have to travel into the village to shop, and Jerah is out hunting with Tomvil. Aiada is making up the bread for the week and Avan would get in her way."

Dek set down the bread and picked up the boy. "How about it, boy? Would you like to spend the afternoon with your Gran-Da?"

Avan laughed and leaned in to plaster a kiss on Dek's nose. "Yah. Gran-Da," he started to say, but ended in a yawn.

"He needs his nap," Nettie said. "He'll be shifting any minute and best he be asleep by then."

Dek glanced at me. "Our people, when we're children, automatically shift when we take naps and go to sleep at night." He handed Avan back to Nettie. "All right, get him situated in the guest room and then be off to do your shopping."

"Thank you, Da," she said, taking Avan and heading through one of the other doors in the cabin.

"I hate to ask, but...do you have..." I blushed. There was no delicate way to say I had to use the bathroom, but Dek seemed to understand.

"The door my daughter went through? You'll find the facilities through the one next to it." He pointed to the second door. "Go down the hall and take the third door on the right."

"Thank you," I said.

The door led to a long hallway, which surprised me, given that when I had first seen the cottage, it looked far smaller than it seemed inside. But I was well aware of magic that created spatial distortions and so I didn't bother trying to figure it out. I merely followed the hallway that stretched out for some ways, and when I came to the third door on the right, I opened it.

Inside was a bathroom that was both luxurious and yet, rustic. A marble bathtub sat against one wall, near a fireplace that took up half the wall. Several pails hung from a pole hung over the logs, and I peeked in them to see water, up to the brim. They were large enough that at first I wondered how Dek would carry them to the tub, but then it occurred to me that he was a bear shifter, and strong enough to manage without a problem.

There was a pitcher of water near a basin, along with a bar of soap, and a towel. In one corner of a room I spied a pump, and thought that must be a luxury—providing indoor water so he wouldn't have to haul it in from outside. In another corner of the room sat the toilet and it looked a lot like the composting toilets over on Earth. In fact, when I examined it, I saw that sure enough, it had been made in China. Laughing, I used the facilities and then washed my hands in the basin.

The soap was a pleasant rose scent, and when I was finished up, I glanced at my image in the mirror hanging over the basin. I smoothed a few stray strands of hair, but otherwise, everything still looked good and so I returned to the main room, resisting the impulse to sneak a peek in the other rooms in this wing of the cottage. First, it was rude, and second—I didn't feel like learning anything that I might not want to know.

I reentered the living room, ready to tackle lunch. Dek had set the table with the stoneware soup mugs that looked hand thrown, and the loaf of bread, cut into thick slices. There was butter and honey and a round of cheese cut into wedges. He had also added a ham, sliced thinly. The smells of the food made my stomach rumble.

"I guess I'm hungrier than I thought I was," I said. "So, you have an interesting house."

Dek snorted. "You are a mistress of understatement. Yes, that wing of the house extends into a private dimension that a witch friend of mine set up. It acts like a panic room does in your world, should anything go awry."

"Ah, I wondered." I slid onto the bench in front of my plate and we began to eat. The soup was a rich tomato-beef stock, with tender shreds of beef, sun-dried tomatoes that tasted like they had been dried at their peak, chunks of creamy white potatoes, and pearl onions. I hadn't tasted anything quite so good in a long time.

"I could bathe in this, it's so good," I said, shaking my head. "What's your secret?"

"Quality ingredients, prepared with care and love, and the perfect amount of char on the meat before you add it to the soup. Then slow cook it for several hours." Dek looked pleased. He pointed toward the cheese. "My daughter made that. Tell me what you think."

I obediently bit into a wedge of the cheese and the creamy tang hit my tongue and almost made me wince, but in a good way. I spread some of it on a piece of bread and ate it and everything blended together into one big orgasm for my taste buds.

"Oh man, I thought I ate well, but this…I could eat like this every day and be perfectly content. I think when I get home, I'll take more care with my meals." I looked at Kipa. "You too, Wolf-Boy. We're going to see what we can rustle up that might rival this."

Kipa snorted. "Yes, ma'am."

When we were settled into our meal, Dek asked, "All right, you said you had some questions about gargoyles?"

"Yes, I do. So, here's my situation. Some time ago, I won a young gargoyle—very young—in a poker game from a demon. The demon had cut off his wings, and the poor baby was hurting. I took him home and I tended to his wounds, and I found a witch who could cast a memory spell on him so he would forget about his early life and forget that he ever had wings. He's been with me over fifty years, and he has…oh…about the mentality of a child around eight years old—using human years." I described his size.

"How do you get along?" Dek asked.

"We've formed an intense bond. I love him and he loves me, and he gets anxiety disorder when I'm away too long. I found out that he's multilingual—apparently he only needs to hear a language to understand it. He also has a power that I've seen twice, and both times he's blanked out and forgotten all about the incidents." I told Dek about the incident with Jim Morrison's spirit, and then the aztrophyllia. "He has...what I call laser eyes. He was able to see the aztrophyllia even though it was invisible, and he shot a beam of light at it and made it let go of me. I need to know if these are common to the gargoyle race, or does he have some special powers that make him unique?"

Dek set down his spoon, propping it against the bowl, and walked over to his bookcase. He trailed his finger over the spines till he came to one volume, and he pulled it out. As he returned, he handed it to me. "Here, you can borrow this."

I opened it up, expecting not to be able to read the language, but it was written in a Fae dialect that I knew. The title page read "Gargoyles In Their Natural Environment" and I flipped to the contents page. The chapters included different types of gargoyles—apparently there were more than one—and the different environments they were found in, the principal traits of each species of gargoyle, their powers and abilities and innate nature, the care and feeding of each species, and finally, essays on what was apparently a great mystery about them.

"From what I know about gargoyles, the ability to speak multiple languages is innate among most of the species. And what you call the laser-eye power is normal among the gargoyle elite. It grows as they grow. I can only think that he must have come from a royal family line. Demons prize owning gargoyles for several reasons. They make effective bodyguards, for one thing, but they're also good ransom material if you can steal one from one of the royal bloodlines in the gargoyle world."

I stared at the book. "Royalty? You mean Raj could be a prince?"

"Probably a minor noble that's connected to the crown. If he'd been a prince, the demon wouldn't have cut off his wings because they'd never recoup their money. In fact, I wonder if the demon tried to extort a ransom and the family refused to pay, leaving your Raj to a life of captivity and torture." Dek scowled. "One thing to know about gargoyles is their society is harsh and they aren't kind to any of their own who are disabled or lacking in any sense of the word."

"That I knew," I murmured. I flipped through the book. "This looks in-depth."

"Yes, and it's all factual. That author is an excellent researcher. He lives in the great city of TirNaNog."

"The one near where I live, or its mother-city?" I asked, flipping through the pages. "Do you mind if I make a copy of this before I give it back to you?"

"Of course you may. And I'm speaking of the mother-city of TirNaNog."

TirNaNog was the city of the Dark Fae, and Navane was the city of the Light Fae. Both were ancient and sprawling, and they were at constant war with one another. But over on Earth, the smaller cities—named after the original—kept their warring in check. *Somewhat.* My friends Herne and Ember were in charge of the Wild Hunt Agency and their main purpose was to ensure that collateral damage—from petty bickering between the two —didn't splash over into the human realm.

"I've never seen the original cities. I'm not sure I want

to, given the depths of their animosity toward one another. And I'm sure they wouldn't hesitate to aim that animosity toward the Ante-Fae, either. They don't like the fact that we're their predecessors and stronger and more cunning than any of them—Light or Dark." I had friends who were Fae but most of them seemed to be on the outs…the black sheep of the family or rejected by their lineage for one reason or another.

"Yes, well, you aren't missing anything unless you like beautiful architecture. Even within the city walls, you can feel the sense of arrogance seeping through the air. They don't welcome my kind there either, so we have something in common." Dek shrugged. "No skin off my nose. But the author who wrote that book lives there, and he's on the outskirts of society. Most of the Fae are unconcerned about anyone who isn't one of their own."

I wanted to begin reading the book right there, but that would be rude. So we finished our lunch, talking about other things, and then Kipa stood.

"I hate to eat and run, but we should get back home and start working on the wards against the aztrophyllia. I know we put up another one this morning, but I'm not sure how well it's going to work." He motioned for me to stand. "I'll get our coats—"

"No," Dek said. "You're my guests, I'll get them. Besides, they're in one of my guest rooms and Avan is asleep in there."

As he slipped out, I turned to Kipa. "You can actually get me in to see Van…what the hell is his name again?"

"Väinämöinen. And yes, he happens to be a friend of mine. He's also one of Tapio's friends and we had a lot of boys' nights until…" He stopped, a sheepish look on his face.

"Until you tried to seduce his wife. You dolt!" I said, smacking him on the arm. "I wish you'd apologize *for real* so that you could go back to Mielikki's Arrow without feeling like you're on probation."

Kipa laughed. "I'll try, love. I'll try."

CHAPTER THIRTEEN

HOLDING THE BOOK AS IF IT WERE PRECIOUS CARGO, I made my farewell to Dek, whom I decided I liked and then we headed back toward the portal through which we had come. I carried the gargoyle guide with me, making certain it was safely stowed away in my backpack.

The snow fell steadily, blotting out most of the sounds. I loved the way snow muffled everything. It felt like nature's bubble wrap, cushioning even the strongest blows. Once we were at the edge of Dek's home, Kipa changed into his wolf form again, and I climbed on his back as his mighty hind legs propelled us along the path, back to the hill and up the slippery surface.

By the time we reached the portal, I was deep in thought. The process to take care of Lenny involved far more than I had thought it would, and for the first time, I questioned whether I enjoyed putting myself out there for others. Dek's cabin had seemed so safe and cozy, and while I wasn't cut out for living out in the wilderness, I had a sudden desire to curl up at home and quit chasing down dragons and demons and ghosts and ghouls.

I must have been too quiet because, once we were at the portal and Kipa transformed back, he turned to me. "Are you all right, love?"

I shrugged. "I'm overwhelmed. I'm still coming to terms with what Pandora did to me, then this mess with the Banra-Sheagh, then my father's betrayal, and now, coping with Vixen's friend. Sometimes I want to get away and forget about everything and everybody except myself, you, and Raj. And the ferrets."

"You need a vacation," he said.

"We *all* need a vacation," I countered. "Look at Herne and Ember—and Angel, losing Rafé. The past year or so has been one big blur of stress and danger." Letting out a sigh, I leaned against the massive oak and crossed my arms, blinking as the snowflakes drifted down to get caught in my hair and my lashes. "Maybe I do need to get away."

"Whenever you want, love," Kipa said. "You don't have to solve everybody else's problems, you know. Vixen can find someone to take care of Lenny—"

"No, they can't. You and I both know that any typical medium wouldn't stand a chance against the aztrophyllia. It would probably go after them as soon as it killed Lenny. How can I turn away when someone's life is on the line and I'm the only one who has the knowledge on how to kill it? And the seal that we need to attach to him so it doesn't come back? Maybe you could find a strong-enough witch to cast it, but chances are it would take too long and he'd end up dying, anyway. I made a promise to Vixen to help if I could. I don't break my promises."

Kipa pulled me into his arms and I burrowed my face against his shoulder as he hugged me to his chest. "And that's one of the many things I love about you. You don't flinch when it comes to doing what you feel is right." He leaned down and kissed my nose, then my lips. "Raven..." There was a strange light in his eyes.

"What?"

He stared at me for another moment, before shaking his head. "Nothing...or rather, not now. But know that I'm so grateful Fate brought you into my life."

"Me too—you," I said, rising on my tiptoes for another kiss.

"Let's go home," he said, gently pushing me back. "Give me your hand."

"That's not necessary. I go through the portals pretty routinely, you know."

"I know. But give me your hand."

And so, hand in hand, once again we stepped through the portal, heading home.

THE SNOW on the other side of the portal had been falling steadily as well, and it was now six inches deep, but that was a far cry from the mounds we had trudged through in Annwn. We hoofed it to my car and settled in, and I turned up the heat. Even with my enchanted jacket, the trip had left me cold inside and out.

"First things first," I said. "We have to stop by Llew's shop so I can pick up the ingredients to create wards against astral creatures. What time is it?"

Kipa glanced at the car clock. "It's nearly seven—Llew closes up at five, doesn't he?"

"Six. All right, can you call him and put him on speaker for me?"

Kipa picked up my phone from where I had placed it in the cup holder. He searched through the contacts until he found Llew and dialed, then punched the speaker option.

"Hey Raven, what's up?" Llew asked. I could hear the sounds of people talking in the background.

"Llew, is there any chance you could meet me at the shop tonight so I can do some necessary shopping? I'd wait till tomorrow, but this is rather urgent."

Pans clanged in the background, and I heard someone —I thought it might be Jordan, Llew's husband—say something. And he didn't sound happy.

"Hold on," Llew said. "Muting for a moment."

"Nope, it's not going to happen tonight," I said as Kipa continued to hold the phone out. "Put us on mute too."

"Done, and what do you mean?"

"That was Jordan complaining in the background."

Jordan was nice enough, but at times he had issues with me. I had the feeling he felt secretly threatened by my friendship with Llew, and he wasn't above pointing out how much time Llew and I spent together. I had been walking a tightrope for over a year, and recently, I had discreetly pulled back, focusing on visiting more with Ember and Angel so that Llew's marriage wouldn't be put to the test.

"You've got to be kidding? Llew's *gay*. You're not a *guy*. What does Jordan have to be threatened by?"

149

"I don't know, but for some reason, he's insecure. I guarantee you when—"

"Raven?" Llew came back on the speaker. "Are you there?"

I unmuted. "Yeah, we're here, Llew."

"I don't think I can make it down there tonight. You have a key—pop in and take what you need. Leave a note if you don't have cash at the moment and you can pay me later."

What I needed was Llew's expertise about wards, but I wasn't going to pressure him. "Never mind. I'll see you later."

"I'm sorry, Raven," Llew sounded apologetic.

The last thing I wanted was for him to feel guilty. "It's okay, everything's fine, Llew."

As we headed home, I decided that I could tinker around and figure out something that would work. When we pulled into the driveway, I noticed the lights were on, but figured Raj had decided to turn them on. He couldn't work switches on lamps, but he could work a light switch on the wall. But as we headed up the sidewalk and around the corner to the walkway along the house, I paused.

"Somebody's here." I glanced at Kipa. "Someone's in there. I know it."

"I'll check. You wait here," he said, motioning for me to move farther down the sidewalk. "Get your keys ready."

I nervously palmed the keys to my car and took a deep breath as I steeled myself to run. Time seemed to stretch out as he edged his way to the door and cracked it open. That was another thing—the door should have been locked, but Kipa opened it without his keys. I tried to keep my nerves in check, praying that Raj was okay.

Please, Great Cerridwen, let Raj be okay—please protect him...

All of a sudden, I heard laughter from inside and Kipa peeked around the door.

"It's your mother—she's home early."

I let out an exasperated sigh. "Why couldn't she have texted me?" I said, marching inside.

"I did," Phasmoria said, standing near the sofa. "You didn't answer."

I pulled out my phone and glanced at it. "Nothing— see?" Then it hit me. "Oh, wait. I was in Annwn—of course your text wouldn't go through while I was over there." My irritation vanished into intense relief. "Never mind."

She grinned. "That's always your answer when you yell at me for no good reason. So, what were you doing over in Annwn?"

"Let me change out of these clothes and I'll tell you. Meanwhile, would you call for a pizza? I'm hungry. Though compared to Dek's lunch, a pizza doesn't sound quite as appetizing." My stomach rumbled and I rolled my eyes. "But I guess it sounds good to my empty gullet."

"What do you want on it?" she asked as Kipa.

I tucked Dek's book away in a fire safe in my office, then headed into my bedroom to change.

"Extra cheese, pepperoni, sausage, ham, pineapple, mushrooms, and make it a thin crust. Order two, because Raj will likely want a piece."

I shut the door behind us and began stripping. "I'm going to take a quick shower. I'm chilled through."

"You want company?" Kipa asked, arching his eyebrows.

I swatted at him. "Shoo, fly. It sounds delightful, but I need food more."

"I can fill you up," he said, slipping over to press himself against my naked body. The feel of his skin on mine made me melt, and he was hard against my thigh. I groaned and turned to him, half lifting my leg so he could slip inside me. He lifted me up, carrying me to the bed, where he laid me down and I wrapped my legs around his waist. As he reached down with one hand to finger me, I pressed my breasts against his chest and let out a soft moan as he stoked the raging fire that built between us.

The chemistry had been there from the beginning, and had grown over the months we had been together. We worked magic with our bodies and our passion.

My breath quickened as Kipa slipped his arms around me and stood, my legs still wrapped around him. He was still deep within me and he carried me into the shower. I reached out to turn on the water as I pressed my lips to his. While the water warmed, he sat me on the sink and stepped away, his eyes glistening as they turned ever so slightly topaz. He was as wolf as he could get without shifting.

"I wish you could feel what it's like to make love as a wolf, my love," he whispered.

"I wish I could too," I said, gasping as he trailed a finger down my chest, tracing the swirls that covered my torso.

And then the water was warm and he took my hand, leading me into the shower. There, I pressed my breasts against the shower wall as the warm water streamed over us, and he began lathering my back with the shower gel. The scent of freshly washed fir and cedar streamed over us, along with hints of rose and peach and vanilla. Kipa lathered me up, every inch, rinsing his fingers before he slid them inside me. Then he turned me around and washed my breasts and stomach before kneeling in front of me.

"Spread your legs," he whispered.

I obeyed, and he pressed his lips and tongue to me, flicking lightly as he unleashed the wild child in me. I began to rub my breasts, circling my nipples as he concentrated his focus. The water streamed down on us like some jungle love scene from a movie, and before I realized it, I came in a sudden, sharp jolt. I gasped, plastering my arms against the slick walls of the shower. Kipa let out a growl, his eyes shining, and I lowered myself to the floor, the water beating down on my back, as he knelt behind me and entered me, thrusting like the wild god he was, filling me so full I could barely breathe. We stayed locked together, his hunger driving into me, until we both came in a blur of passion.

I QUICKLY DRIED MY HAIR, my towel wrapped around me as Kipa slicked his hair back into a wet ponytail and fastened it with a hair tie. He dressed in jeans and a V-neck sweater.

"What do you want to wear?" he said, poking around in my closet.

I glanced at the clock. It was almost eight. "You know, pull out my pajama shorts and a tank top, would you, and my robe. I'm tired and I don't want to get dressed."

"All right." He did as I asked, finding a pair of the soft

knit boy shorts I used for when we had company and I couldn't walk around commando. He held up an oversized camisole, also in a soft knit. "This work?"

I glanced at the violet cami. "Yeah, that's good. And my fuzzy robe, not the silk one." I finished drying my hair, took off my makeup, and dressed, then slid my feet in a pair of cushioned slippers. With Kipa's arm draped around my shoulders, we headed out to the living room.

My mother was paying the delivery boy, and she carried three pizzas to the kitchen table, where I saw she had brought out paper plates and napkins.

"Oh thank you, I didn't feel like eating formally tonight." During the time my mother had lived with my father and me, she had insisted on place mats and china every night, and on rare occasions she had allowed me to eat in the living room. Of course, back then the world had been more formal, in many ways, and there was no TV to gather around.

I filled my plate with three slices of pizza and headed for the living room, stopping to grab a bottle of water from the fridge. Kipa followed me, his plate stacked high. The gods didn't technically need to eat—not much—but they enjoyed it, and when they did eat, they had good appetites.

"So," I said, settling in on the sofa, placing my plate on a tray on the coffee table. "Did you talk to Da and Dougal?" I both wanted to hear and yet didn't want to hear what went down. I was afraid that my relationship with my father might be permanently terminated. If he really *had* disowned me, then I'd have to get used to it, and though I knew I could adapt, the hurt was still a bitter pill lodged in my throat.

Phasmoria sat down in the rocking chair with her plate. She placed a glass of wine on a coaster, then cleared her throat. "Yes, I talked to your father, Raven. And to that curmudgeon of a grandfather you have. I found out what happened and I let them have an earful, trust me."

"What do you mean? What happened?"

My mother pursed her lips. "I never trusted the old man—when I first met him, I knew he was going to cause problems. That was before you were born. As you know, Curikan and I were just having fun, and then boom, I was pregnant. I wasn't sure what to do, but my instincts told me I needed to have you. We went over to Scotland so I could meet Curikan's family, and they treated him like dirt, but the old man fawned on me. He was sure I was going to have a boy and that the child would take after him. He wanted Curikan to stick to the Black Dogs for a love match and he wasn't thrilled with me, but if there was a chance he could get his hands on a boy..."

"Just how strong is Dougal?" Kipa asked.

"Stronger than you might think, but he's getting older. While his other sons would probably do a fine job leading the clan, Dougal wants Curikan to take over because Curikan is the smartest. But he wants Curikan to toughen up, and that's not Curikan's style. Curikan made the mistake of talking about the mess with Blackthorn to his father—he was horrified that Ember was almost killed by the King of Thorns. Dougal saw a chance to exert some control over the family. He was the one who went to the Banra-Sheagh and told her that she was losing control of her subjects."

"I didn't even know she *existed*. How can she lose control over people who have never heard of her? I don't even know how the Ante-Fae have a queen. We're all a bunch of anarchists, when you think about it." I bit into my pizza and suddenly, as good as Dek's lunch had been, the memory of it faded into a mouthful of hot cheese, yeasty crust, tomato sauce, and all those yummy toppings. I suddenly didn't mind as much that we weren't making our own bread.

"That's one of the issues at stake. The Banra-Sheagh is beginning to realize that she's outlived her time. The Ante-Fae have never been a cohesive people. You're right in that we all pretty much lead our own lives and don't give a flying fuck about the government. Anyway, I think Dougal saw a way to try and make Curikan behave with the promise of bringing you over to live with the family— and to ensure that you had to—he mistakenly thought that a word from the Queen would take care of your connections here. Dougal's intent on building a dynasty, and that would be fine except that he's banking on the wrong people."

I tried to sort out what my grandfather's goal was. "But what's his endgame? Why have me come over, since I'm not one of the Black Dogs?"

"To keep your father there. Curikan misses you, sweetie. Curikan was about ready to come home and your grandfather was frantic about it. He's convinced that if he can bring out your father's harsher nature, he will be the strong son that Dougal wanted him to be. You see, your uncles are dolts. They're the perfect temperament to lead the clan, but they don't have two brain cells to rub together to their names. So…"

I began to understand. "So, if Dougal can make Curikan more like them, then that—combined with his brains—would make for a powerful leader. But I still don't understand why he needs to strengthen the clan."

"Because there are other Black Dog families that are as old as Dougal's. Rivals, if you will, and they don't get along. Dougal is worried that in the future, his clan will die out or fade into a ragtag group. He's looking for power, Raven. And he sees your father as the one son who can build that power." Phasmoria picked up a slice of the pizza and bit into it. "Mmm, good. Dougal realized that you were the key to getting Curikan to stay. But when you refused to knuckle under, he decided that the only other way was to get Curikan to let you go. So he manipulated the Queen into making you a pariah. I think they had the plan worked out before you ever got there—what to do if you refused, that is."

So I had been a pawn. A carrot to dangle in front of my father's face, and then when that didn't work, he unceremoniously ripped my father and me apart. "Fucking bastard," I muttered.

"I have to agree," Kipa said. "That's a low trick, and somebody should take him to task."

I was almost afraid to ask the next question, but I had to know. "So, what did my father say to you about everything?"

Phasmoria gave me a gentle smile. "He knows what Dougal is up to, *now*. And he's heartsore about what happened. He's turning in his formal resignation from the clan and returning here in a week. Curikan is coming home, and he's asked me to speak on his behalf with you. He's asking for forgiveness, for not standing up for you in front of the Banra-Sheagh and your grandfather."

That was all I needed to hear. My father still loved me

and he hadn't been part of the trickery. I burst into tears, relieved and yet saddened that this had happened. And all the while, in the back of my mind, I knew that things would never be quite the same, and that I—and any of the Ante-Fae who supported me—would still be excommunicated from our people, and that might last forever.

CHAPTER FOURTEEN

After that, I was useless for the rest of the evening. All the conflicting emotions, along with the scare about the aztrophyllia, raced through me. I needed to relax, and as much of a release as sex had been, I wasn't feeling relaxed.

I finished my pizza, adding in a fourth slice, then brought over my handpan and stand and set it up. "Do you mind if I play for a bit?" If anything could relax me, it was the haunting notes of Laralea—my handpan's name. The music from the complex, UFO-shaped instrument resonated on an ancient level, sending me into a soft trance. I often worked magic with Laralea, but some days, I played her for fun or for joy or—like tonight—to relax.

"Please do," Kipa said. "I love it when you play."

My mother stared at it. "I don't think I've heard you play. Please, go ahead."

As they finished eating, I set to a pattern, closing my eyes and thinking of the mountains around here, the volcanoes and the massive forests and then the ancient groves over on the Olympic Peninsula. I played their music—the music of the watchful ones, the music of the sentinels of the earth who held sway over the land, whose deep roots burrowed so far into the ground that they had become entwined with the stones and fossils found below. I played the solitude of the forest, and then the wild cresting waves of the Pacific as she swept ashore, crashing in foamy white breakers, hauling driftwood logs to the beaches to toss them around like she was playing pick-up sticks.

And after I played the ocean's strength, I began to play magic, welling it up to surround me, feeling it thread into every note, in every echoing sound the reverberated out of the metal shell. The magic grew, surrounding me as it swelled and spilled out of the notes—and then, I opened my eyes to find the living room was alive with dancing lights, in shades of pink and yellow, blue and green, and they darted around like dragonflies, crackling with the energy I had woven.

"Beautiful," my mother whispered. "I've never heard anything so beautiful before. I had no idea you were musical."

"I found this instrument when she was first being made—it wasn't that long ago, actually, what…twenty years or so? And I fell in love with her. I realized I could make magic with her. And so, we began the journey together, with me figuring out how to weave the music into magic. Mostly, I use her for trance work, but there are times she's helped me sort out spells." I rubbed my hand over the metal. "I never play her when I'm wearing rings, because it could damage her."

"You would fit so well within my society," Kipa said.

"In my homeland, music is prized. Bards hold magical battles by singing their spells. I can see you in the deep forests of the north, by one of the thousands of lakes, playing your music and weaving your charms."

"Well, maybe I'll bring her when we go to Kalevala tomorrow."

"What's this?" Phasmoria asked, perking up.

"We're headed to my homeland tomorrow so I can introduce Raven to Väinämöinen, one of the Force Majeure. She needs to know how to perform a powerful spell because of—well, you tell her," Kipa said.

I told my mother about what we had found out about the aztrophyllia that was attached to Lenny and how it had attacked me. "If I don't dislodge it and protect him, he'll die."

"And if you do dislodge it, it may come for you. Have you thought about what to do in that case?" My mother didn't seem entirely overjoyed about the idea.

"I need some powerful wards for the house to prevent it from gaining entrance. Best-case scenario would be to prevent it from ever entering the physical realm again. So maybe Väinämöinen can help me learn how to do that, as well." That might be stretching good will a bit, but if you didn't ask, you never got an answer.

"We should get to bed early," Kipa said. "The journey to Kalevala requires going through a portal to Finland, and then through a portal there, which is actually in Mielikki's Arrow."

"Which portal will we be taking?" I asked.

"The one in the park next to Herne's house. I let him know we were going, and he's alerted Orla, the portal keeper, so she'll be waiting for us. She'll set the coordinates." Kipa yawned and stretched. "I want to sleep tonight."

Phasmoria frowned. "Well, if you're going to Kalevala, I'm coming along." She stood, picking up our plates. "I'll put the pizza away and make sure Raj is fed. You two go on to bed."

I gave her a kiss on the cheek as I passed. "Thanks… you're a good mother, you know that?"

"No, but I'm a functional one," she said. "I know I'm not the kind of mother that daughters hope for, but I hope that I'm the kind of mother that stands by her children."

"You're the mother I want with me when I'm in a jam," I said. Sleepy, I rested my head on her shoulder for a moment, then motioned to Kipa. "Come on, Wolf-Boy. Let's go to sleep." As we headed into the bedroom, I thought again about my father, and how he was coming home. I didn't know when, and I wasn't sure what was going to happen, but I fell asleep almost before my head hit the pillow, and I slept through until morning.

EARLY MORNING, Kipa woke me up by throwing open the bedroom window and letting the icy air invade the bedroom. I stared at him, blurry eyed. He seemed all too chipper and cheerful.

"What the hell?"

"Get up, woman! We have places to go and people to see." He grabbed my hand and launched me out of bed. I grabbed for the covers but too late—I found myself standing in front of him stark naked, my nipples greeting the cold air with a high-and-mighty salute.

"It's colder than a witch's tit, and mine are proving it," I grumbled, trying to worm my way out of his hold.

Kipa pulled me to him, wrapping me in his arms as his hands slid over my back and my butt. "Oh, woman, I love it when you talk that way," he murmured, laughing. "Kiss me, wench, and then get dressed before I rethink our trip and bed you again."

"You can bed me later, though it would be a lot warmer than standing here in the icy air." I was about to ask him why he was in such a good mood, but then it dawned on me—he was going *home*. He was going to see his homeland, and that always brought a smile to his face. I relented. It wasn't that I wasn't looking forward to the trip, but being woken up so rudely wasn't high on my list. "Okay, love, kiss me and then let me dress."

He did, long and slow and sultry, my hair in his fist, and then he slapped me on the ass again. "Get dressed. I'll go help your mother make breakfast."

As soon as he was out the door, I shut the window and slid into my robe. Figuring out what I wanted to wear was easy. Kalevala in winter was even colder than Annwn in winter, and there would probably be even more snow. I opted for a thick pair of leggings, a pair of gauchos—long out of style but still in my wardrobe—their hem an inch below my knee, a turtleneck sweater over a cami for extra warmth, and a pair of knee-high lace-up boots that were flat-soled, non-skid, *and* waterproof, since we'd no doubt be wading through deep snow. I also packed an extra pair of socks and underwear in my backpack, along with some hand warmers that could fit in my gloves. Finally, I added earmuffs, and a ski hat that had purple and black stripes.

When I entered the dining room, I saw that Phasmoria

and Kipa had made breakfast. Oatmeal with dried cranberries and brown sugar, and sausage, along with copious amounts of coffee. Raj came over and nudged me and I gave him a hug. I thought about calling Apollo to see if he could stay with Raj for the day, but then decided no, because if the aztrophyllia decided to return, Apollo wouldn't be able to fight against him. His talents and powers lay in the Prince Charming department, not the fighting side. But…

"I'm calling Trinity to see if he'll sit with Raj. He can fight against that creature if it returns or get Raj out of here if he needs to," I said, pulling out my phone.

"Good idea," Kipa said. "Trinity can take care of himself."

I wasn't sure if he'd answer—Trinity worked on his own schedule—but he picked up on the second ring. "Hey Trinity, I need a favor, if you have time."

"What's going on?" Trinity had one of those soft, seductive voices that always made me shiver. He was known as the Keeper of the Keys and the Lord of Persuasion. So he, like Vixen, was a Charmer, in many ways.

I explained what I needed and why, and he immediately agreed. "I'll be over in half an hour," he said. "Raj will be fine with me." Trinity might be shady in a number of ways, but when he gave his word to me, I knew that I could trust him.

Feeling much more secure, I dove into my breakfast. Raj would be safe while I was gone. "Is there anything I should know about traveling to Kalevala?"

"Watch out who you piss off," Kipa warned me. "Louhia comes from that area—though she's in Pohjola—

and there are a lot of sorcerers, bards, and witches in Kalevala. A number of them aren't very nice."

Phasmoria snorted. "Telling Raven to watch what she says in front of other people is a lost cause, and actually, after the other night in front of the Banra-Sheagh, I'm rather proud of that. But having said that, my daughter, Kipa knows his homeland the best. So try to watch yourself."

I stuck my tongue out at her. " 'No more wire hangers!' "

She looked bewildered. "What did you say and why do I have the feeling that's an insult?"

I laughed then. "*Mommie Dearest*. A movie. And it was sarcasm, not an insult. Yeah, I'll watch my tongue. I don't want any more problems than we already have." I paused. "Say, you can't take care of the aztrophyllia for me, can you?"

It was Phasmoria's turn to laugh. "No, I can't. My screech might do it in, but it would also kill your friend and I don't think that's your end goal."

"True enough. My end goal is to keep him alive. I keep forgetting you're not a one-woman army. Though sometimes it seems that way, and *that*, Mother, is a compliment." I leaned back, staring at my plate. I had finished everything but I was still hungry. "Is there any more?"

Kipa laughed. "Yes, there are more sausages and more oatmeal, if you want." He reached for my plate and bowl.

I handed them to him. "I do want. Thank you." I turned to Phasmoria. "So, seriously, all joking aside, you can't do anything?"

She shrugged. "I could try, but I could also make it worse. I'm powerful, but some astral creatures are more than a match for me. Bean Sidhe—even the Queen—are not all-powerful. And we do have specific functions we use in service to the Morrígan, so it's not like we're out there tooling around the world. As I said, I could try, but I have a feeling things might go south, and that's the last thing you want."

"Right. Okay, well, I guess that doesn't matter. I'm looking forward to learning something new anyway, if Väinämöinen will teach me. And I'm also looking forward to seeing Kipa's homeland." I paused as Kipa brought in my plate and bowl. The oatmeal was creamy, and the cranberries gave it a lovely tang that was countered by the savory sweetness of the brown sugar. And the sausages mirrored the brown-sugar flavor with an addition of sage and whatever else they used. All in all, it seemed like the perfect breakfast.

By the time we were done, Trinity arrived. He was his usual goth boy chic, with jet black hair pulled back into a braid and guyliner that made him look mysterious and sexy and yet, very slightly feminine.

He gave me a hug and waved at Kipa and Phasmoria. "Hey. Where are you off to?"

"Kalevala," I said. "I'm going to meet one of the Force Majeure, if he's willing to talk to me. If you could watch Raj, and make sure nothing comes through. There's an astral creature called an aztrophyllia that attacked me the other night—"

"I know what those are. I've tangled with one before. I finally managed to kill it, but it took a lot of time and energy. Hey, I have something I'd like to ask your advice on, but it can wait."

I glanced at Kipa and Phasmoria. Kipa was digging

through his pack while Phasmoria was carrying dishes into the kitchen. "I have a few minutes."

"Are you sure?"

I nodded, walking him into the living room away from the others. "Sure, what's up?"

Trinity blushed—and I never knew him to blush. In low tones, he said, "All right, here's the problem. I think I've met someone I really like."

"What's the problem with that? Unless…" I paused, wondering if his incubus nature had kicked in. "Is she married? Or…he?"

Trinity shook his head. "No, but that's part of the issue. Not that she's married, but the fact that… You know I'm half incubus."

"Right," I said.

"I really like this woman and I think she likes me. But what if I get together with her and then I… I'm a virgin, Raven. And I know that the incubus/succubus natures kick in—not necessarily at puberty, but the first time an incubus has sex. What if we get together, and then I turn into my father? That's why I never slept with anybody—not because I didn't want to, but because I'm afraid that I'll turn into some gluttonous, greedy perv who won't be able to sustain control. What would that do to a relationship?"

I managed to keep a deadpan face, but the realization that Trinity was a virgin, and the fact that he had deliberately avoided having sex because he was terrified his father's nature would come out and turn him into a sex addict who used people told me just how much he actually did care about people.

"Trin," I said, sitting down beside him and taking his

hand. "I don't know the answer to that, but there has to be somebody who can help you." Then it hit me. "Sejun—my counselor. If he can't help, then he should know someone who can. Maybe Ferosyn can help. I can call Herne and ask if he can get you an appointment. Ferosyn's the most powerful healer I know."

Trinity grimaced. "I guess. I feel like a fool. It's hard enough to talk about my parents—given neither of them want anything to do with me. And to admit that, at my age, I'm still a virgin? But I'm so afraid of triggering something I can't put back in the bottle."

"I'll call Herne and give him your number. Either way, it's better that you know what might—or might not— happen." I gave him a quick hug. "Thank you for trusting me. That's a hard secret to carry around."

Trinity leaned close enough to whisper. "Raven, you know that if it weren't for Kipa, it would be you—don't you? And if anything ever goes wrong between you, I'll be here, waiting."

I ducked my head. "I know," I whispered back. "I will never hurt Kipa…but if things *were* different…" I let the words stay unsaid. Better not to dangle the hope of too much in front of a hungry man. Especially when that man carried a powerful lineage behind him. I cleared my throat and said, "I'll talk to Herne for you. But now, we really have to leave. Thank you for taking care of Raj today."

Trinity held my gaze and it felt almost as though he were kissing me, but then the sensation dropped away and he said, "I'll spare asking you why you're heading over to the land of fire and ice until you get back, but I want to hear the whole story later." He waved us toward the door. "Go on, now. I'll watch over the place."

"There's some leftover oatmeal and sausages in the kitchen, if you'd like them," Kipa said.

For a while, he'd been jealous of the friendship that Trinity and I had, but I had finally convinced him that, even if I was attracted to Trinity, I wasn't going to act on it. Kipa had been there for me when I needed him, and we had such good chemistry and the love was there, and I couldn't see throwing away what we had for a fling.

Because as much as I liked Trinity, I knew that was all it would ever be and I had the feeling that, after talking to Ferosyn, Trinity would confirm it. He was half-incubus, and one thing I knew about the incubi was that they had trouble forming long-lasting love relationships. Friendships? Yes. Partnerships? Not so much.

Once we were outfitted, we headed for the door. Trinity was watching cartoons with Raj, and everything seemed settled and in order, so I tried to leave my worries at the door, and we settled in my car for the trip over to the park next to Herne's house. I texted Herne on the way, asking him to call Trinity, and then tried to put the gorgeous goth boy out of my mind.

CHAPTER FIFTEEN

GOING THROUGH PORTALS MIGHT BE LIKE STEPPING INTO A tornado and out again, but the effects weren't necessarily cumulative, unless you went jumping through them one after another in a short period of time. So the trip to Kalevala wasn't taxing, even though we'd been in Annwn the day before.

Finland was icy cold this time of year. We were nearing the Winter Solstice and the temperature had settled in around twenty-three degrees. It was snowing, and dark as pitch. Though it had been morning when we stepped into the portal, it was nearly nine P.M. when we stepped out of it. I glanced around.

"Where are we? And how far away is Mielikki's Arrow?" I asked. "It's freezing."

"I called ahead. She's sending someone to meet us," Kipa said. "It's too cold to walk. We're in a park. This is Merikatu Street."

I glanced around, trying to make out the lay of the

land, but even the street lights couldn't brazen their way through the blowing snow and the inky night.

"How do we address Her Ladyship?" Phasmoria asked.

Next to me, Kipa shivered, but I didn't think it was from the cold. "You call her Lady Mielikki. Or Lady of the Hunt, or Queen of Fae. Probably Lady Mielikki is best. She's got a sense of humor, but don't push it. And don't make a mess in her office. She hates clutter."

I snorted. "I can keep myself from throwing mud around."

"I'm not kidding," Kipa said. "Mielikki is a neat freak, for all her wandering she does in the woods. I think, though, Tapio will be relieved to meet you, if he's around."

"Why?" Then it dawned on me as to why Mielikki's husband would be happy to see me. "Oh, that's right. You made a pass at her right in front of her husband once, didn't you?"

Kipa sobered. "Yeah, and it's a mistake I'll never make again." At that moment, a black sedan pulled up, with tinted windows.

"What, are they vampires?" I tried to see who was driving but couldn't.

"Yeah, don't joke about that either. Mielikki doesn't care for vampires, though she does rule over a number of the Leannan Sidhe, so…energy vampires she's not so down on." Kipa opened the front door and spoke to the driver for a moment, then opened the back door and motioned for Phasmoria and me to slide in. He rode shot-gun. The driver was a muscular man in a chauffeur's outfit who didn't even acknowledge Phasmoria or me. I wasn't sure what I had expected, but he wasn't it.

The car glided through the streets, silent in the muffling snow. I could barely see anything through the tinted windows, but soon, we pulled into a parking lot next to a three-story stone building. The driver opened the doors for us, and motioned toward the building's doors.

The first floor housed a medical clinic. Odd, I thought, because the first floor of the building the Wild Hunt was in also homed an urgent care clinic. We took the elevator to the second floor, stepping into the lobby of Mielikki's Arrow, a sister organization to the Wild Hunt. The receptionist—a blond bombshell who reminded me of some Norwegian goddess—was sitting behind the counter. She smiled, and the entire room lit up.

"Welcome to Mielikki's Arrow. Lord Kuippana, it's so nice to see you again."

I glanced at Kipa but he didn't seem fazed by her beauty and ample assets, which were straining at her low-cut dress.

"Good evening, Katia. Will you let Lady Mielikki know we're here?" he said.

She rose from her chair. It was then I realized she wasn't just built, she was *built*. Her biceps and shoulder muscles were well toned and broad, and her calves looked like she was a professional body-builder. I knew she wasn't one of the Fae, but I wasn't sure *what* she was.

Kipa motioned to the sofa and chairs in the waiting area. The entire room was painted in a soft green, and two windows overlooked the street below, their shades a creamy ivory. As we settled in, Kipa draped his arm around me.

"You nervous?" he whispered.

I shrugged. "It's not like I haven't met the gods before

—I know Herne, and Morgana and Cernunnos, and of course, Arawn and Cerridwen. But there's a magical feel to this agency that I don't think I've noticed in the Wild Hunt."

"That's probably because Mielikki works magic in a way that Herne never has. She's a goddess of the Fae, and you'd probably notice this sort of magic more at—say—Morgana's castle. She and Mielikki inhabit the same sphere and mirror each other in a number of ways."

I was about to ask another question when Katia returned.

"Please follow me," she said.

We followed her to a back room—it looked like a break room, with a microwave, a refrigerator, and a sink —very much the standard setup. Standing behind a long table was Mielikki. I recognized her immediately, though I had never met her.

Like most of the gods, Mielikki was tall—she stood probably about six-four and her black hair flowed in waves down to her ass. She was very pale, almost a pale green, and her eyes sparkled like pale amethysts. She was wearing a long violet gown, almost sheer so that at first I thought I could see her naked body beneath the material, but then, upon looking again, I realized I could see her curves, but not her actual body.

She was blinged out like nobody's business—gold and silver chains around her neck and her wrists, rings on her fingers. A circlet of silver, with silver leaves and gemstones embedded within the leaves, surrounded her head, and in the very center over her forehead, the circlet contained a shimmering moonstone that radiated an icy blue from deep within. But despite the feminine gown

173

and the jewelry, behind all of that, beat the heart of a huntress. I could feel her, ready to stalk and hunt and pounce. Instinctively, I knew that if Mielikki aimed an arrow at anyone, she would never miss.

She graciously motioned for us to be seated. Kipa inclined his head in a semi-bow and it suddenly hit me, they were both from Kalevala. They were both from the world of the gods. I was so used to Kipa my boyfriend that sometimes I forgot that he was also a god, and that he was wild and powerful beyond what I saw every day.

"Lord Kipa, introduce me to your companions." Mielikki's voice trilled over the words and I found myself enchanted. I could listen to her read a grocery list, if she always spoke like that.

"Lady, may I introduce my consort, Raven BoneTalker, and her mother, Phasmoria, Queen of the Bean Sidhe?"

If she was surprised, Mielikki didn't show it. She turned to me and held out her hand. "Well met, Raven BoneTalker. You walk the roads of the dead, do you not?"

I took her hand, surprised by how strong and cool her fingers were, like a summer brook on a chilly night. "I'm a bone witch, yes."

"Then we've traveled through the same lands at times. And this is your mother?" She bent her head, acknowledging my mother. "Queen Phasmoria, well met. I've heard of you and I'm grateful to be able to put a face to the name." Again, she held out her hand.

My mother shook hands, though I could sense some sort of hesitation there. I wasn't sure why, but then the energy vanished and we were all sitting down.

Mielikki motioned to Katia, who was still waiting.

"Coffee, please." She glanced at us. "What would you like to drink? We can make almost anything."

I gave her a tentative smile. "A triple peppermint mocha?"

"'Tis the time of the year for good cheer," Mielikki said, laughing. "Yes, we can make that happen. Phasmoria? Kipa?"

My mother asked for a black coffee, and Kipa asked for a caramel macchiato. Mielikki turned back to Katia. "Two peppermint mochas, one large black coffee, and a caramel macchiato."

Katia headed over to the counter and began to fix our drinks. Mielikki leaned back in her chair and it struck me how incredibly beautiful she was. There was a magnetism about her and I began to understand why Kipa had made such a stupid move. I was mostly straight, but seeing Mielikki made me wonder about what it would be like to — *Whoa, hold on there, cowgirl.*

I stopped that train of thought the moment I realized I was thinking it. It wasn't that I thought fantasy was wrong, but I wasn't sure if she—or her assistant—could read minds.

"So," the goddess said, "Kipa said you need to use our portal to Kalevala. What are your plans for your trip, if you can share?"

Katia brought over our drinks—she was quick and efficient—and then returned to stand near the sink, waiting for Mielikki's orders.

I glanced at Kipa. "We're going to Kalevala to talk to Väinämöinen. I need to learn a spell from him, if he'll teach it to me."

That was the first time Mielikki looked surprised.

"Well, then, that's an undertaking. What do you need to learn?"

I told her about the situation and what Dek had said about the aztrophyllia.

"Those are dangerous creatures—I know of them. I'd offer to come take care of it but I'm heavily involved in the war against the Dragonni and am on my way to a meeting in a few minutes. But if you can't find the help you need, have Kipa contact me again." She stood. "Now, if you'll excuse me, I must fly. But Katia will take you to the portal. Merry meet, and good fortune to you all."

As she started to leave the room, she paused, glancing over her shoulder. "Kipa, don't lose this woman. She's a match for you. I mean it." And with that, she vanished out the door.

HALF AN HOUR LATER, after we'd had our coffee and the chill had dissipated, Katia returned to the break room to lead us down to the bottom floor, then out the door and around back of the building. There were two massive fir trees, and I could sense that there was a portal between them, but it was well cloaked.

"We keep this protected so that humans don't stumble onto it," she said. "But I've programmed it for Kalevala, so go in good peace. You'll be able to return without a problem from the other side. I've contacted the portal keeper there and she'll program the portal so you arrive directly back in Seattle without having to go through this direction. I've contacted Orla and given her the coordinates for the Kalevala portal so that you won't need to make an intermediary jump again."

"You're efficient," I said, realizing that I had been on the verge of categorizing her as a "bunny-blonde," as I called them. But she was anything but that.

"Thank you," she said, beaming. "I do my job the best I can."

We waved to her. Then, with Kipa holding my hand, we walked through the portal into Kalevala.

I DON'T KNOW what I expected, but when we stepped through into Kalevala, it took my breath away. I looked up to see the night sky scintillating with lights—green and blue and shades of plum rippling across the horizon.

"The Northern Lights? But I thought they were products of the solar flares, and—we're in another realm," I said.

"The Northern Lights are much more than that. Yes, that's part of the explanation, but here you see the spiritual side of them. What you see is the Ancestral Road and the Bridge of the Gods. The gods—myself included—have used the aurora for thousands of years as a way to cross the sky, and the ancestors walk this road when they die, returning home to the realms whence they originally came." Kipa gazed up at them, a reverent look on his face.

Phasmoria was watching, too, her face lit up by the glimmering show overhead. "It's so beautiful. I've seldom seen such raw beauty and power."

"What do you think?" Kipa asked me.

"I'd love to walk that road, to see what it's like." I found myself breathless, the sheer energy of the land and sky hammering at me. Kalevala was magical, a force so powerful that I wanted to run into the energy and lose myself.

"Maybe we will, one day," he murmured. "I will bring you back when we have time to vacation. But for now, we must move. I've done some snooping, and Väinämöinen has been spotted deep within the Forest of Honey."

"The Forest of Honey? Is that its name?" Phasmoria asked.

"If I told you the Finnish name, you wouldn't be able to pronounce it. It's close enough. The forest belongs to Mielikki and Tapio, and runs through their land of Tapiola. We must cross through a portal to get there—you cannot get to it from a portal outside of Kalevala. But the vortex is near, and we'll be in Tapiola within less than half an hour."

Kipa motioned for us to follow him and so we began the climb up the snow-laden slope, slogging through knee-deep snow. Halfway up, he noticed I was having problems.

"Here, let me shift into my Wolf and you can ride on my back. Phasmoria, are you having any problems?"

She blew on her hands. "Not terribly, but I'm not going very fast."

"I'm big enough to carry both of you," he said. Within seconds, he had transformed into his massive wolf-self. I climbed on his back, then my mother behind me, and with her holding my waist and me holding onto Kipa's ruff, he loped up the slope. Having two women riding his back didn't seem to slow him down. We reached the top of the slope a lot faster than we would have if Phasmoria and I had attempted to trudge through the snow on our own.

At the top of the slope the ground leveled out into a field that seemed to have no end. The snow shimmered under the aurora, picking up colors from the flickering lights and reflecting them back. Vast silhouettes dotted the horizon, and when I squinted, I realized the shapes were massive thickets dappling the land. It was a frozen wonderland, so postcard-perfect that it was almost too beautiful to look at.

Nearby, there was a small copse of fir and to one side of the path, stood two massive cedar trees. I could see the energy popping and sizzling between them. The portal was waiting for us. I slid off Kipa's back after Phasmoria dismounted, and stood watching the trees as Kipa transformed back into himself. The energy between the trees sparked, arcing like miniature lightning bolts, and somehow, the portal made me nervous in a way the other portals never had.

"There," Kipa said, pointing to it. "That's the portal that leads to the Forest of Honey."

"It looks different from other portals," I said.

"It is. I warn you, it's a bit more jarring than the others. The energy feeds directly in from the storm gates of Ukko —don't ask. Trust me, you *don't* want to know right now. But yeah, it can be a bit more prickly. It won't hurt you, but I sure wouldn't go through there if I was wearing a pacemaker." Kipa pointed to my pack. "You didn't bring your phone, did you?"

"I left it in the car at Orla's. I've learned the hard way to avoid taking electronics into Annwn, and I assumed that Kalevala wouldn't be any different," I said.

My mother nodded. "I left mine behind, too."

"Then we should be good. Come on, then, let's get to it. Väinämöinen never stays in one place for long and I'd hate to have to track him down again. He's not all that easy to find."

Kipa led us over toward the two cedars. The snow was so thick I worried we'd sink to our thighs once we started walking, but as I took a step forward, I realized that it was crusty, frozen over like a layer of ice. I sank, all right, but only an inch or so before it compacted into a hardened path.

"Whoa, I expected to end up hip-deep in snow," I said, testing my footing.

"That's because this area of land is always cold. During the winter, the snow falls and freezes, then it falls and freezes again. There are layers of ice beneath our feet that won't melt off until…well…what you would consider mid-May."

"So what's it like here during the summer? Is there even a summer?" I had visited realms that were perpetually autumn and summer.

"Even during the late spring and summer—which goes fast—the temperatures barely hit the seventy-degree mark. It's warm enough to grow a few quick-growing crops, but the people of Kalevala mostly grow root vegetables, and they hunt and fish and forage during the summer months to fill the larders. There's a lot of game in the woodlands here, and in the summer, the open meadows are laden with herbs and berries." Kipa glanced around and sighed, a wistful note in his voice.

"You miss it, don't you?"

By the look on his face, I knew he did. "I admit, I do. I

miss the northlands, and running over the frozen snow at night with my SuVahta at my heels. I miss the high mountains, which you can't see from here, but far in the distance, they rise like jagged teeth into the sky."

"It's beautiful," Phasmoria said. "I've mostly been in Annwn, and while that's wild and overgrown, it seems almost tame compared to this land."

"This is the land of fire and ice," Kipa said. "There are volcanoes in this realm that rival the description of Mt. Doom in *Lord of the Rings*. And then there are the frozen wilds that never thaw—that forever live beneath the Northern Lights."

"I want to see them," I said, surprised by the longing that swelled up in my heart. "I want to visit there."

Kipa glanced down at me, smiling. "We will, my love. We will." He leaned down to kiss me, his lips cool from the chill of the air. "But for now, let's find Väinämöinen and get you that spell. If he's willing. He's generally in a good mood, but I can't vouch how he's currently feeling."

"We'll never know unless we give it a try," I said. "Lead on."

He held out his hands. "Best we travel linked, just in case."

I didn't want to ask what the "just in case" might entail, so I took his right hand and Phasmoria took his left hand. We approached the portal and the closer we got, the more my hair felt like it was standing on end. Then, taking a deep breath, Kipa counted to three and we stepped through the blurred lines of blue and white that crossed the space between the trees.

CHAPTER SIXTEEN

As I stepped out of the portal, I was gripping Kipa's hand tighter than ever. The energy had sent my hair all cattywampus and it felt like every nerve in my body had been tickled, teased, or singed. I wasn't sure whether it had been pleasant or I never wanted to experience that feeling again.

"That...was *different*," I said.

Kipa laughed. "I warned you. You two okay?"

I tried to shake off the feeling of cobwebs attached to my body. "Yeah, I'm all right. Mom?"

Phasmoria snorted. "I'm fine, but yes, that was unexpected."

I glanced around. We were still in deep snow, but we were now inside of a forest, off of what looked like a main road. The road was also covered with snow but it passed through the trees, carving a trail that looked well used. In fact, I thought I could hear music from up ahead.

"Do I hear...music?" I asked, not sure if my ears were still ringing from the portal.

"You do. There's an inn up ahead, and they get quite a good clientele coming through."

I wasn't sure why that surprised me so much. There were inns in Annwn, but somehow, Kalevala had seemed much more remote and less populated.

"I'm looking forward to a good fire, if they have one," Phasmoria said. "Will we be stopping there?"

"That's where we're headed. You didn't think we'd find Väinämöinen sitting under a tree, butt in the snow, did you?"

I blushed, grateful he couldn't see me. I had thought exactly that. Or that he'd be in a cave, hiding out with the crystals. *No wait, that was the Merlin.*

But my mother was the one to say it. "He's part of the Force Majeure. I wouldn't be surprised to see him trying to walk on lava on the floor of a caldera."

I snorted. "What she said."

Kipa laughed. "You two take the cake. But…I know what you mean. The Force Majeure scare the hell out of me. They're so far beyond their roots that sometimes the gods seem closer to human and Fae-kind than the Force Majeure do." He pointed toward a bend in the road about thirty yards away. "The inn is right around the corner. Let's go."

As we started along the path, the music grew louder, and I felt my stomach shift. Meeting one of the Force Majeure—for a witch, *any kind* of witch—was like meeting a god for most people. I hoped I wouldn't make a fool of myself in front of Väinämöinen.

THE NAME of the inn was Cloudberry Inn. I knew that cloudberries were found in Finland, so that made sense. The three-story inn was built of stone, and windows overlooked the front. There were lights from within, and also shining out from some of the smaller windows on the upper floors. Even from here, I could smell baking bread and some sort of stew, and the music was lively and made me want to tap my foot.

Kipa opened the door, then stood back to usher us in. My mother went first, and the moment she stepped into the room, the music paused. I followed her, and then Kipa brought up the rear. All eyes were on us as we stood by the door.

The inn was spacious, and a long polished hardwood counter ran in front of the bar. Bottles of booze lined the shelves behind the bar. Three long tables with benches on either side filled the dining area, and each table looked capable of seating sixteen people total. To the right there was an archway into what looked like a kitchen. The delicious smells were wafting from there. Against the back right wall, behind the bar, a staircase led to the upper floors.

To the left was an open area with a group of musicians sitting there, with their long-handled stringed instruments and two wooden drums. The instruments were ornate, intricately carved. The men manning them were gorgeous, with long brown hair and swarthy skin and eyes so black they looked like rich soil. They were dressed in blue tunics and brown trousers, and as for their ages— they could have been thirty or sixty.

The man behind the counter was a beefy man, with muscles on his muscles. He was bald, his head shining.

But for as menacing as he could have looked, his eyes twinkled and a smile creased his face.

He caught sight of Kipa and rounded the corner of the bar as Kipa stepped up to meet him. The men clasped hands, then hugged, and Kipa said something I didn't understand. The man turned to us. He said something else and I felt a shift—whatever it was had been an incantation.

"Well met, Lady," he said, bowing to my mother. "We are graced to have a Daughter of the Morrígan in our presence."

My mother seemed to be caught off guard for the moment, but then she laughed and said, "Well met to you, as well. I'm afraid I don't know your name."

"Kipa, introduce us, you wolf, you." The barkeep arched his eyebrows. "Such a lack of manners with this one, always."

Kipa laughed. "Bear, you need to stop bemoaning my lack of social graces. You do this every time we meet." He held out his hand to me. "Bear, I'd like you to meet my mate, Raven BoneTalker. She's one of the Ante-Fae. Raven, this is Bear, my cousin."

Startled, I turned to him. "You're related to Kipa? Then, you're a—"

Bear nodded. "Yes, I'm a god. What you might call a minor god. My given name is far longer than I care to use, so you may call me Bear. You are a lovely woman, and I can tell your spirit has a good, sharp edge to it. Well met, Lady Raven."

"Phasmoria is Raven's mother," Kipa said.

It was Bear's turn to look surprised. He glanced from

Phasmoria to me. "I can see the resemblance. Then you are not following your mother's path?"

I shook my head. "No, I'm not born to be one of the Bean Sidhe. I'm a bone witch."

"Ah, a speaker for the dead. You come from a revered tradition." Bear paused, then pointed to the table that was empty. The other one had eight travelers gathered around it, and they were all eating and drinking. The music started up again, softer, but as beautiful and haunting as it had been before.

"Sit, take your weight off your feet. I'll call for food and drink—and don't even bother protesting. Even a short jaunt through the realm of ice will leave you out of energy." Bear motioned to a woman I had assumed to be a serving maid. "Food, drink, plenty of it and quickly, girl."

The girl curtsied and vanished into the kitchen.

"Your daughter is growing into a lovely young woman," Kipa said.

Bear laughed. "She is at that. I would have tried to get you to take her hand, but you have found another lovely for yourself." He turned to me. "No worries, milady Raven, I will not interfere. I would have loved to have Kipa for a son-in-law, but then again, he has been known to play fast and loose with the hearts of many a woman throughout Kalevala, and I would never wish that on my daughter, Aiedal." He paused then, blushing. "Not that I think he would do so to you—"

"Give it up, Bear. You always end up with foot-in-mouth disease." But Kipa laughed and draped his arm around my shoulders. "Don't worry, love," he said to me. "You know I've left my wandering eye behind."

"I should hope so," Phasmoria said.

Bear snorted and slapped his thigh. "Best beware, Wolf. You know how mothers can be."

"Oh yes," Kipa said. He gave a reverent nod to my mother. "Phasmoria knows I won't ever play her daughter fast and loose."

I remembered Kipa telling me that, among the Finns, the true heroes were the mothers of the heroes. They often bailed their sons out of trouble and managed to unravel the messes they made. So that meant my mother had some clout here.

"What brings you to our neck of the woods?" Bear asked as Aiedal carried in a serving tray that was almost as round as she was tall. She set it on a folding stand and began to fill the table with dishes. There were bowls of soup, a basket of warm, fresh rolls, a crock of butter, a round of soft cheese, what looked like a whole fish that had been roasted in the oven, a cranberry tart, and a ham, sliced and ready to eat.

"I'll return with your drinks," she said, vanishing again.

I stared at the spread, once again ambivalent about the food in my world. As I tasted the potato soup, my body began to wake up and I realized that the extreme cold had made me feel like I was shutting down and going to sleep.

"We're seeking Väinämöinen and last I heard, he was staying here, in your inn." Kipa picked up a roll and tore it in half, slathering it with the spreadable cheese.

Bear went into a coughing fit, accepting a stein of ale from his daughter, who had returned with several bottles of wine, two steins of ale, and two goblets. She set the goblets in front of my mother and me, and handed Kipa the other stein. Bear guzzled down the ale, wiping the foam off his lips as he cleared his throat. He handed the empty stein to his daughter. "More, please."

She carried the stein away.

"So, you're here to see the old coot?"

"Don't talk like that. You owe him some honor for all he's done," Kipa said. "I'm irreverent and even *I* give Väinämöinen his fair due."

I watched the interplay with interest. I had seen Kipa around Herne, and around Cernunnos and Morgana, but until today I hadn't seen him around other gods of his kind. And given Bear was his cousin and some sort of god, it fascinated me to see how he interacted with him.

"True that, my brother. True that," Bear said. "He can be frightening. But yes, he's here. He's in a room on the second floor, but I will tell you this—he seems surly today. I'm not sure what happened but he stormed in, ordered that he's not to be disturbed, and had four bottles of wine sent up to his room."

Kipa stared at his plate. "That's not comforting."

Phasmoria broke open one of the rolls and added butter, ham, and the cheese to make a sandwich. I wasn't that hungry because I'd been eating potato soup, but the ham beckoned to me, too, and so I added several slices to my plate.

"Come walk with me," Kipa said, motioning to Bear. "We'll be right back," he added, turning to me.

As they walked off toward the corner where we couldn't hear them, I glanced around. "This is a pretty inn," I said.

My mother bit into her second sandwich. "So, what do you think?" she asked, keeping her voice low. "Would you ever live here?"

"Maybe," I said, blinking. "Why?"

"Because if you and Kipa stay together, eventually he may want to return here and then you'll have a choice to make. You'll have to ask yourself if you're willing to give up city life for a life here."

"I doubt he'd want to stay, though. He seems to like the 'modern' era," I said.

"I know, but you can never be entirely sure of what's going to happen." She paused, then added, "The Dragonni are making inroads and the gods aren't having much luck turning them back. I know all about…their secret weapon, and we can hope that it will turn the tide, but you need to seriously give some thought to what happens if Typhon and his kind manage to take over. You need a place to retreat to, Raven, a place you'll be safe. Because anyone—*anyone*—aligned with the gods in trying to repel the Father of All Dragons will be marked for execution. I've seen wars like this before. And I will *not* have you murdered in your sleep, even if I have to drag you off to the Morrígan's castle."

I pressed my lips together, suddenly grasping her meaning. If Echidna—the Mother of All Dragons—wasn't able to beat Typhon back into the realm in which he had been trapped, then the world would be doomed. There was no option for compromise. With Typhon, it was all or nothing. Even now, the Father of Dragons was working on two fronts—one offensive, and the other, much more insidious.

"I suppose I could go to Annwn. That's where my gods are, and that's where Herne and Ember and Angel would be," I said.

"If it comes to that, don't wait too long. Whether it be

Annwn or here. I'm so proud of how you've stepped up to helping with the war effort, but don't put your life on the line." She went back to her dinner, leaving me to think over her words.

A moment later, Kipa and Bear returned. Kipa motioned to us.

"Bear's arranged a meeting with Väinämöinen. Come, we don't want to risk him changing his mind." He slid his arm around my waist and, with Phasmoria following, led us toward the stairs. On the way up, he added, "Bear's right. Väinämöinen is a crusty old salt, but he's also one of the most powerful bards in the world and he's crafty and sly. So watch your words, mind your manners, and maybe we'll come away with what we need."

As we ascended the stairs to the second floor, I found myself getting nervous. As a witch, I instinctively revered the Force Majeure. They worked some of the most powerful magic in the world—sort of the rock stars of the bewitching set.

We stopped at the second door on the left side of the hallway, and Kipa knocked. A moment later, a young man opened the door. He looked muscled and strong, and young, and though I knew that magic could enhance the illusion of youth, I was startled by how real the illusion seemed. That is, until the youth led us into the sitting room area of the inn's suite, and I realized that he wasn't Väinämöinen.

An older man was sitting in a rocking chair beside the fireplace. His face was lined with wrinkles, a topographical map of his life, and he wore a long pale blue robe. His hair hung in braids down to his back—shining white and smooth—and there was a quiet aura of power surrounding him that almost muffled the entire room. My stomach fluttered and I found myself frozen as I stared at him and doubt began to emerge. Who was *I*, a mere bone witch, to ask such a powerful bard to teach me his magic? I blushed, my cheeks red and hot as I bit my lip.

Phasmoria was standing behind me, and she poked me in the ribs and whispered, "Say something."

I stumbled forward and awkwardly curtseyed. "Merry meet." I realized I had no idea what to call him—I didn't know what title he used. But Kipa took care of that for me.

"Raven, Phasmoria," he said, "I present you to Väinämöinen, keeper of the oldest kantele, Lord of the Runos. Lord Väinämöinen, this is Raven, my consort, and her mother Phasmoria, Queen of the Bean Sidhe."

The old man looked up and his eyes flickered, a brilliant blue that was unclouded and untouched. His look alone told me that the wrinkles and the age were all the true illusion. Oh, the bard was as old as time, but magic kept him young, and it kept him going.

He slowly stood, and as he did so the magic in the room shifted, rising up as he stood to cloak him in a swath of sparkling energy.

"Well met, young daughter of the Ancient *Verkko*." He smiled at me, then, and it felt like I had been blessed by some holy man. Being in Väinämöinen's presence made me feel special.

"What's Verkko?"

"The web," Kipa said. "The energy that binds us all together."

I turned back to Väinämöinen. "Thank you for seeing

us." Pausing, I turned to Kipa. I felt utterly tongue-tied and unsure of how to ask what I needed to ask.

Kipa stroked my back. "Ask your question."

"It's true, girl, I don't bite," the ancient bard said. "Unless you prefer it that way."

I bit my lip again.

Right then, my mother stepped up. She inclined her head and said, "Lord Väinämöinen, my daughter is star-struck. But she needs a boon from you, Ancient Father."

Väinämöinen glanced at her, his eyes glimmering. "So I gather, Queen of the Bean Sidhe." Turning back to me, he said, "Ask, girl. What do you want? You never get anywhere in life if you don't ask for what you want."

I steeled my courage. "I need to know how to seal someone from being attacked by an astral predator." I explained what had happened and what we had learned about the aztrophyllia. "So, even if we blast it back to the astral plane, that's no guarantee it won't try to reach Lenny again."

Väinämöinen stroked his beard, which was down to his chest, and sat back down, motioning for us to join him. There were two loveseats as well as the rocking chair he was sitting in. "Let me think for a moment. There are several possibilities."

As he leaned back and closed his eyes, we sat down to wait. I tried to curb my impatience, but honestly, just being in his presence made me calmer. I felt something akin with him—like we were connected by our love of magic. In an odd way, it felt like he was the Buddha and I was one of his disciples. And I had never felt that way about anybody before.

After a while, I began to feel sleepy. My mother was

sitting beside me. She had taken off her boots and was now sitting cross-legged on the sofa. Kipa was on the other loveseat and he was stretched out, his eyes closed as well. I rested my head against the back of the cushion, and before I realized it, I had dropped off to sleep.

CHAPTER SEVENTEEN

I WAS DREAMING THAT RAJ AND I WERE GOOFING AROUND IN my backyard, playing in the snow. Raj kept kicking showers of it at me. I was freezing and getting irritated, wanting to go in but he kept urging me to stay. I was about to order him inside when a voice pierced the dream, echoing through the sky, asking me to wake up.

Blinking, I slowly pried my eyes open, and the images of Raj and the snow blended into my mother's face as she shook me by the shoulders. "Wake up, Raven. Raven?"

I tried to fend off the cobwebs that came from taking a nap. I glanced around, trying to place where we were, and then I saw Väinämöinen, watching me. I thought he was smiling but it was hard to tell behind the trailing beard and mustache.

"I must have dozed off." As I shifted, my neck protested with a sharp stab from sleeping all cockeyed. "Ow." I rubbed my shoulder. "I must have turned into a pretzel. Sorry I fell asleep. That was rude."

"We *all* took a nap," Kipa said.

"Indeed," said Väinämöinen. "Some of my best ideas come from when I'm out on the Dreamtime." He stood, stretching and yawning. "I suggest you all follow suit and then we'll discuss your request, Raven."

I eased out of the tangle I'd apparently made of my body and hesitantly stretched, taking it easy until I finally felt like I'd unknotted myself. "How long were we asleep?"

"Time is relative," the bard said. "But for practicality's sake, around two hours."

I rubbed my eyes. I could have sworn it was far longer, and I realized that I felt more rested than I had in a long while. "Well, then, shall we get on with it?"

"You're a hasty one, aren't you?" He chuckled. "Was she always like this?"

My mother snorted. "As far as I know, yes. But she's still young in our world—barely off the leash, you might say, and impatience is a trait of youth."

"True enough," Väinämöinen said. "Very well, then. I will teach you the spell you need, but for a price."

My heart sank. I didn't have much money left, given I had tried to pay my mother back for giving my father the money he had spent on my house. And even if we became friends again, I wasn't at all sure I'd ever trust him enough to accept another gift. At least, not anything like paying for my home.

"I'm afraid I'm broke at the moment—"

"No, not that kind of payment," he said.

Instantly my mind went where it probably shouldn't. "I don't offer my services for—"

"Guess again," Väinämöinen said. "I have no interest in you that way. No, my price is this—and it is unnegotiable. You will come back here and train with me for a year's time.

You have a spark in you, girl, which I checked out once you were asleep. And that spark portends greatness. But you'll never reach that level without someone to train you."

I stared at him. What he was offering was a priceless gift, one I'd never even dreamed of. The chance to train with one of the Force Majeure? There was no dollar figure you could place on it.

"You're not joking, are you? You're offering to *train* me?"

"Yes, but under these conditions: you obey my instructions. You don't shirk the work. Once you begin the training, you will complete it. And when you complete your year's training, you will then enter an internship with me for a period of one year, here, in Kalevala. Do you understand?"

I caught my breath. The price was steep, but the rewards would be incredible. "Can I bring my gargoyle Raj with me? I never go anywhere without him. And Kipa…" I glanced over at my Wolf Lord. "What about him?"

"Both are welcome, and you will be given breaks several times through the year where you may travel home and make certain everything is all right." Väinämöinen sat back down in his chair and unconcernedly picked up a huge dark red apple from the end table next to him. He bit into it, waiting for my answer. "Take your time. We have all the time in the world, here."

I glanced at Kipa, who said, "I cannot decide for you, love. This has to be your choice."

Phasmoria agreed. "He's right. This is your path to decide."

A thousand thoughts whirled through my head, but my gut said, *Jump on it, while you can. You may never have another opportunity like this.* "All right, I'll do it. When will we start?"

"After the beginning of the year. But now, I will teach you this spell. You can't learn it the regular way, not in the time we have here. So I'll need to implant it into your mind. You'll be able to keep the spell after it's cast—you won't lose it. So use it wisely."

I caught my breath and sighed. At least this was going right—so much better than what I had imagined. "All right. How do we do this?"

"You'll need to be asleep so that I can enter your mind without resistance. And by sleep, I mean I need to put you into an extremely deep sleep state." He motioned to the door leading into the bedroom. "Why don't you go in there and prepare. You'll want to use the facilities, take off any constricting clothing because this process will take several hours, and get under the covers. Don't worry about trying to fall asleep—I'll make that happen. And if you want someone to watch over the process, I have no problem with that."

It was at that moment that I realized we'd been speaking English all along. "Say, will I be able to learn the translate spell? You must be using one." I wanted to be like Raj and understand everybody.

"During your internship with me, yes." His eyes crinkled and I could tell he was amused. "Now hurry. The sooner we get this done, the sooner you can leave and I can get back to the problem I was working on."

And with that cryptic statement, he shooed me into

the bedroom. My mother followed me in, leaving Kipa to talk to the bard.

I SETTLED UNDER THE COVERS, both nervous and excited. I loved learning new magic.

"I wonder what he's going to do," I said.

"Are you nervous?" my mother asked.

I thought about it for a moment, then said, "No, honestly, I'm not. At least I'm not afraid. I trust him—he's crafty and cunning, yes, but there's an innate goodness in his heart that I can feel. And do you realize what this means for my future? I've never had an opportunity like this, to actually train with someone. My magic has been self-taught. All of it except that which was given to me by the gods."

I was jumping out of my skin with anticipation. Magic ran through my veins, like ink through a writer's veins. It made me who I was. I was a born witch and any chance to increase my abilities was an opportunity I couldn't resist. It also occurred to me that, with Väinämöinen training me, Pandora might think twice about ever trying a second attempt on me.

My mother leaned over me, stroking my hair out of my face. "I'll be here, watching over you. I won't let anything bad happen to you, to my very best of abilities."

I knew why she qualified that. She hadn't been able to save me from Pandora—no one had. Trinity did, at the end, but by then, the damage had been done. I preferred it when people didn't overpromise. It seemed more genuine when someone promised the moon instead of the stars—because that meant they weren't just over-reaching.

"Thank you," I whispered. Then I looked into her eyes and said the words we seldom said to each other, but we knew were true. "I love you, Mother."

"I love you, too, Raven. You know that whatever I can do for you, I will." Phasmoria patted me on the cheek and then stood back as the door opened and Väinämöinen entered the room.

He motioned for her to sit in a chair on the other side of the bed. As he approached, my nerves rose again, but I tried to calm myself.

"How will you put me to—" I started to say, but he waved his hand over my face and…

…I was standing naked in a field under the night sky.

The ground was covered with snow, but I didn't feel the cold, and the stars overhead wheeled in a massive arc around us. I could see both Arianrhod's silver wheel, as well as the trail of Northern Lights. The aurora shimmered, scintillating as it flowed across the sky, waves of neon green and blue.

The next moment, I was standing on the bridge of lights, staring down at the world as it circled beneath my feet. The aurora sparkled and crackled around me like synapses of the brain, like lightning arcing across a forest, jumping from crown to crown.

I wanted to bathe in the energy—it flowed like a wild river around me, and as I stretched out my arms, it licked the tips of my fingers, jolting me with its touch as it beckoned me to join its dance. I wanted to run off, to play in it, but a whisper floating at the edge of my ears warned me against getting lost in the energy. Instead, I looked around and saw Väinämöinen standing on another part of the bridge. I cautiously tested my step but the lights were firm beneath my feet and so I made my way across the length to where he waited for me.

"Are you ready?" he asked and he seemed to not notice I was naked—or if he did notice, he ignored the fact.

Feeling at ease with him, and like a greedy child who was absorbing as much of the energy as I could, I said, "I'm ready. I could stay out here forever."

"Get lost and you might do that. It's easy to let the aurora carry you out into the depths of space," Väinämöinen said. "It's seductive, and hard to resist. You're doing remarkably well."

"What do I do now?"

He raised his hands and began to weave a glyph between his fingers, a gold thread of light forming the symbol. After a moment, he lowered his hands and the glyph remained in the air. He motioned to me.

"Reach up and touch the glyph on both sides, using both your hands. This will transfer the ability to use the spell to you. Usually, I would set about teaching you how to use it, but that would take a lot more time than we have at this moment, and your friend would be dead before then. This will give you the power to use the spell on a permanent basis. I warn you, the transfer might jolt your system. So be aware that during the next few days that you may experience a number of side effects, but they shouldn't be too disruptive."

I focused on my astral body—moving on the astral was

different from walking around a room. If you weren't careful, you could shoot off to where you were thinking about, so it required a strong focus. Although I suspected we weren't even on the astral, but out farther than either the astral and etheric realms reached. This felt far removed from the energy I was used to.

My gaze intent on the glyph, I reached up and placed my hands on either side. The energy of the symbol almost blew me backward, but I forced myself to continue. The golden threads began to unravel and burrow into the center of my palms. It both tickled and hurt—as though it were drilling its way into my aura. Kind of like the dentist drilling into a tooth, and patching it with a filling.

Bringing my mind back to my main focus, I jumped as the glyph vanished into my hands. The next thing I knew, a massive bolt of energy slammed into me and I was falling—dropping off the bridge of lights and plummeting into a void below. I screamed, but then Väinämöinen was there, catching me by the wrist. He was hurtling headfirst down toward the abyss as well, but as soon as he caught me, he did a U-turn and we were traveling back up, and then past the aurora into a mist that hovered off to one side. I began to get sleepy and, as we entered the mist, I dozed off, drifting in the swirling white fog, until I felt myself settle into my body.

Another moment, and I opened my eyes.

CHAPTER EIGHTEEN

It took me a few moments to fully wake—I had been so far out on whatever realm Väinämöinen had taken me to that even though I was back in my body, I still felt disoriented. I groaned, slowly sitting up as I rubbed my head. I had the headache from hell and my temples and the top of my head throbbed like I'd been hit with a two-by-four.

"Head hurt?" the bard asked.

"Head hurts bad. *Really* bad." My stomach lurched and I groaned and lay back down. "Can someone douse the light in this room? I don't feel so good."

"That's normal. Think of it like getting a shot full of magic juice that you don't normally work with—all at once. You'll feel under the weather for another day or so, but by tomorrow, you should be back on your feet, at the least." He leaned back, staring at me like I was a monkey in a zoo. "This should be interesting. This is the first time I've done something like this in several centuries. I'm a loner by nature and I avoid people as much as I can."

"And you want *me* to be your acolyte? Boy, are you going to regret that," I said, squeezing my eyes closed. "I want to go home and sleep it off." As I turned over on my side, my eyes were growing heavier and it was easier to tune everything out and go back to sleep.

I SLEPT the sleep of the dead—at least the dead who were at peace. When I next opened my eyes, I was in my own bed, in a comfortable nightie, and Raj was sitting next to the bed, staring at me. The curtains were closed and I had no clue whether it was night or day, or what time it was, or how I had gotten there.

My head still hurt, though not as much, and my stomach had calmed down enough to where I was actually hungry. I slowly eased my way up into a sitting position, groaning slightly. My muscles were stiff from lying down.

"Hey, can Raj tell Raven what day it is?" I said, squinting at him.

Raj grinned. When gargoyles smiled, it was disconcerting until you got used to it. "Today is Thursday. Raj knows because *Acrobert and the Alphas* were on TV last night. And they're always on Wednesday evenings unless preempted by special programming."

I suppressed a laugh. He sounded like a game show announcer. But that was Raj. "Raven thanks Raj," I said, wincing as another pang hit my head. But it wasn't as bad as before and I could tell the headache was winding to a close.

"Can Raj go get Phasmoria or Kipa for Raven?" I asked,

shading my eyes from the light that filtered in between the cracks in the curtains.

"Raj will get Kipa." He turned to bounce out of the room.

I lay back down, pulling a pillow over my eyes to block out the light. Curious, I reached for the spell that Väinämöinen had given me and sure enough, there it was. I could see it—feel it—and, I knew—cast it. So it was part of my arsenal now.

"Raven, you're awake?" Kipa's voice echoed through the muffled folds of the pillow.

"Can you get me a blindfold so I can take this fool pillow off my face?" I asked.

"Of course." Another moment and he placed a blind-fold in my hands. Technically, it was a sleep mask, but we usually used it for play time rather than sleeping. But today it would work other than as a sex toy. It did what it was supposed to do—block out the light.

I slid the mask on, then pushed the pillow away and very slowly sat up again. I was dizzy and disconcerted, but the lack of light helped settle the queasiness that had started in again when I began moving around.

"I need food. What's today? Raj said it's Thursday?"

"Yes," he said, sitting on the bed beside me to take my hands. "You were out from Tuesday when you crashed in Kalevala. Väinämöinen warned us you might sleep for over twenty-four hours, and you did—around thirty-six, to be precise. It's nine o'clock on Thursday morning. Are you hungry?"

My stomach rumbled. "Now that I've blocked out the light, yes. I was when I first opened my eyes but the light started making me queasy again. But it's not bad like it was on Tuesday night after the ritual. Do you know where he took me? I don't think it was the astral—"

"No, it wasn't the astral. He took you to Ukko's realm, which is out on the web not too far from where the dark matter of the universe exists. It's on the realm where the soul of the aurora lives. While the actual physical manifestation of the lights are created by the sun, the energy behind them is found in Ukko's realm, among a few others, and the heart of the bridge they form is found there."

"You make it sound like the Northern Lights are entities, not just a connecting bridge."

"That's because they are. Or rather, *it* is—the aurora is a hive-minded being. It acts as the bridge for the gods, but it's also a sentient creature that exists in energetic form. And Ukko has forged an alliance with it."

"Is it the same thing as the Rainbow Bridge—Bifrost?"

"No, that's connected to Heimdall, from the Norse, and Iris from the Greeks, and a few other deities. However, the Rainbow Bridge does act similarly to the aurora, though it's more bound to Earth than the aurora is."

He let out a sigh, squeezing my hands. "I'm so glad you came through this. I was worried."

I thought about all that had happened. "I'm going to be training with Väinämöinen. I never would have guessed that would happen, not in a million years." I paused, then brought my knees up and rested my chin on them. "Did you know?"

"That he was going to require you to train with him? No, I had no clue. In fact, I thought he would probably turn us away, given the mood Bear told me he was in.

But…do you think you can actually follow through? It means that next month you'll be leaving to live in Kalevala for a year. Two years, actually, given the internship afterward. I'll go with you, of course, and we'll take Raj. I can find us a snug-enough home. But can you live without modern technology, or access to your friends for that long?"

I shivered. The thought was daunting. But I had given my word and one thing I was good for: following up on my promises. Also, the opportunity was too great to ignore.

"Yeah, I'll do it. I'm looking forward to it, in many ways, and who knows where this will lead. My mother asked me Tuesday, while you were talking to Bear, if I thought I could ever live in Kalevala. That one day you might want to return home and then I'd have to make the decision whether to go or stay."

I rested my forehead against my arms, feeling worn out and yet strangely alert. The thought of training under a bard who belonged to the Force Majeure was like candy sitting on the counter with no one watching. It was impossible for me to resist.

"Väinämöinen wouldn't have offered you the chance if he didn't think you had the talent to go far. He's not that generous. He's also not into young girls, and to him, that's what you are. So never think it's because he wants something untoward from you. I've seen him train two other people in all the time I've known him. And that goes back long before I ever came to this realm."

"Good to know. I'm steady enough to eat." I slowly took off the sleep mask and winced. Once again the light hit hard, but each time the effects were subsiding. I tossed it on the bed. "Help me into the kitchen. I'm hungry, and I want food."

As Kipa swept me up in his arms—with me protesting that I could walk—my thoughts were a swirl of chaos. I still had to take care of Lenny, but mostly I was thinking about what a shift my life was coming to. I was facing a crossroads in my life, and nothing would ever be the same.

By EVENING, I was mostly feeling back to myself. I tried to sort through whether I felt any different other than knowing a new spell, and to some degree, I did. There was something that felt like it had been triggered, in a good way, as though a part of me had woken up after being asleep for a long time. I felt stronger, and Väinämöinen's energy signature had left a trail that—when I examined it —left me reeling with how much power the bard had. In some ways, I'd swear he was stronger than the gods.

"What are you thinking about?" my mother asked while we were eating dinner.

I cut into the lasagna with my fork, trying to think of how to answer her. "It's as though a part of Väinämöinen came back with me, and it makes me feel more confident." I looked up at her. "I'm looking forward to training with him, though the thought of staying in Kalevala is daunting."

"I'll be there with you," Kipa said. "I may have to leave now and then to help Herne, but I'll be there with you for at least the entire first month. I talked to Väinämöinen before we left and we agreed that he'll train you in Tapiola

—Mielikki's realm. I called her while you were asleep and she agreed that we could live in one of the grounds cottages while we're there. So there will be people around, and we can keep a cow and chickens for milk and eggs."

I stared at him, then broke out laughing. "What the hell am I supposed to do with a *cow*? I've never milked a cow."

"You'll know how by the time we return," he countered, grinning. "But seriously, I know how to do all of that, and you won't have much time for it given your training. So I'll hire a servant to clean the house and cook for us and—yes—take care of the animals."

"Have you thought about what you're going to tell your father about all of this?" Phasmoria asked.

I helped myself to more garlic bread. "I don't know and I don't care. He doesn't get an opinion." I glanced at her. She merely gave me a questioning look. "He's going to have to earn my trust again. And given all that happened, that's not going to be easy. He helped me get expelled from my own community, he turned his back on me, and he said he disowned me to please his own father. Those aren't actions I can easily forgive."

"I'm glad to hear you say that," she said. "Honestly, I'm surprised you're giving him another chance, but I am glad for it. You may have thought you took after your father, but the fact is that you've always been more like me. That's one reason I knew I could obey the Morrígan and leave you with him. You had the strength of will to handle it. I prepared you for it from the beginning, and the fact that your nature lent itself to being decisive was a help. I hope you know I've always been proud of you."

I stared at my plate. My mother wasn't shy about

giving out praise, but she was stern and no-nonsense and when she said something, she meant it. She never tiptoed around matters when people fucked up, and she was ready to let them know it, too. So for her to say she was proud of me meant the world. In some ways, it would have been much easier if I had been born with her Bean Sidhe blood taking precedence and followed in her path. But then I would have missed out on so many things.

"You're introspective today," Kipa said, poking my arm.

I glanced up at him. "Yeah, well…so much has happened the past week that I'm not sure what to think, in some ways. I've gone from holding a Winter Solstice party to being kicked out of the Ante-Fae community to my father disowning me to suddenly facing that I'll be training with one of the Force Majeure for a year to my father returning to ask me to forgive him. That's a lot to take in for one week."

"You're right, of course. That's a lot of change for one person, let alone all in one week. I guess Fate decided to take her foot off the brakes." Kipa reached for the lasagna pan. "More?"

I held out my plate. "Yeah, thanks. I suppose I should call Vixen and schedule a time for us to deal with the aztrophyllia. To think that this whole training thing started with me helping out a friend." I paused, another thought striking me. "What about the ferrets? I can bring them to Tapiola, can't I?"

He nodded. "That won't be a problem. Maybe Väinämöinen might even have a suggestion for you on how to break their curse."

That perked me up. "You're right—if *anybody* might

know the answer, it would be one of the Force Majeure."
Feeling hopeful—and anxious—about the coming year, I
settled into finishing my dinner, trying to enjoy the time
in my house while I could. Because once I returned from
training, I wasn't sure who I would be—or how I would
feel.

I CALLED VIXEN THAT NIGHT. "How's Lenny doing? I've
been detained figuring out how to take care of the attachment that's latched onto him, so I'm sorry I haven't been
able to call earlier. But I know how to deal with it now."

I didn't feel like telling them what had happened—not
yet. Not till I had at least told Ember and Angel. It struck
me that I'd be away from my friends for a year, and that
made me realize how close we had gotten during the past
sixteen months I had known them.

Vixen let out a satisfied sigh. "I'm so glad. Lenny's
getting worse, I can tell it. He barely showed up for our
meeting yesterday about the website and he looks gaunt—
like he hasn't eaten for a long time. But I know he has.
Can you tell me what's going on?"

Biting my lip, I said, "Yeah, I can, but you cannot
approach him about it or you'll make yourself a target.
What has a hold on him attacked me in my home Sunday
night and tried to kill me. It can detach from him, which
is why I don't want you going after him. The creature's
called an aztrophyllia, and it's an astral entity that feeds
off life force. I'm going to have to knock it back into the
astral plane with Kipa's help and then I have to seal Lenny
against it ever getting hold of him again."

Vixen was silent for a moment, then they cleared their throat. "That sounds bad. Will he survive?"

"Yeah, it is bad. As for whether we're catching this in time, I hope so. It will be hard to say until we detach it from him and are able to calculate how much energy it drained from him. Theoretically, he should recover if he's still alive and on his feet. But I've never dealt with one of these creatures, so it's rather hard to say." I paused. "Can you arrange for him to come over to your place tomorrow? Kipa and I will be there and even if we have to strap him down, we can attempt to remove the aztrophyllia."

"I'll try. I'll call you back. I might be able to persuade him to come over, but he's resisting more and more." Vixen sounded concerned and I realized that they cared about Lenny more than I thought.

"Do what you can. If you can't get him to come over, we'll have to go find him." As I hung up, I felt restless. Everything was coming tumbling down at once, it seemed like, and while I was looking forward to the sudden change in my future, I was also scared.

I slid on my coat and found Raj's leash. "I'm taking Raj for a walk in the park," I said.

"You want company?" Kipa asked.

I thought about it. Mostly when he asked, I was grateful because I hadn't liked walking alone ever since Pandora. A lot had changed because of her, and I knew she was still out there. But tonight, I had a lot on my mind and I wasn't sure whether I wanted company or not.

Kipa must have noticed my ambivalence because he said, "I can walk behind you, just to make sure you're okay. Or we can go together and not talk."

Finally, I said, "All right. Maybe we can walk him and not talk so I can think?"

Kipa shrugged on his jacket. "Sounds good. Hey, does Raj want to go for a walk with Raven and Kipa?" he called.

Raj came bouncing over. "Raj loves walks. Raj go to the park?"

"Yes, Raven and Kipa are taking Raj to the park. Now, Raj needs to sit still while Kipa puts his leash on." Kipa leaned down and fastened the leash to the collar while Raj darted impatient glances at the door.

"I need to read that book Dek lent me," I said, staring at Raj. "Somehow, I don't think that…well…this situation is quite normal, if you know what I mean."

"Yeah, but I wouldn't worry. Very little ever goes by the book in life."

We headed out into the snow, toward the trailhead into UnderLake Park. I lifted my head to the sky, letting the snowflakes settle on my face. All around us, the world was muffled and frozen, but frozen or not, my life was moving forward in a direction I had never anticipated. I hadn't even consulted my gods about it.

We know. Do you think we don't know these things?

The words echoed in my brain as I felt Cerridwen stir her cauldron, catching up my fate and destiny with her. Suddenly feeling at peace—my gods were behind me on this, and that made me feel much more secure—I tried not to think about the coming fight with the aztrophyllia while we silently walked down the trail and into the park, under the veil of snow.

CHAPTER NINETEEN

Friday morning came early. Our walk had been helpful, letting me calm my thoughts and focus them solely on being in the present. In fact, I slept deeply, my dreams taking me to Tapiola, where I saw a cottage covered with ivy and climbing roses, and in the dream, Kipa was making fried eggs and bacon for breakfast while I stood outside, breathing air so clear that it felt like my lungs might freak out. Raj was playing with a dog that looked almost twice his size, and a cat sat in the window next to the box of magical herbs. It was so calming that I woke to an anticipation I seldom had in the mornings.

It dawned on me that maybe this move had already been in my destiny. Maybe it wasn't just happenstance. Wondering about Fate and what part she played in our lives, I slid out of bed.

Kipa was already up and I could hear him laughing in the kitchen with my mother. I was grateful the two of them got along so well. At first, there had been a part of myself afraid he might find her more attractive than me—

213

after all, she was as wild as he was—but he never showed any sign of seeing her as anything more than my mother, and that set me at ease. I knew he wasn't her type, but sometimes, having a mother who was Queen of the Bean Sidhe made for insecurity.

I decided to be festive and slipped on a Santa red bra and panties, then fastened a garter belt to match around my waist, using the garters to hold up green, red, and white striped thigh-high socks. The next layer was a green tulle petticoat and then, a red satin circle skirt. Zipping up my red brocade corset over the top, I then added a green bolero jacket, and I was ready for makeup.

I quickly did goth-chic eyes with green metallic eye shadow and heavy liner and mascara, and decided to leave my lips a pale pink for a change. After brushing out my hair, I put on platform calf-high boots and headed toward the kitchen, feeling ready to face the day.

My phone jangled as I entered the dining room and I glanced at it. Vixen had convinced Lenny to be there by one.

"Hey, Lenny will be at Vixen's by one, so we should be there at least an hour early." I entered the kitchen to see Kipa ladling out oatmeal with raisins into bowls while Phasmoria was stacking bacon and sausage on a platter. They both froze, staring at me.

"Where's your Santa hat?" Kipa asked, smirking.

"You look…festive," Phasmoria added. "I don't think I've ever seen you looking quite so…festive?"

I stuck my tongue out at them. "I love both of you, too. Hey, I felt like celebrating the season, so keep your opinions to yourself if you're going to play Scrooge."

Kipa laughed, setting down the bowl and the ladle. He

pulled me to him and kissed me soundly. "I didn't say I didn't *like* it—you make a most comely elf—though frankly, most Elves are insulted by their portrayal as non-unionized toy makers employed by a man who probably doesn't even give them good health benefits."

I snorted. "I never thought about that."

"You're lovely," my mother chimed in. "I'm not used to seeing you wear much besides black, purple, and green."

"I have my moments," I said. "So, did you hear me?"

"We'll be there early. I want to get this over with. We need to strategize, though." He set the bowls on a tray and, with Phasmoria carrying the platter of sausage and me picking up the bowl of fruit salad, we carried our food to the dining room table. Kipa had already set out the plates and bowls, and I returned to the kitchen for the cream and brown sugar for the oatmeal.

Raj was waiting at his dish and Kipa set a bowl of plain oatmeal down for him, along with a plate with several sausages on it. Raj began to lap up the oatmeal, using his paws to eat the sausages. He hated using forks and spoons. As long as he wiped his paws on the mat after eating anything that could leave a mess on the floors, I was fine with however he wanted to eat his food.

"So, how are we going to do this? We go over there… are you going out on the astral before they get there?" I asked.

"I don't think that's a good idea," Kipa said. "Since the aztrophyllia is on the astral, it might sense me if I'm out there when Lenny arrives. We will probably have to restrain him because the moment the creature realizes what's happening, it will try to get him out of there."

A thought struck me. "What if it leaves? What if it tries to save its ass and vanishes?"

"Then we're so much the better. You can seal Lenny off from it, because if it leaves, it won't have a hold on him for that moment. And then we use that spell to seal it from ever getting back to your house." Kipa paused, then said, "I know that look. What's wrong?"

"I wish we could get rid of it for good. I can't help but think it's going to search for another victim." I hated unfinished business, and that's what this felt like.

"It will, love." Kipa softened his voice. "One thing you have to come to terms with is that we'll never be able to stop *all* the bad guys—or monsters—in the world. We'll never be able to make the world safe. There will always be monsters and pain and victims. But there will always be beauty and joy, as well. And kind hearts. Do you understand?"

I didn't want to agree, but he made sense. "Yeah, I get it, I do. I'd rather not believe it, but you're right. All right, now, to dislodge it you'll need silver—how do you even take that over to the astral realm?"

"I don't, but we'll take a good length of silver chain and…" Kipa paused, frowning. "You know, if we bind Lenny with a silver chain, the energy will resonate through his aura. Crystals and metals—they all have an energetic component, and when someone holds a crystal, that energy blends with their own. The same for metal. So if we bind him with silver, it may disrupt the aztrophyllia enough so that I can go after it on the astral plane, while you seal Lenny with the spell so it can't reattach."

That made sense. "All right. I agree, you're on to something. We'll try it that way because I don't have any better solution than that."

"What do you need to cast your spell?" my mother asked.

"Nothing. Väinämöinen uses very few spell components. I get the feeling that the Force Majeure don't need anything but their own energy to cast spells, and the way I see the spell working, it's a matter of manipulating energy. I often wondered if they keep a room full of bones and feathers and so forth, and I get the impression through him touching my mind that he does have something like that, but it's not always necessary."

I had also discovered that the saying was true: The Force Majeure were more removed from humankind than the gods were. When Väinämöinen had met me out in the depths of space, he had seemed far more alien than Kipa had. It was as through something had happened to him—shifted his DNA. In fact, I would never have pegged him for being one of the magic-born. He seemed so far beyond that.

"Good, then. What do we have to do before we leave?" Kipa finished his breakfast and wiped his mouth on his napkin. I had taught him a few manners, at that.

I pushed back my dishes, finished. "I need to tend to the ferrets, and I should meditate for a bit. I need to build up my focus for casting the seal."

"I'll do the dishes and mind the house while you're gone," Phasmoria said, standing.

We scattered to finish our tasks. Even as I fed the ferrets and told Elise about our impending move, my mind was hanging out in space, remembering Väinämöinen's mind-touch. It had been perhaps the most intimate thing that had ever happened to me, and one of the greatest gifts. I had looked into the mind of brilliant power, and returned alive and unblinded.

VIXEN WAS WAITING for us at the door. They were in a feminine mood today, wearing a linen pantsuit that curved to their form with a smooth ease. They were holding a handkerchief and I could tell they were feeling anxious, because they were knotting it in their hands, using it like a worry stone.

"Hey, Vixen," I said, leaning in to plant a kiss on their cheek. "Kipa and I think we can free Lenny of the creature."

"I know, but I'm nervous. Will this hurt him? What if the... What did you call it?"

"Aztrophyllia?"

"Yes, what if the aztrophyllia decides to attack one of us?"

Vixen was in a state and I couldn't quite pinpoint why. Yes, the aztrophyllia was scary, but Vixen was a powerful snake shifter, and they shouldn't be as afraid as they were.

"Why are you upset?" I blurted out. "I know this is nerve-wracking and you're afraid for Lenny, but you seem a lot less sure than you did the other day."

Vixen met my gaze, and I saw something shift in their eyes. "I was visited by an emissary from the Banra-Sheagh yesterday. I wasn't going to tell you, but..."

I frowned. "But what? What happened?"

"They've threatened to not only exile me from the Ante-Fae, but they said they'd find a way to close down my club for good if I…stay friends with you." Vixen let out a sigh. "They're going to expel me from the Ante-Fae community, which I would be able to handle except they've also threatened to tear my club apart and to target every client I have, Raven. Basically, every client who comes to the doors of the Burlesque A Go-Go will find themselves targeted by the Banra-Sheagh for excommunication."

My stomach dropped. The club was Vixen's life. They had fought long and hard to open it, first against the city itself who didn't want an Ante-Fae nightclub around, especially a burlesque club, and then against the older members of the Ante-Fae who thought that Vixen was inviting too much of the human element in. It had taken them a long time to resolve both sides of the issue, and now it could be wiped out in one sweep if Vixen stayed friends with me.

I sat down, realizing that it was time to be selfless. Vixen was my friend, and I wouldn't let them be ostracized and their dreams destroyed because of me.

"Tell them you'll fall into line."

When Vixen started to protest, I held up my hand. "Vixen, I'm heading to Kalevala for a year next month. I'm going to train with one of the Force Majeure and after that year, I'll be interning with him for another year. Maybe in that time, things will change so that this will all be moot. Regardless of what happens, I won't let you lose everything you hold dear just because the Queen's got her knickers in a wad."

Vixen was nothing if not pragmatic. They sat down and took my hand. "You really mean it, don't you? And second, how the hell did you come to meet with one of the Force Majeure and insinuate yourself into a two-year internship?"

"First, it's a year in training and then a year's internship. And second, I met Väinämöinen thanks to Kipa, when we were researching what Lenny's attachment is. The bard thinks I have promise and his price for giving me the spell that can protect Lenny from the aztrophyllia was that I train with him for a year." I swallowed, feeling teary-eyed, but I blinked the tears away. "So, I'll be gone anyway, and I can sneak notes to you through Ember and Angel."

Vixen shook their head. "Thank you, Raven. You don't know what this means to me. But I mean it—say the word and I'll give up the club. What they're doing isn't right. The Queen's encroaching too much on our lives."

"Be that as it may, we might as well fly under the radar and preserve what we can while we sort all of this out." I sighed, leaning back. "I'll miss so many things, but you'll be in the top five."

Kipa cleared his throat. "I hate to break this up, but when's Lenny due? We're going to need to tie him up and you can be sure the aztrophyllia won't want any part of that."

"I have something that might be useful, darling," Vixen said. "I have a chair that has automatic cuffs. Lenny's never seen it. Only select members of my personal life know about it. It looks like any normal armchair, but it's made for sex play."

Kipa stared at Vixen like they'd grown another head. "Well, then...as long as it's not going to inflict anything else on him, we can use that and then wrap the chain around him. It will be less violent than me restraining him without help."

"I'll have my man bring it up." Vixen summoned the butler and requested he bring up the "Restraint Chair"… and apparently the butler knew exactly what they were talking about. When he returned with two of the house-maids who were carrying the chair, he arranged it in place of the rocking chair, which he moved out of the room.

True to what Vixen had said, the chair looked like a sculptural piece, but one that was functional. The arms were curved and ornate, and the chair was padded with a velvet cushion. Vixen showed us the almost invisible slits on both sides of each arm that housed retractable cuffs.

"You'll have to move fast," they said. "I'm not program-ming the leg cuffs because that requires more precision, and most of the people who've sat in this chair were willing participants. But you should be able to get the chain around his waist before he goes berserk."

"*Most of?* No, don't tell me. I don't want to know." Kipa eyed the contraption. "Where did you get this?"

"I have a friend who makes furniture, mostly for dungeons—and I'm not talking about the dank ones, but the ones that are oh so fun. He made it for me." Vixen winked. "Want his number?"

Kipa quickly declined. "No, we'll pass."

Vixen laughed, glancing at me. "What about you? You think you could use his number?"

Snickering, I said, "What Kipa said. Our bed play is wild enough. I'm dating the Lord of the Wolves, remember."

At that moment, the doorbell rang.

"Lenny," Vixen said, sobering instantly.

"Well, then…it's go time. Let Kipa and me hide so he doesn't see us." As we left the room and hid in Vixen's office, which was right next to the parlor, Vixen motioned to the butler and instructed him to escort Lenny in.

"Ready?" Kipa asked as we stood near the door to the office, cracking it so we could hear when Vixen called for us.

"I hope so. Once we take care of this…I guess that's the last I'll see of Vixen for a year. Or maybe two." I paused, then added, "I'll tell you one thing, the Banra-Sheagh has made an anti-monarchist out of me. I'm angry, Kipa. So angry I wish I could—"

"Don't say it," he quickly said. "You don't know who's listening."

I started to answer but stopped as the sound of Lenny talking to the butler echoed from the foyer. Lenny was bitching about not having the time to coddle Vixen and the butler was remaining politely silent. Kipa and I waited, straining to hear what was going on. There was muted conversation from the parlor and then, a moment later we heard Lenny shout.

"Hurry! Got him!" Vixen screamed.

We rushed back to the parlor, Kipa first, silver chain out and ready. We entered the room to see Lenny struggling against the cuffs holding his arms to the chair.

"You fucking freakshow bitch!" he was screaming at Vixen. "Let me go!"

As we came in the room, he glanced at me and shouted again. "Get away from me, you witch!" But when Kipa approached him, silver chain in hand, he gritted his teeth and his eyes grew narrow. "No—don't you dare!"

"Shut up or we're going to have to do this the hard way," Kipa growled under his breath.

I said nothing, watching as Kipa bound the chain around Lenny's arms, cinching him tight against the back of the chair. I felt oddly detached as I began to prepare the spell. I began to spin the webs of energy in my head, focusing on building the structure of the spell. It was like a puzzle, moving a thread of fire this way, a thread of earth energy that way, weaving it like I might weave a lattice.

Kipa fastened the chain so Lenny couldn't get away and turned to me. "I'm ready to go out and—"

At that moment, something coiled around my neck and I couldn't breathe. The aztrophyllia had jumped from Lenny to me. Struggling for air, I clawed at my throat but the creature had a firm hold and was squeezing hard, and I couldn't see it to attack it. It had a tighter hold on me than the first time, and I was quickly running out of air, without Raj there to help me.

Before Kipa could react, Vixen was at my side and they morphed into a massive snake, almost ten feet long and a beautiful golden brown. Vixen reared, mouth open to show long fangs. Petrified, I watched the snake weaving back and forth, using their tail for balance with their head at eye level with me. And then, even as the room started to blank out and my mind grew hazy, Vixen struck.

I wanted to dart away, to fall back, but the aztrophyllia held tight, not letting me move. I braced myself for impact, but the fangs never touched my skin. Instead, through my fading eyesight, I could tell that Vixen had hold of the creature with their fangs, trying to drag the aztrophyllia off of me. There was a sudden flash, and then

I could see what Raj had described—the bat-like creature. Its tail was wrapped around my neck, but Vixen had stuck their fangs into the body and was tugging hard.

Kipa shouted, leaping over the chair to land beside Vixen and me. He brought out a silver dagger and, doing his best to avoid Vixen, plunged the blade into the body of the aztrophyllia.

I could barely keep my eyes open. My lungs were burning and my head was pounding like it was going to explode. Wondering if this was it, I started to fall. The next moment, everything went black.

CHAPTER TWENTY

I FOUND MYSELF STANDING IN THE MIDDLE OF A crossroads under a wheeling sky of stars, and in front of me stood Arawn, Lord of Death. Everywhere, billowing mist tumbled along. I couldn't tell whether I was in a field because the ground was covered with the rolling fog, and overhead was black as night, black as pitch, studded with stars.

I turned back to Arawn. The massive god was cloaked in shadow, and he wore an indigo-colored cape with a hood that covered his face. All I could see were diamonds where his eyes should be. His arms were visible through the slits on the cape, but he was wearing silver gauntlets ornately embellished with Celtic knotwork. He held a tall scythe, silver blade attached to a jet black handle that must have been ten feet tall. Arawn himself had to be over eight feet, and he rose above me, staring down imperiously.

"And so...we come to a point of fate in the timeline of

your life," he said. His words echoed out over the fog, then were immediately sucked into the mist and vanished.

I stopped. "Am I dead?" I didn't *feel* dead, and I worked with ghosts so much I should be able to tell. But then, I had never been dead—at least not in this lifetime.

"No, Raven, you are not. But you stand on a turning point in your life. You stand at the crux. If you choose to live, your life will never be what it was. It will never be the same. That timeline has been wiped out by the past few days and the past few decisions you've made."

I thought back, nodding. "What about Väinämöinen? I was supposed to study with him for a year." I felt myself suddenly frantic, and realized how much I wanted the opportunity. I hadn't realized it meant so much to me until now. It had still seemed so fresh and frightening that I hadn't realized it was also the fulfillment of a dream for me—the chance to train under one of the great sorcerers of history.

"Do you have any clue where that path will lead you?" It wasn't a judgment, but a very real question. "You will be embarking on a journey that will lead you far into the magical realms and you might not ever return."

I crossed my arms over my chest. "I don't have a clue what it means for the long run, but…I want it."

"You have not used his spell yet. I could remove it and free you from your obligation. But even then, your life will never be the same." The god of death waited. I felt like he would wait forever if it took me that long. Death knew no time, he knew no constraints, and in the end, he always won.

And now, Death was offering me a chance to change my life again. But even if I took him up on the offer, he was right. Nothing would ever be the same. Whether Typhon was driven back into stasis or took over the world, nothing would be the same. Because *I* wouldn't be the same.

Less than a week ago, I had been happily tooling along, but now, so much had shifted. My father had fallen off the pedestal I put him on. He had feet of clay. My mother had become my champion. I had been evicted from a community that was my very blood. My friends had put themselves on the line for me and now had to turn their back on me. Kipa had paved the way for an opportunity that might come once in a lifetime. And Raj had saved my life, once again playing my knight in gray wrinkly leather armor.

Arawn was correct. I was at a crossroads. Nothing would be the same, regardless of which direction I chose.

"I choose to go forward, to keep my vow and train under Väinämöinen," I said. "It's the right path for me. The one that makes sense. If you let me live, that is my choice." I felt something settle inside. I had made my decision.

"You may live, yes. Your time isn't done yet, though I could change that if you had chosen to walk with me into the mist. But you will return, and you will go to Kalevala and train with the bard, and by doing so, you unfold a new destiny and a new future. This is your will?" He sounded almost proud, I thought.

I agreed, sure this was what I wanted to do, even though I had no clue what I was getting into. "It's my will."

"Then return to your body, Raven, and don't forget— just because you have a new beginning, that doesn't mean that you are free from Cerridwen and me. We will always be your heart and soul, and you will always bend your knee to us."

Before I could answer, the mist swirled up, engulfing me to where I couldn't see anything. And then, another blink later, I opened my eyes. I was on Vixen's sofa, and Kipa was holding my hand as I slowly moved, trying to sit up.

"Where am I?" I felt groggy as I sat up with Kipa's help. My voice was almost nonexistent, and my throat felt so raw that I swore I tasted blood. "What..." I looked around. Lenny was sitting on one of the ottomans, staring at me, but the fire in his eyes was gone and he looked melancholy and lost.

Vixen was standing behind the sofa, watching over me. "Raven, love, are you all right?"

I was trying to organize my thoughts. I remembered the entire discussion with Arawn, but I had no clue what had happened here. But then, my gaze fell on a *very* bloody creature on the floor. The aztrophyllia.

"You managed to kill it?" I squeaked, pointing toward it.

Vixen nodded. "Yes, actually. Apparently it couldn't handle being stabbed by silver *and* impaled by venomous fangs. It actually died."

"I didn't think we'd be able to kill it—" I paused, my throat hurting so much that I couldn't talk anymore. At that moment, a maid entered the room, carrying a warm cup of fragrant tea. Vixen added a splash of brandy and handed it to me.

"Drink. It's not hot enough to burn your throat, and it's got honey and lemon. It's warm hibiscus tea, and the honey is wildflower honey." They lifted the cup into my hands and I clutched at it, feeling dizzy and lightheaded and sore and all sorts of things swept up into one big knot.

I sipped the tea, thinking about Vixen. I'd never seen them in their snake form till now, and the sight had daunted me. I realized that Vixen was far more powerful than I had thought. And then, Arawn's conversation with me kept running through my head. I had set into motion a new destiny for myself. I didn't flatter myself by thinking I had created the entire situation just for me to move forward. But whatever the case, the future was now different.

As we sat there, Kipa and Vixen talking, and Lenny offering a few words into the conversation, my mind wandered. This would be the last time for a while that I'd be talking to Vixen directly. I also knew that my time here was limited. I had no clue what would happen after my training with Väinämöinen, but I knew that it was where my future rested, and so I tried to extend the conversation, talking as best as I could, so that when we went home, I wouldn't feel like I had left things unsaid to Vixen. After all, it wasn't every day that I had to bid farewell to a good friend.

Two Weeks Later...

The house was decked out in brilliant lights, the tree even brighter because I had bought more ornaments.

The food overflowed the table, and I was nervously waiting for our guests. I had stuck to inviting Ember and the Wild Hunt gang, because I didn't want to put any of my Ante-Fae friends in danger. The Banra-Sheagh had been thorough, working her way through all of my acquaintances, and I had a feeling that Dougal was helping her. And speaking of Dougal, my father was also due in and I wasn't sure at all how that was going to go.

I paced back and forth until Raj tugged on my skirt.

"Raven seems nervous. Is Raven okay?"

I glanced down at him and knelt beside him to give him a hug. "Raven's fine. Raven just has to tell her friends something that is both sad and exciting. In fact, Raven needs to tell Raj something—"

"Raven is going to have a baby?" Raj burst out with a grin.

Taken aback, I sputtered. "No, Raven is *not* going to have a baby. Whatever gave Raj that idea?"

"Raj saw a show last night where Timbert's girlfriend told Timbert that she was going to have a baby and she was sad and excited." Raj blinked, and once again, all I could think of was a big, gray, leathery Scooby Doo.

"Well…no. No baby. Raj, come sit with Raven." I led him to the sofa and sat down. He climbed up beside me and sprawled back on the sofa. Gargoyles looked remarkably like big dogs, and that included their genitals. Though I'd never seen Raj excited, for which I was grateful. But then, he sat up, his eyes solemn.

"What does Raven want to tell Raj? Will it make Raj sad?" He leaned forward, looking nervous.

"Next month, Raven, Raj, and Kipa are going on a long

vacation to a different world. Have you heard of Kalevala?"

"Kipa has spoken of it," Raj said. "Raj knows the name is the name of Kipa's homeland."

"Raj is correct. Raven and Raj and Kipa will be in Kalevala for at least a year. Raven will be training with a powerful wizard, and so we'll all be living there. I'm afraid Raj will have to get used to living without a TV for a year. But there will be a lot of fun things to see and do."

At the words "No TV," Raj's shoulders slumped and he let out a whine. His expression twisted, as though he wasn't sure what to think.

"*No TV*? Whatever will Raj do?"

"Raj can play outside, look through comic books, and make friends, maybe?" It occurred to me we'd better take a lot of creative supplies with us. "Raj can paint and do jigsaw puzzles and lots of other things. Raven and Kipa will figure it all out so Raj shouldn't worry." Maybe it would do Raj good to be away from the TV for a while. I had created a couch potato, when he should have been out exploring things and having fun.

"Raj will miss TV. Raj has lots of friends on TV."

I paused, suddenly realizing that Raj had been lonely. Even though I loved him dearly, and he loved me, I wasn't a constant companion. Maybe there was some way to remedy that. "The ferrets will come with Raven too. The whole family is moving. It will be a big adventure. But Raven's not selling this house. When the vacation is done, we'll probably come back here." Even as I said it, I wasn't sure. Maybe I'd love it over there. Maybe the Dragonni would take over this world. Maybe the universe would implode.

Raj mustered a smile. "Raj will have fun. Raj likes seeing new places."

I hugged him, even though I knew he was putting on a brave face for me. "Wait and see. Raven thinks Raj is going to love it there far more than he thinks he will." And I prayed that was true.

EVERYBODY SHOWED UP ON TIME—EMBER and Herne, Viktor and Sheila, Angel, Yutani, and Talia. They gathered around the tree as the fire crackled cheerfully in the hearth. The food was good, the ambiance warm, and I basked in the glow of having my friends around me. I decided to wait for an hour or so before telling them Kipa and I were leaving.

The doorbell rang and I went to answer it. There, on the doorstep, covered with fresh-fallen snow, was my father. I stared at him for a moment, wondering what to say. What *could* I say after the past couple weeks? How could I confront him without sounding like I wanted to slap him silly? And yet, I did want him to know what he put me through. I wanted an apology, I wanted an explanation, but I knew full well that even if he had the most sincere of excuses, I still couldn't trust him the way I used to.

Curikan hung his head under my scrutiny. "Raven, I'm so sorry. I don't know what to say except I didn't mean to… Oh hell, there's no good way to excuse my actions. I'm so sorry. I hope you can one day forgive me."

I wanted to reach out, to hug him, but I couldn't. Not yet. I took a deep breath and let it out slowly. "At least you're not trying to justify what you did. Dougal would never have used me that way and got me kicked out of the Ante-Fae community if you hadn't given him the idea it might work. He never thought two licks about me before."

"I know," Curikan said. "I know. May I come in?"

I stood back so that he could enter. "I want you to know something before we go in the living room where everybody else is. I'm going to try to forgive you, but it will take time. I want to trust you again. I love you, but I feel so betrayed. And even though I realize you thought maybe I'd come over to live—"

"No, don't try to rationalize why I did what I did. My father always makes me feel like dirt, and the time I spent with him over in Scotland brought up all those painful childhood memories. He's never going to love me. He's never going to be proud of me and nothing I do will ever be good enough. And that, I have to learn to live with."

Even as he spoke, I could feel the centuries of disappointment weighing on his shoulders. And it made me realize that no matter what, until this mess, my father had always shored me up and made me feel special. He had never made me feel like he was disappointed in me. And a voice inside me whispered, "He's allowed to make a mistake. He's mortal, he's not perfect, and he's allowed one error in all the time he took care of you."

He held up an envelope. "I have a check here for your mother. She paid me back for your house and I'm giving this back to her. I love you, Raven, and I will never forgive myself for hurting you."

That broke the dam. I fell into his arms, sobbing. "I love you, Da. I was so hurt by what you did. You've always meant the world to me."

He held me, patting my back. "We'll sort this out, girl. We'll sort this out."

I stood back. "You were going to move to Y'Bain, but I talked you into going to Dougal's—Mother and I did. Now...how would you like to live in Kalevala?"

Curikan looked puzzled. "What do you mean? Why would I go there?"

I dried my eyes. "Come in, and I'll tell you."

He followed me into the living room. Phasmoria gave him a long look as he leaned down to place a kiss on her cheek. He whispered something to her I couldn't catch, then said hello to everyone else.

He turned to Angel as I introduced them. "This will be the only time we can meet," he said. "If we meet again, you'll be in danger from my nature. So this evening will be the only time we will ever be able to say hello. Ember, you too—though my effect on the Ante-Fae is minimal."

Angel nodded, eyes wide. "Well, it's nice to be able to say hello to you this one time, then."

He sighed. "I wish it were under better circumstances. I suppose you all know what happened with me and my daughter," he said. "We're working on resolving that, and I've... I'll prove that I'm worth forgiving."

"Since you're all here, I have something I want to tell you," I said, standing in the center of the room. Kipa moved over to my side and wrapped his arm around my waist.

"You're getting married?" Angel let out an excited squeal that made me snort.

"No, we're not getting married. But...we are moving."

Everyone except Herne and my mother looked shocked.

Kipa whispered to me, "I told Herne that I'd be taking a year off except for when I'm needed because of the Dragonni. I don't technically work for him, but I've been helping a lot."

That explained why the Lord of the Hunt didn't look surprised.

"What...where are you moving? Another state?" Ember asked.

I held her gaze for a moment, realizing that the moment I spoke, it would all be real. "No, actually. I'll be training with Väinämöinen for a year." That brought a tumble of questions and I finally held up my hand. "One at a time. But first, let me tell you how this happened." I explained everything that had happened during the past couple weeks, from what went down the night of my last party, to what happened with the Banra-Sheagh, to the aztrophyllia and Vixen and Lenny, to Väinämöinen's offer.

Ember and Angel looked dumbstruck. "But you *can't* move. We're in the middle of a war," Ember said, then blushed. "I know that sounded ridiculous, but...I'll *miss* you. We'll miss you."

I ducked my head. "I know, and I'll miss you all, too. But I'll be over here for special occasions and, like Kipa, if you need my help during something big going down with the Dragonni, let me know and I'll come back. It's only for a year for training and then the internship—after that..."

"After that, who knows?" Phasmoria stood. "Life moves on, everything changes. Change is life, stagnation is a form of death. We all grow and advance or we slide into obscurity with too many regrets. Ember, you'll be stepping up to goddesshood soon, you'll be changing. Angel, you took the life-extending elixir, you've chosen a different route. Everything moves as the cycles of the world turn on and on. My daughter's making an informed choice. She's choosing to brave the unknown because she knows this will lead to a new path, with new options, and it's an opportunity most magical workers would kill for. I'm proud of you, Raven."

I smiled at her, tears running down my face. "I'll miss you all, I really will. But it's not like you can't come over to visit. And I'll be back." I turned to my father, who had remained silent all the time I was talking. "Do you see why I asked if you'd like to come with us to Kalevala?"

He nodded, looking grateful. "If you and Kipa will have me, I'll come. I can help around the house and grow a garden and help with Raj and the ferrets. I might even write a book about my life."

After that, everyone jumped into the conversation and we discussed the future, which was coming full throttle, and we discussed the changes we were all making. And the evening wore on, a kaleidoscope of friends, food, and fun, even as outside, the snow was falling, and the world was turning, and time would not stand still for anyone.

CHAPTER TWENTY-ONE

ON NEW YEAR'S EVE, KIPA AND I STOOD AT THE EDGE OF the portal. My father had gone ahead with the ferrets and was waiting for us on the other side, so he wouldn't endanger Ember. I was holding Raj's leash. We had moved all of the furniture and other goods we would need over during the past couple days and the cottage was set up and waiting for us. Now, all that remained was for us to take the final step.

Behind us, a few steps away, were Herne and Ember. They were holding hands, looking so much in love that my heart swelled for them. She was going to make an incredible goddess, I thought. And then another thought struck me—if Kipa and I ever broached the subject of marriage, I'd have to make the same choice Ember did—to embrace goddesshood, and a life forever changed till the end of time.

I took a deep breath. On the other side, the rolling fields of Kalevala awaited. Orla had programmed the portal directly for the Northland, rather than the portal in Finland.

"Are you ready, love?" Kipa asked.

Was I ready to give up everything I had ever known and dive into a future that was unsure, a future that I had no clue of where it was going? I took a deep breath.

"Yeah. I'm ready." I turned back to Ember. "I'll miss you, lady. You've become a friend of mine in ways I didn't think possible."

She had tears in her eyes when she hugged me. "And you, too. Herne and I will come visit, and we'll bring Angel with us."

I knew that the fight between Typhon and the gods was in the offing. "When you can, just let us know in advance so my father can be out of the house. And as I said, if you need me, call me. Kipa and I'll be coming back next month, anyway, for Viktor and Sheila's wedding."

Viktor and Sheila had shifted their wedding date to mid-February to avoid a conflict with Imbolc celebrations and I was one of Sheila's bridesmaids, along with Ember and Angel and Talia. Kipa had agreed to be one of the groomsmen.

I looked around. The snow had vanished, as per typical Seattle weather, but a silver rain sprinkled down and I could see my breath in front of my mouth. "I guess this is it."

"We'd better go," Kipa said gently.

I hugged Ember again, and then Herne. He slipped something into my hand. It looked like a silver dollar with a stag leaping on it. "What's this?"

"If you need me and Kipa's not there to help, hold this

and send me a message. The coin will vanish but I'll hear you and come as soon as I can."

I stared up at him. So much had happened since I had first walked into his office to ask for help with my missing fiancé. So much water under the bridge. I turned back to Ember and held out my hand. She took it.

"This is it," I said. "I'm scared."

"I know," she said. "So am I. But you can do this, and think about what you'll be learning. So much about magic. I bet someday you'll be invited to join the Force Majeure."

"Oh, I doubt it, but…" *But,* I thought, *you never know.* I kissed her cheek. "Thank you, for everything. And I'll see you next month, if not before."

"Next month!" Ember knelt next to Raj. "Ember hopes Raj has fun."

Raj snorted. "No TV," he said sadly, but then he perked up. "But Kipa promised Raj many long walks."

And so we turned back to the portal and, deciding I wasn't going to look back because the future held so much promise I didn't want to miss any of it by mourning the past, we crossed through the vortex into Kalevala, and into my new life.

IF YOU ENJOYED **WITCHING FIRE**, then you might want to read the rest of **The Wild Hunt Series**. Begin with **The Silver Stag**, **Oak & Thorns**, and **Iron Bones**. Book 17: **Veil of Stars**, is available for preorder now. Heat level: steamy at times.

If you like ooo-spooky fiction with an older female

lead, check out **Starlight Web**, **Midnight Web** and
Conjure Web. January Jaxson returns to the quirky town
of Moonshadow Bay after her husband dumps her and
steals their business, and within days she's working for
Conjure Ink, a paranormal investigations agency, and
exploring the potential of her hot new neighbor. You can
also preorder the next book in the series: **Harvest Web**.
There will be more to come of January's adventures after
that. Heat level: mildly steamy.

If you like paranormal mysteries/paranormal women's
fiction, try my **Chintz 'n China paranormal mysteries**.
The series is complete with five books and two novellas.
Begin with: **Ghost of a Chance**. Heat level: mild.

Return with me to Whisper Hollow, where spirits
walk among the living, and the lake never gives up her
dead. I re-released **Autumn Thorns**, and **Shadow Silence**
along with a new book—**The Phantom Queen**! Come
join the darkly seductive world of Kerris Fellwater, spirit
shaman for the small lakeside community of Whisper
Hollow. Heat level: steamy.

If you prefer a lighter-hearted paranormal romance,
meet the wild and magical residents of Bedlam in my
Bewitching Bedlam Series. Fun-loving witch Maddy
Gallowglass, her smoking-hot vampire lover Aegis, and
their crazed cjinn Bubba (part djinn, all cat) rock it out in
Bedlam, a magical town on a magical island. Start with
Bewitching Bedlam. There are six books and several
novellas in the series. Hot vampire nookie!

I invite you to visit Fury's world. Bound to Hecate,
Fury is a minor goddess, taking care of the Abominations
who come off the World Tree. Books one through five are

available now in the **Fury Unbound Series**. Start with **Fury Rising**. Heat level: steamy at times.

For a dark, gritty, steamy series, try my world of **The Indigo Court**, where the long winter has come, and the Vampiric Fae are on the rise. There are five books and one novella in this series and it is complete. Begin with **Night Myst**. Heat level: dark steamy.

For all of my work, both published and upcoming releases, see the Bibliography at the end of this book, or check out my website at **Galenorn.com** and be sure and sign up for my **newsletter** to receive news about all my new releases.

QUALITY CONTROL: This work has been professionally edited and proofread. If you encounter any typos or formatting issues ONLY, please contact me through my **Website** so they may be corrected. Otherwise, know that this book is in my style and voice and editorial suggestions will not be entertained. Thank you.

CAST OF CHARACTERS

Raven & the Ante-Fae:

The Ante-Fae are creatures predating the Fae. They are the wellspring from which all Fae descended, unique beings who rule their own realms. All Ante-Fae are dangerous, but some are more deadly than others.

- **Apollo:** The Golden Boy. Vixen's boytoy. Weaver of Wings. Dancer.
- **Arachana:** The Spider Queen. She has almost transformed into one of the Luo'henkah.
- **The Banra-Sheagh:** Queen of the Ante-Fae.
- **Blackthorn, the King of Thorns:** Ruler of the blackthorn trees and all thorn-bearing plants. Cunning and wily, he feeds on pain and desire. Deceased.
- **Curikan, the Black Dog of Hanging Hills:** Raven's father, one of the infamous Black Dogs. The first time someone meets him, they find

good fortune. If they should ever see him again, they meet tragedy.

- **Dougal:** Raven's grandfather. Leader of the Black Dogs Highland Clan.
- **Phasmoria:** Queen of the Bean Sidhe. Raven's mother.
- **Raven, the Daughter of Bones:** (also: Raven BoneTalker) A bone witch, Raven is young, as far as the Ante-Fae go, and she works with the dead. She's also a fortune teller, and a necromancer.
- **Straff:** Blackthorn's son, who suffers from a wasting disease requiring him to feed off others' life energies and blood. Deceased.
- **Trinity:** The Keeper of Keys. The Lord of Persuasion. One of the Ante-Fae, and part incubus. Mysterious and unknown agent of chaos. His mother was Deeantha, the Rainbow Runner, and his soul father was Maximus, a minor lord of the incubi.
- **Vixen:** The Mistress/Master of Mayhem. Gender-fluid Ante-Fae who owns the Burlesque A Go-Go nightclub.
- **The Vulture Sisters:** Triplet sisters, predatory.

Raven's Friends:

- **Bear:** One of Kipa's friend—a god, in Kalevala—who owns an inn.
- **Dek:** Another friend of Kipa's, a bear shifter who, with his daughter, lives in Annwn.
- **Elise, Gordon, and Templeton:** Raven's ferret-

bound spirit friends she rescued years ago and now protects until she can find out the secret to breaking the curse on them.

- **Gunnar:** One of Kipa's SuVahta Elitvartijat—elite guards.
- **Jordan Roberts:** Tiger shifter. Llewellyn's husband. Owns *A Taste of Latte* coffee shop.
- **Llewellyn Roberts:** One of the magic-born, owns the *Sun & Moon Apothecary*.
- **Moira Ness:** Human. One of Raven's regular clients for readings.
- **Neil Johansson:** One of the magic-born. A priest of Thor.
- **Raj:** Gargoyle companion of Raven. Wing-clipped, he's been with Raven for a number of years.
- **Wager Chance:** Half-Dark Fae, half-human PI. Owns a PI firm found in the Catacombs. Has connections with the vampires.
- **Wendy Fierce-Womyn:** An Amazon who works at Ginty's Waystation Bar & Grill.

The Wild Hunt & Family:

- **Angel Jackson:** Ember's best friend, a human empath, Angel is a member of the Wild Hunt. A whiz in both the office and the kitchen, and loyal to the core, Angel is an integral part of Ember's life, and a vital member of the team.
- **Charlie Darren:** A vampire who was turned at 19. Math major, baker, and all-around gofer.
- **Ember Kearney:** Caught between the world of

Light and Dark Fae, and pledged to Morgana, goddess of the Fae and the Sea, Ember Kearney was born with the mark of the Silver Stag. Rejected by both her bloodlines, she now works for the Wild Hunt as an investigator.

- **Herne the Hunter:** Herne is the son of the Lord of the Hunt, Cernunnos, and Morgana, goddess of the Fae and the Sea. A demigod—given his mother's mortal beginnings—he's a lusty, protective god and one hell of a good boss. Owner of the Wild Hunt Agency, he helps keep the squabbles between the world of Light and Dark Fae from spilling over into the mortal realms.

- **Rafé Forrester:** Brother to Ulstair, Raven's late fiancé; Angel's boyfriend. Was an actor/fast-food worker, now works as a clerk for the Wild Hunt. Dark Fae. Deceased.

- **Talia:** A harpy who long ago lost her powers, Talia is a top-notch researcher for the agency, and a longtime friend of Herne's.

- **Viktor:** Viktor is half-ogre, half-human. Rejected by his father's people (the ogres), he came to work for Herne some decades back.

- **Yutani:** A coyote shifter who is dogged by the Great Coyote, Yutani was driven out of his village over two hundred years before. He walks in the shadow of the trickster, and is the IT specialist for the Wild Hunt Agency.

Ember's Friends, Family, & Enemies:

- **Aoife:** A priestess of Morgana who guards the Seattle portal to the goddess's realm.
- **Celia:** Yutani's aunt.
- **Danielle:** Herne's daughter, born to an Amazon named Myrna.
- **DJ Jackson:** Angel's little half-brother, DJ is half Wulfine—wolf shifter. He now lives with a foster family for his own protection.
- **Erica:** A Dark Fae police officer, friend of Viktor's.
- **Elatha:** Fomorian King; enemy of the Fae race.
- **George Shipman:** Puma shifter. Member of the White Peak Puma Pride.
- **Ginty McClintlock:** A dwarf. Owner of Ginty's Waystation Bar & Grill
- **Louhia:** Witch of Pohjola.
- **Marilee:** A priestess of Morgana, Ember's mentor. Possibly human—unknown.
- **Meadow O'Ceallaigh:** Member of the magic-born; member of LOCK. Twin sister of Trefoil.
- **Myrna:** An Amazon who had a fling with Herne many years back, which resulted in their daughter Danielle.
- **Sheila:** Viktor's girlfriend. A kitchen witch; one of the magic-born. Geology teacher who volunteers at the Chapel Hill Homeless Shelter.
- **Trefoil O'Ceallaigh:** Member of the magic-born; member of LOCK. Twin brother of Meadow.
- **Unkai:** Leader of the Orhanakai clan in the forest of Y'Bain. Dark Fae—Autumn's Bane.

The Gods, the Luo'henkah, the Elemental Spirits, & Their Courts:

- **Arawn:** Lord of the Dead. Lord of the Underworld.
- **Brighid:** Goddess of Healing, Inspiration, and Smithery. The Lady of the Fiery Arrows, "Exalted One."
- **The Cailleach:** One of the Luo'henkah, the heart and spirit of winter.
- **Cerridwen:** Goddess of the Cauldron of Rebirth. Dark harvest mother goddess.
- **Cernunnos:** Lord of the Hunt, god of the Forest and King Stag of the Woods. Together with Morgana, Cernunnos originated the Wild Hunt and negotiated the covenant treaty with both the Light and the Dark Fae. Herne's father.
- **Corra:** Ancient Scottish serpent goddess. Oracle to the gods.
- **Coyote, also: Great Coyote:** Native American trickster spirit/god.
- **Danu:** Mother of the Pantheon. Leader of the Tuatha de Dannan.
- **Ferosyn:** Chief healer in Cernunnos's Court.
- **Herne:** (see The Wild Hunt)
- **Isella:** One of the Luo'henkah. The Daughter of Ice (daughter of the Cailleach).
- **Kuippana (also: Kipa):** Lord of the Wolves. Elemental forest spirit; Herne's distant cousin. Trickster. Leader of the SuVahta, a group of divine elemental wolf shifters.

- **Lugh the Long Handed:** Celtic Lord of the Sun.
- **Mielikki:** Lady of Tapiola. Finnish goddess of the Hunt and the Fae. Mother of the Bear, Mother of Bees, Queen of the Forest.
- **Morgana:** Goddess of the Fae and the Sea, she was originally human but Cernunnos lifted her to deityhood. She agreed to watch over the Fae who did not return across the Great Sea. Torn by her loyalty to her people and her loyalty to Cernunnos, she at times finds herself conflicted about the Wild Hunt. Herne's mother.
- **The Morrígan:** Goddess of Death and Phantoms. Goddess of the battlefield.
- **Pandora:** Daughter of Zeus, Emissary of Typhon, the Father of All Dragons.
- **Sejun:** A counselor in Cernunnos's employ. Raven's therapist. Elven.
- **Tapio:** Lord of Tapiola. Mielikki's Consort. Lord of the Woodlands. Master of Game.

The Fae Courts:

- **Navane:** The court of the Light Fae, both across the Great Sea and on the east side of Seattle, the latter ruled by **Névé**.
- **TirNaNog:** The court of the Dark Fae, both across the Great Sea and on the east side of Seattle, the latter ruled by **Saílle**.

The Force Majeure:
A group of legendary magicians, sorcerers, and

witches. They are not human, but magic-born. There are twenty-one at any given time and the only way into the group is to be hand chosen, and the only exit from the group is death.

- **Merlin, The:** Morgana's father. Magician of ancient Celtic fame.
- **Taliesin:** The first Celtic bard. Son of Cerridwen, originally a servant who underwent magical transformation and finally was reborn through Cerridwen as the first bard.
- **Ranna:** Powerful sorceress. Elatha's mistress.
- **Rasputin:** The Russian sorcerer and mystic.
- **Väinämöinen:** The first and most famous Finnish bard.

The Dragonni—the Dragon Shifters

- The Celestial Wanders (Blue, Silver, and Gold Dragons)
- The Mountain Dreamers (Green and Black Dragons)
- The Luminous Warriors (White, Red, and Shadow Dragons)
- **Ashera:** A blue dragon.
- **Aso:** White dragon, bound to Pandora, twin of Variance.
- **Echidna:** The Mother of All Dragons (born of the Titans Gaia and Tartarus).
- **Gyell:** Shadow dragon, working with Aso and Variance to bring chaos to Seattle.

- **Typhon:** The Father of All Dragons (born of the Titans Gaia and Tartarus).
- **Variance:** White dragon, bound to Pandora, twin of Aso.

TIMELINE OF SERIES

Year 1:

- May/Beltane: **The Silver Stag** (Ember)
- June/Litha: **Oak & Thorns** (Ember)
- August/Lughnasadh: **Iron Bones** (Ember)
- September/Mabon: **A Shadow of Crows** (Ember)
- Mid-October: **Witching Hour** (Raven)
- Late October/Samhain: **The Hallowed Hunt** (Ember)
- December/Yule: **The Silver Mist** (Ember)

Year 2:

- January: **Witching Bones** (Raven)
- Late January–February/Imbolc: **A Sacred Magic** (Ember)
- March/Ostara: **The Eternal Return** (Ember)

End of the First Series Arc

- May/Beltane: **Sun Broken** (Ember)
- June/Litha: **Witching Moon** (Raven)
- August/Lughnasadh: **Autumn's Bane** (Ember)
- September/Mabon: **Witching Time** (Raven)
- November/Samhain: **Hunter's Moon** (Ember)
- December/Yule: **Witching Fire** (Raven)

Year 3

- February/Imbolc: **Veil of Stars** (Ember)
- March/Ostara: **The Antlered Crown** (Ember)

End of the Second Series Arc

I will be writing a few novellas and a short story collection at some point, while I take a break to decide whether there will be a sequel series.

PLAYLIST

I often write to music, and WITCHING FIRE was no exception. Here's the playlist I used for this book.

- **3 Doors Down:** Kryptonite
- **Airstream:** Electra (Religion Cut)
- **AJ Roach:** Devil May Dance
- **Adam Lambert:** Mad World
- **Air:** Moon Fever; Napalm Love; Playground Love
- **Alexandros:** Milk (Bleach Version)
- **Alice in Chains:** Man in the Box; Sunshine
- **Amanda Blank:** Something Bigger, Something Better; Might Like You Better
- **Android Lust:** Saint Over; Here and Now
- **Arch Leaves:** Nowhere to Go
- **Awolnation:** Sial
- **Band of Skulls:** I Know What I Am
- **Beastie Boys:** Rhymin & Stealin; She's Crafty; Paul Revere

- **The Black Angels:** Currency; Evil Things; Don't Play with Guns; Young Men Dead
- **Black Pumas:** Sweet Conversations
- **Black Sabbath:** Lady Evil
- **The Bravery:** Believe
- **Broken Bells:** The Ghost Inside
- **Camouflage Nights:** (It Could Be) Love
- **Crazy Twon:** Butterfly
- **Death Cab For Cutie:** I Will Possess Your Heart
- **Depeche Mode:** Blasphemous Rumours
- **DJ Shah:** Mellomaniac
- **Eastern Sun:** Beautiful Being (Original Edit)
- **Eels:** Souljacker Part 1
- **Everlast:** Black Jesus; I Can't Move
- **Faithless:** Addictive
- **FC Kahuna:** Hayling
- **The Feeling:** Sewn
- **Fluke:** Absurd
- **Foster The People:** Pumped Up Kicks
- **Garbage:** Queer; #1 Crush; Push It
- **Gary Numan:** When the Sky Bleeds, He Will Come; Dominion Day; The Angel Wars; Hybrid; Petals; Walking with Shadows; Ghost Nation; My Name Is Ruin; The End of Things; I Am Dust; Splinter; We're The Unforgiven
- **Gorillaz:** Dare: Demon Days; Hongkongaton; Clint Eastwood; Stylo
- **Imagine Dragons:** Natural
- **Low:** Witches; Plastic Cup; Half Light
- **Marconi Union:** First Light; Alone Together; We Travel; Weightless
- **Matt Corby:** Breathe

- **Orgy:** Social Enemies; Blue Monday
- **Outasight:** The Boogie; The Bounce
- **A Pale Horse Named Death:** Meet the Wolf
- **Pati Yang:** All That Is Thirst
- **People in Planes:** Vampire
- **Puddle of Mudd:** Psycho
- **Robin Schulz:** Sugar
- **Rue du Soleil:** We Can Fly; Le Francaise; Wake Up Brother; Blues Du Soleil
- **Screaming Trees:** Where the Twain Shall Meet; All I Know
- **Shriekback:** The Shining Path; Underwaterboys; Go Bang; Big Fun; This Big Hush; Agony Box; Bollo Rex; And the Rain; Wiggle and Drone; Now These Days Are Gone; The King in the Tree
- **Tamyrn:** While You're Sleeping, I'm Dreaming; Violet's in a Pool
- **Trills:** Speak Loud
- **Vive La Void:** Devil
- **Warchild:** Ash
- **Wendy Rule:** Let the Wind Blow
- **Zero 7:** In the Waiting Line

BIOGRAPHY

New York Times, *Publishers Weekly*, and *USA Today* best-selling author Yasmine Galenorn writes urban fantasy and paranormal romance, and is the author of over seventy-five books, including the Wild Hunt Series, the Fury Unbound Series, the Bewitching Bedlam Series, the Indigo Court Series, and the Otherworld Series, among others. She's also written nonfiction metaphysical books. She is the 2011 Career Achievement Award Winner in Urban Fantasy, given by RT Magazine. Yasmine has been in the Craft since 1980, is a shamanic witch and High Priestess. She describes her life as a blend of teacups and tattoos. She lives in Kirkland, WA, with her husband Samwise and their cats. Yasmine can be reached via her website at Galenorn.com. You can find all her links at her LinkTree.

Indie Releases Currently Available:

Moonshadow Bay Series:
  Starlight Web
  Midnight Web
  Conjure Web
  Harvest Web

The Wild Hunt Series:
  The Silver Stag
  Oak & Thorns
  Iron Bones
  A Shadow of Crows
  The Hallowed Hunt
  The Silver Mist
  Witching Hour
  Witching Bones
  A Sacred Magic
  The Eternal Return
  Sun Broken
  Witching Moon
  Autumn's Bane
  Witching Time
  Hunter's Moon
  Witching Fire
  Veil of Stars

Chintz 'n China Series:
  Ghost of a Chance
  Legend of the Jade Dragon
  Murder Under a Mystic Moon
  A Harvest of Bones
  One Hex of a Wedding

Holiday Spirits
Well of Secrets
Chintz 'n China Books, 1 – 3: Ghost of a Chance,
Legend of the Jade Dragon, Murder Under A
Mystic Moon
Chintz 'n China Books, 4-6: A Harvest of Bones, One
Hex of a Wedding, Holiday Spirits

Whisper Hollow Series:
Autumn Thorns
Shadow Silence
The Phantom Queen

Bewitching Bedlam Series:
Bewitching Bedlam
Maudlin's Mayhem
Siren's Song
Witches Wild
Casting Curses
Demon's Delight
Bedlam Calling: A Bewitching Bedlam Anthology
The Wish Factor (a prequel short story)
Blood Music (a prequel novella)
Blood Vengeance (a Bewitching Bedlam novella)
Tiger Tails (a Bewitching Bedlam novella)

Fury Unbound Series:
Fury Rising
Fury's Magic
Fury Awakened
Fury Calling

Fury's Mantle

Indigo Court Series:
   Night Myst
   Night Veil
   Night Seeker
   Night Vision
   Night's End
   Night Shivers
   Indigo Court Books, 1-3: Night Myst, Night Veil, Night Seeker (Boxed Set)
   Indigo Court Books, 4-6: Night Vision, Night's End, Night Shivers (Boxed Set)

Otherworld Series:
   Moon Shimmers
   Harvest Song
   Blood Bonds
   Otherworld Tales: Volume 1
   Otherworld Tales: Volume 2
   For the rest of the Otherworld Series, see website at Galenorn.com.

Bath and Body Series (originally under the name India Ink):
   Scent to Her Grave
   A Blush With Death
   Glossed and Found

Misc. Short Stories/Anthologies:
   Once Upon a Kiss (short story: Princess Charming)
   Once Upon a Curse (short story: Bones)

Once Upon a Ghost (short story: Rapunzel
Dreaming)

Magickal Nonfiction:
    Embracing the Moon
    Tarot Journeys

Made in the USA
Monee, IL
06 October 2021